Who by Water

Voices of the Dead: Book One

Victoria Raschke

Who by Water: Voices of the Dead - Book One

For further information, please contact:

Thousand Volt Press

info@1000voltpress.com

www.victoriaraschke.com

Cover design and book layout: keifel a. agostini.

Find him at keifelagostini.com.

The book is typeset in Brisio Pro. The font was chosen specifically for the shape of the letters and support of Slovene character sets.

SECOND EDITION
ISBN: 978-1-7347422-0-6

ACKNOWLEDGEMENTS

If I've learned anything on this adventure, it is that novels, like children, take a village.

I've had the great good fortune to learn from and work with teachers and writers who shaped my writing and voice in ways both obvious and mysterious. Caroline Eldridge, Anthony Keko, Roma Lingerfelt, Naomi Davis, Ralph King, Richard Jackson, Ken Smith, Earl Braggs, Boris Novak, Lori Berryhill, Aleš Debeljak, Art Smith, and Marilyn Kallett, thank you all for your knowledge, encouragement, instructive criticism, and your many kindnesses.

For Keifel, Julian, and Ishara. Thank you for putting up with the neurotic outbursts and general weirdnesses that come of living with a writer and for remembering to feed the cats, Orion and Vega, and yourselves when I was trying to finish a chapter.

The village that has tended the birth of this book is an especially large one. From the beginning my sister Lynne Rose and my friend Janet Neely have been the best beta readers a writer could have. In working with Griffyn Ink, I gained a second family of writers and readers who hold each other up and want nothing more than for all of us to be successful in following our crazy dreams. Thank you to Eli Jackson - indie publisher badass, A.J. Scudiere, D. B. Sieders, and Steve Bradshaw. I am honored to be both on your team and in your company. A thousand thank yous to my editors, Beth Terrell for helping me craft a better story and Christina Wilburn for making it polished. Any mistakes you encounter are mine, because these women are incredible pros. Another huge thank you goes to R.D. Morgan who took me under her wing when it dawned on me that writing a book is about a third of the work of getting the story into your hands. And finally, thank you to all of the folks at Wild Love Bakehouse in Knoxville. Fully two thirds of the writing of this book took place there, fueled on some of the best almond croissants to be had on this side of the Atlantic.

For the second edition I would also like to thank Jennifer Goode Stevens for re-proofing — we'll coin a word — to bring it stylistically in line with the books in the series she edited and to correct a couple things that got missed in the original printing.

The setting for this book is a world I had the privilege to live in a very long time ago. I've relied on kind friends and new acquaintances to fill in details and try to do justice to a place that will always feel magical to me. Thank you to Irena Šumi, Tit Škerget, Polona Debeljak, Matjaž Praprotnik, Matjaž Lulik, Erica and Aleš Debeljak, Rok Gros, and many others who've helped in small ways they may not have even realized during my travels. A special thank you to Aleksander and Tiha Šenekar and their daughters, Brina, Bistra, and Tisa, for their friendship and for believing in this project.

And a final shout out to Dean Stamoulis, wherever you may be. I told you I was writing a novel; it just took a lot longer than I thought it would.

for A.

A note on Slovenian pronunciation

Slovenian uses a few extra characters.

č is pronounced like the ch in church

š is pronounced like the sh in shirt

ž is pronounced like the second g in garage

Familiar letters are pronounced differently.

e is most often pronounced like a in bay

i is most often pronounced like the e in be

j is pronounced like a y

r without a paired vowel is pronounced like the ir in skirt

"In time and with water, everything changes."
Leonardo DaVinci

CHAPTER 1

Gustaf had only himself to blame. When he told Bettine she needed to assign an Observer to Slovenia, he hadn't anticipated her retaliation: for telling her how she should do her job, she sent him back to the place he'd hated.

Hated, past tense. Ljubljana had grown on him in a decade's time. Much of its architecture was the work of Jože Plečnik and reminded him of his beloved home of Vienna. Begrudgingly at first, and largely for the sake of his sanity, he had embraced the change. A decade later, his appreciation was real. The jewel box capital city belonged to him, or he to it.

The walls of Gustaf's garret flat were lined with shelves and covered in maps. A battered door divided his living and sleeping area from his closet-sized bathroom. He stood in the larger room, in a sea of dust motes electrified by the early morning light that burst through the wavy panes of the dormer window.

His focus for the past hour had been the cup of coffee cooling in his hand and a large map of the city stuck with color-coded pins. The green ones marked historic sites of supernatural interest: Plečnik's church in the marshes, Prešeren's statue and the bust of his love Julija across the square, the Trnovo church, Roman sites known and unknown to the general public, and various spots along the river. The red pins, each with a flag and a date, were the incidents that had threatened the Veil. The flagged blue pins noted the names and the addresses, or lairs, of people and beings of supernatural origin or ability.

On the map, the lines of the city looked sinuous, as if it were molten, trying to ooze between two green boulders and carry all his carefully placed flags with it along the path of the river. The old part of the city, the part the Romans named Emona and the modern residents call Staro Mesto, sat between the castle hill and the city's lungs, orderly Tivoli Park and the wilder Rožnik hill beyond it. On either end of this pinch, modern Ljubljana spread into the river valley and the marshes, a mix of sparkling glass and marble and somber Brutalist architecture.

On the Tivoli side of the river, the pedestrian-only streets of the old town ran largely perpendicular to the water. Buildings huddled together along the streets, differentiated by the colors of the new or peeling paint on the façades. Each building had its own arched wooden door that opened into a cobblestone courtyard. Shops and restaurants occupied the ground floors, and *Ljubljančans* held the flats above.

The address on the map for his building had four blue pins. One for him. One for Vesna Kos, the scion of a family of Witchfinders. One for Goran, a university professor and antique dealer who was more than he seemed. And one for Jolene Wiley.

CHAPTER 1

Gustaf had only himself to blame. When he told Bettine she needed to assign an Observer to Slovenia, he hadn't anticipated her retaliation: for telling her how she should do her job, she sent him back to the place he'd hated.

Hated, past tense. Ljubljana had grown on him in a decade's time. Much of its architecture was the work of Jože Plečnik and reminded him of his beloved home of Vienna. Begrudgingly at first, and largely for the sake of his sanity, he had embraced the change. A decade later, his appreciation was real. The jewel box capital city belonged to him, or he to it.

The walls of Gustaf's garret flat were lined with shelves and covered in maps. A battered door divided his living and sleeping area from his closet-sized bathroom. He stood in the larger room, in a sea of dust motes electrified by the early morning light that burst through the wavy panes of the dormer window.

His focus for the past hour had been the cup of coffee cooling in his hand and a large map of the city stuck with color-coded pins. The green ones marked historic sites of supernatural interest: Plečnik's church in the marshes, Prešeren's statue and the bust of his love Julija across the square, the Trnovo church, Roman sites known and unknown to the general public, and various spots along the river. The red pins, each with a flag and a date, were the incidents that had threatened the Veil. The flagged blue pins noted the names and the addresses, or lairs, of people and beings of supernatural origin or ability.

On the map, the lines of the city looked sinuous, as if it were molten, trying to ooze between two green boulders and carry all his carefully placed flags with it along the path of the river. The old part of the city, the part the Romans named Emona and the modern residents call Staro Mesto, sat between the castle hill and the city's lungs, orderly Tivoli Park and the wilder Rožnik hill beyond it. On either end of this pinch, modern Ljubljana spread into the river valley and the marshes, a mix of sparkling glass and marble and somber Brutalist architecture.

On the Tivoli side of the river, the pedestrian-only streets of the old town ran largely perpendicular to the water. Buildings huddled together along the streets, differentiated by the colors of the new or peeling paint on the façades. Each building had its own arched wooden door that opened into a cobblestone courtyard. Shops and restaurants occupied the ground floors, and *Ljubljančans* held the flats above.

The address on the map for his building had four blue pins. One for him. One for Vesna Kos, the scion of a family of Witchfinders. One for Goran, a university professor and antique dealer who was more than he seemed. And one for Jolene Wiley.

CHAPTER 2

Jo untangled herself from Milo and the sheets. She sat up and squinted at the phone display to see two messages from Vesna. The first message was "Where are you?" The second was "No. Really. Where are you?"

"Dammit." Reaching for Milo's shoulder to wake him, she shook off the remnants of a dream. Something about home. It was probably best not to remember.

She texted Vesna back. "Sorry. Thought he was coming later. Clear the bed, clothes on, and I'll be down."

Vesna replied immediately, "Milo or Rok?"

She wouldn't dignify that question with a reply. She snorted and shook Milo's shoulder again. This time he at least grunted.

"M, you really need to get going. I've got to meet Vesna. Now."

Milo mumbled something uncharitable toward Vesna and Christ's balls. "You're just going downstairs, and it's Saturday morning. Can't I sleep for a bit?" He rolled over and put his hand on her thigh.

"No." She moved his hand. "You know the rule." She gave his shoulder another push for good measure.

"If you're not here, I'm not here." He followed that with a disgusted grunt and sat up, reaching for his glasses on the white drum table on his side of the bed.

"What if one of my many paramours came by to find you curled up in my bed? Think of the awkwardness." She was only half kidding.

He wasn't under any delusion about being the only person who ever shared her bed, but she really didn't want any of them meeting and comparing notes over her crockery. Ljubljana was small, and keeping things quiet, let alone secret, was hard enough. And it weirded her out to think of Milo in her place alone. That would be more intimate than anything they'd done in her bed.

He waved his hand at her dismissively and stood to dress. She watched him; it was like watching a particularly lanky cat putting on pants. He looked at her as he buttoned the wrinkled shirt he'd worn the day before.

"Are you enjoying the show this morning?" He wasn't being sarcastic; his baritone had an invitation in it.

If she hadn't already been in the doghouse with Vesna, she would have greedily pulled him back into bed. "Don't test me, you tempter." She shook the duvet out in his direction for punctuation.

He laughed as he wound an elastic around his dark hair, making a ponytail at the nape of his neck. It was deeply unfair that a forty-year-old man should look that good after rolling unwillingly out of bed.

He patted his pockets for his wallet and keys. "Can I at least get a coffee? You can't be in that much of a hurry."

"Not this morning, I need to run." She pulled an ancient Nick Cave T-shirt over her head. Why was he dragging this out?

Milo plopped on the futon in the main room while she finished getting dressed. His gaze followed her as she moved through the flat, putting in small silver hoop earrings. She checked her messenger bag for the sketches she'd made for the graffiti artist and went back to the wardrobe in the bedroom for a black cardigan to pull on over the T-shirt. All the while she was humming, though she couldn't place the tune. Something from a television show?

When she stayed at Milo's place, there was none of the weirdness that came with booting him out so she could go to work, but he preferred to stay at her place now that he was seeing someone else. She'd asked several times if his new friend knew about their arrangement. He assured her everything was aboveboard. She believed him, for the most part.

They left together, bumping into each other as they tried to put their shoes on in the small closet that passed for the entryway to her flat.

He stood from tying his shoes, then wrapped his arms around her waist, burying his face in her neck. "When do I get to see you again?" His hand slipped down and cupped her ass.

"Right now I have no idea. Call me tonight. Or text." She kissed him on the mouth and shooed him down the steps. She bounded down behind him with the laces of one boot trailing.

Vesna opened the door to the shop before Jo could get her key in the lock. Her friend was dressed for a business meeting in a black skater skirt and tights and a red cowl-neck sweater. She'd even put on makeup. Her eyeliner was perfect.

Jo hadn't even remembered to brush her teeth. "I'm sorry. I really thought he was coming at noon." She closed the door behind her and breathed into her hand to make sure she didn't have dragon breath.

"He was. Then he texted us both last night, could we do eight instead. Didn't you see it?" Vesna looked at her with equal parts concern and frustration.

"No. Milo came over, and we went at it like minks until the wee hours of the morning."

Vesna snorted at her and threw a napkin from one of the tables at her head.

Jo feinted left to avoid the napkin. "Hey, you're the one who was asking me about my sex life at the crack of dawn."

"Eight o'clock is hardly the crack of dawn. And I was testy because you were late."

"Still. I don't get all up in your sex life business."

"That's because I don't have any sex life business. I'm too busy keeping this place together."

Vesna had a fair point. Jo was the creative partner. She handled the décor, music, and menus. Vesna handled anything that involved money or the government. And for that, Jo was truly grateful.

"Anyway. At least he's a little late, so I don't look totally flighty." She ran her hands through her hair, trying to at least smooth it to one side. It tended to have a mind of its own, especially the gray parts.

There was a determined knock on the glass of the front door. They both looked to the door, where Igor, Ljubljana's premier graffiti artist, announced his arrival with a single wave.

Vesna tucked her dark hair behind one ear and walked over to let him in, the heels of her ankle boots clicking on the wooden floor. Just before she turned the lock, she looked back over her shoulder at Jo and gave her the please-don't-sleep-with-vendors face. Jo pointed to herself and mouthed, "Who, me?"

She had expected a whippet-nervous, behoodied twentysomething. Igor was instead tall and wiry, probably in his mid-forties, with longish dirty blond hair going gray. He also had those piercing, glacial blue eyes Slovenes so often had and was dressed more cafe-poet than parkour-graffiti-artist, in black from head to high-tech hiking boots. She liked the unexpectedness of him, and Vesna seemed to have suddenly warmed up to the idea of working with "another flaky artist."

"I'm going to make us some tea, and then we can get down to business." Jo excused herself and headed toward the kitchen. She paused and turned to ask how Igor preferred his tea.

"Strong and sweet." A fleeting bolt of energy flew between them. Jo smiled even though she could almost hear Vesna rolling her eyes.

Vesna called after her. "Hey, Jo, if you're making black, may I have some milk? Warmed. Please."

Jo futzed at the tea station and grabbed a few things from the tiny restaurant kitchen. She filled an infuser with an English breakfast style tea and put some of the teahouse's signature mismatched china cups and saucers on a tray with a small earthenware bowl of irregular brown sugar cubes and a creamer filled with warmed milk. She added a plate with a few sandwiches left over from yesterday's service and a cookie or two. When the tea was ready, she deftly balanced the tray and turned to carry it out to the table. A glint of metal from the kitchen caught her eye. One of the plate racks they used for a full tea was lying in the middle of the floor.

That was weird. It hadn't been there a minute ago.

She set the tray back on the tea counter and turned back to the kitchen. The rack was gone.

She looked around, but it definitely wasn't there. She counted the racks on the shelf over the dish sink. Maybe she just needed some caffeine. She scooped the tray up and headed back out to Vesna and Igor.

They were seated at a four-top near the empty bakery case that separated the seating from the service area at the back of the shop, deep in conversation about which wall was best for the mural. Jo was set on the back wall behind the service area, where it would be the first thing customers saw when they walked in. Igor seemed to prefer the right-hand wall that separated the teahouse from the new-age shop next door. Vesna agreed with him. And she was flirting. It was very subtle, but it was definitely flirting.

So Vesna still knew how to flirt. Happily surprised, Jo

poured tea for everyone and sat back quietly in her chair without interrupting their conversation. The plate rack still puzzled her. Things didn't just move or disappear.

Vesna looked up at her a little sheepishly. "Thanks. Oh! Jo, did you bring the sketches?"

"What? Yes." She popped up to grab the messenger bag she'd flung onto the first chair inside the door when she'd arrived. After a short rummage on her way back to the table, she produced three tea- and possibly wine-stained sketches she'd done sitting at her dining table/desk upstairs while Vesna had paced and talked brand-speak at her. Jo's main concern was that the mural look cool and fit in with the teahouse's vibe.

Jo handed the sketches to Igor, who made a bit of a show flattening them out on the table with his forearm. He laughed softly. "At least they aren't on napkins."

Vesna was indignant. "We don't use paper napkins. It's wasteful."

"No disrespect to your Greenpeace membership." He smiled at her.

"It was a joke. I'm sorry." She looked like she'd just told the coolest girl in ninth grade about her extensive Barbie collection.

"Vesna's a little concerned about the money we're spending. As you can imagine, it's more than we usually spend on décor." Jo waved her arm around in a sweep to indicate the walls surrounding them. She slid Igor a plate with two sandwiches and a shortbread cookie.

"I can imagine. I think it's smart though. Not to brag —

well, maybe a bit — but it might bring in more tourists interested in street art." Igor took a bite of the cookie and then looked at it, surprised.

"It's pink peppercorn shortbread." Jo continued, "And that was kind of what we were thinking. Plus, the place needs a facelift."

She looked around at the aging punk and metal gig posters they'd hung when they'd first opened the shop almost a decade earlier. The wear and tear of restaurant traffic and kitchen heat had battered them. The place had a definite aesthetic, but it was time to evolve.

Igor held up her sketch of a clipper ship rendered like an old-fashioned sailor's tattoo and looked at the wall. "Just out of curiosity, why aren't you all in Metelkova? It seems more suited to what you're going for here."

Vesna answered, "Our silent partner owns the building."

Gregor, their other partner, was one of the friends Jo met when she'd first arrived in Ljubljana. She'd hit on him at a club, not realizing it was Pink Night. He was kind to the lost American, and they became friends and then business partners. His family owned the building that housed Renegade Tea and all of the flats upstairs, where both she and Vesna lived. There were other tenants, as well — a university professor and a guy in the tiny flat on the top floor whom Jo saw maybe once or twice a year.

"That would be reason enough." He looked at the second sketch of waves mimicking the style of Hokusai's *The Great Wave of Kanagawa*, but filled with burning crates of tea.

"Boston Tea Party?" Igor looked to Jo.

Vesna nodded. "Jo said the Boston Tea Party was punk as fuck."

Igor laughed. "I can see that."

Jo poured more tea in his cup. "Is that your favorite? I mean, can you work with it?"

"Yeah. I think I can work with that."

———

"Okay. So, we're closed tomorrow. We can move everything away from that wall after we close tonight. I'll come help after this thing with Gregor." Jo tied her long French waiter-style apron over her clothes to get started on the day's setup with Maja and Frédéric, who'd arrived soon after Igor left.

Someone had flipped on the sound system, and Roky Erickson's "I Have Always Been Here Before" was loud enough to block out the words Maja and Fred were chattering at each other. Jo heard Maja laugh. That was a rare thing, but Fred seemed to be the one to bring it out. She wondered if he knew their baker had it bad for him.

Vesna gathered up the stack of bills and paperwork she'd been leafing through to return them to her esoteric filing system in the desk drawer. "Can you let Igor in tomorrow morning?"

"Hot date?"

Vesna looked up at Jo, her brown eyes glinting with a bit of murder. "No. I promised my mother I'd have lunch at home. I have to catch the early bus."

"Special occasion?"

"Miha is engaged." Vesna's face fell as she said it.

Miha was her younger brother, and Jo knew that tomorrow's lunch was less a celebration of Miha's engagement than a prime opportunity for Mother to remind Vesna that she'd neglected to marry and produce grandkids.

"I don't know whether to say 'congratulations' or 'I'm sorry.'" Jo slid against the wall to get behind the desk with Vesna as she stood. Towering over her pixie friend, she put her hands on Vesna's shoulders and looked her in the face.

Vesna glanced down at the desk and then back up at Jo. "I think it's time to tell her enough is enough. I'm a successful business owner. The whole marriage and kids thing ... That's not me."

It was a good speech, but it was only half true: Vesna didn't want children, but Jo's unattached life didn't appeal to her in the least. And even if she did treat them like her children, Antony and Cleopatra, her cats, weren't all the companionship she ever wanted.

"Go for it, honey," Jo said. "Just remember, she guilts because she loves."

"I know."

"If she listens, she might even stop trying to fix you up with fifty-year-old bachelor accountants."

A rueful smile turned up the corner of Vesna's mouth. She finally laughed. "You really are the best."

Jo gave Vesna an extra squeeze and slipped out from behind the desk and into the kitchen to join her brigade prepping for service.

The three shifted into overdrive to pump out the day's menu. Frédéric made curried chicken salad sandwiches for the tea special.

Maja was efficient, as always. Vanilla bean shortbread cookies were already cooling on a speed rack jammed in the corner of the kitchen as she worked on their signature decadent brownies. That left Jo to get on with the verrines and tartlets. She filled shot glasses with yogurt while Frédéric threw together some odds and ends to make an eggy torta as the hot dish. They'd serve it with some Tuscan kale for a side salad.

Despite the eclectic punk ambiance of the teahouse, it was important to Jo that their food be high quality, sustainable, and seasonal. She hated the idea that kids, the teenagers and students who were the bulk of their clientele, just wanted pizza and crap food. The Renegade Tea menu was a mashup of English teatime tradition, Jo's American roots, and Frédéric's Algerian background, all interpreted in local produce.

The shop opened at three-thirty. Frédéric ran the kitchen. Maja had a second job bartending at a trendy place on the river, so Vesna did table service and made tea along with Damijan, a philosophy student at the university. Jo floated between front of house and the kitchen, doing whatever needed to be done to keep them out of the weeds. That night, though, she was on tap to be Gregor's date at a schmooze-fest at the City Museum, so Vesna and Damijan would be running the show without her.

Frédéric was taking their sidewalk menu board out onto a table to write the day's specials. He poked his head back into the kitchen.

"Jo, did you do a soup?"

"Fuck. No."

Maja stepped out of the kitchen. "In the freezer there's a gallon of that minestrone base Fred made for the catering last week. We can boil some orecchiette and add some of the kale and maybe throw in a couple herb bombs to freshen it up."

"Sounds like a plan. Good thinking." Frédéric nodded his approval and went back to his task.

Maja took the three steps back into the kitchen and pulled a gallon Lexan and a bag of herb bombs out of the little reach-in freezer jammed between the speed rack and the door to Vesna's broom closet of an office.

Herb bombs had been Maja's idea. At the end of service, any fresh herbs that looked the worse for wear got chucked in the food processor with some olive oil to produce a green gunge. The gunge was frozen in ice cube trays for adding to soups or sauces. They were also good for masking the lawn-clipping flavor of Maja's wheatgrass hangover smoothies, a concoction Jo needed less frequently these days, noticing as she had that fortysomething couldn't drink like twentysomething.

Soup handled and everything else prepped and ready for service, Jo de-aproned. Vesna joined them, standing in the door of the office: four people in that kitchen at the same time was an impossibility.

"All ready?" Vesna tried to peer over Jo's shoulder to the counter where Frédéric was cutting the crusts off the last batch of smoked salmon sandwiches. He handed her one of the sandwiches over Jo's shoulder. "Mmmm. These are my favorite."

"You guys should get a plate and have staff meal. I need to head upstairs and ponder what I'm wearing tonight." Jo rolled her apron into a ball and threw it for a goal toward the hamper next to the desk in the office. She missed and took the six steps to pick it up and place it in the hamper. "And that, ladies and gent, is why I never played basketball."

Frédéric went into the dining room to add the soup to the menu board. He had, by far, the best handwriting of any of them. He'd come to Ljubljana to study architecture in the mid 1980s. His half-French, half-Algerian background had made him stand out in Slovenia's largely homogeneous capital. That, and the fact he was gorgeous. He'd inherited his Algerian mother's complexion, dark hair, aquiline nose and full mouth along with his French father's deep blue eyes.

When Frédéric's midlife crisis hit in a big way, he'd walked in and quit the firm he'd been with since graduation. A few days later, he'd shown up at Renegade Tea asking for a job. Jo hired him on the spot, even though Vesna thought she was crazy. Jo figured anyone ready to make that kind of change needed an outlet and a chance.

Maja walked out with Jo so she could have a cigarette, pausing to point out something on the chalkboard to Fred. She laughed again and touched his arm before joining Jo in the courtyard and offering her a cigarette, which Jo declined. She'd quit years ago, though she would occasionally have a social smoke. Shit. She'd probably quit smoking before Maja was born, or close. That was sobering.

Maja held her cigarette between two fingers tattooed with astrological symbols and exhaled a perfect smoke ring. "What's this thing you're going to?"

"It's to celebrate the success of the Emona exhibit." It was the 2,000th anniversary of the founding of Emona, the Roman city that would become Ljubljana. The summer had been filled with activities around the celebration, including this exhibit at the City Museum and tours to all the Roman sites in Ljubljana, complete with costumed characters. "There's drinks and schmoozing at the City Museum, and Gregor asked me to join him at the Emona house excavation for an even schmoozier gathering with more expensive drinks, for donors or something, afterward."

"Doesn't much sound like your kind of thing." Maja took another long drag off her cigarette. Her gaze kept straying back to the shop windows.

"Not really. But Gregor needed a date, and I enjoy people-watching."

Maja laughed. "And no way in hell could Gregor take his actual love interest and still be one of the elite."

Jo arched her eyebrow at Maja. "What are you talking about?" She kept her tone light, but she was fiercely protective of Gregor.

"Keep your shirt on, boss lady. I don't care if Gregor's gay. I just know that he is, and despite the more liberal attitudes of those elites, he'd still have a hard time in that crowd with another dude on his arm. Everyone knows you're his beard. They just don't care because Gregor plays along with their bullshit."

Jo was surprised Maja was so frank. She usually kept herself to herself, did her work and ducked out, but her other job probably made her privy to a lot of gossip. Jo didn't really know what to say.

Maja bent over to stub out her cigarette in the ash can hidden behind the planter full of herbs at the front door. "The thing most people don't know is that Gregor is kind of your beard too." She pulled the elastic out of the bun on top of her head, and a curtain of neon blue hair, black at the roots, fell to her shoulders.

"Okay. What?" Jo didn't even pretend lightness this time.

"We all see you almost every day. I could set my watch by when you come downstairs and by when Milo or Rok or whoever that goddess is you've been seeing heads out in the morning. Otherwise, you do a pretty good job of keeping your private shit private. Being Gregor's public companion probably helps with that. I did overhear my boss one night talking with someone at the bar about being surprised you don't know or don't mind that Gregor's gay."

Jo was rarely at a complete loss for words.

Maja slapped her playfully on the shoulder and laughed. "Hey, it's no big deal. I like you and don't give two shits about who you, or Gregor, are sleeping with, as long as someone signs my paycheck."

Jo smiled. She couldn't quite bring herself to laugh, but she figured her not-so-secret secret was probably safe with Maja. Maja turned to go back inside, and Jo crossed the courtyard to the stairwell that led back up to the flats.

She saw the top of Goran's salt-and-pepper head bent over in the antique shop's windows as he selected an item from the display that faced the courtyard. As always, the window was dark and the "Zaprto" sign was on the door of the accountant's office next door to the antique shop. In all the time Jo had lived in the building, she'd never seen it open.

She'd asked Gregor about it. He said he didn't worry too much; they paid rent by bank draft and kept the place clean.

Did she really need a beard, as Maja had suggested? She wasn't ashamed of her life. Her son knew she dated around, and they were no more likely to discuss her sex life than they were his. Faron was first among the handful of people whose opinions mattered to her. The others she could count on one hand: Gregor, Vesna, Rok, and her Aunt Jackie. Rok because they'd been friends, with benefits, for almost fifteen years. And Jackie because she was the only "old life" family Jo kept in touch with.

It didn't do much good to dwell on these things, or on things in general. Jo's life suited her temperament. She liked the way things moved along in an orderly fashion, with just the little bit of turbulence and rush that came with restaurant life and none of the crap she'd left back home. Jo liked her personal excitement scheduled. Rok and Milo had days assigned to them, in her head at least. Helena, the "goddess she'd been seeing," was always a surprise, as she'd been from the beginning.

Not that she had never been attracted to women; she had just consistently preferred men. Her biggest concern about getting involved with Helena was stepping into unknown territory. She didn't want to hurt someone inadvertently by not wanting anything serious. Helena had put that fear to rest as quickly as she'd gotten Jo into bed. Romance wasn't her thing either. She was more feral and demanding than any man Jo had ever been with, and she wasn't even remotely sentimental. Helena would soon tire of her, so she intended to enjoy the ride while it lasted.

CHAPTER 3

Gregor met her in the courtyard downstairs. He wore an impeccably fitted suit. His dark hair was newly clipped but long enough to tousle if he, or someone else, ran fingers through it. The gray at his temples gave him just enough gravitas, but it was his eyes that had drawn her to flirt with him all those years ago. They were a soft brown, kind, and hid almost nothing.

He took her hand and twirled her about. "Don't you clean up well, Ms. Black T-shirt?"

She laughed. Her day-to-day work uniform was jeans or a long black skirt with a black T-shirt and a cardigan, also black. She liked her wardrobe simple enough to get dressed in a power outage without clashing. She'd also put on a little weight over the years and had lost some interest in flaunting her sturdy but curvier ass.

She knew how to dress herself well when the occasion called for it though. Her cocktail dress was a peacock blue she thought brought out the blue in her eyes. She paired it with silver, low-heeled sandals — too many years of chef clogs and Doc Martens to go teetering over Ljubljana's cobblestone streets in sky-high ankle breakers. Her hair was wrapped into a low bun, with a few loose pieces to avoid the ballerina-bunhead look. She wore the tiny pearl earrings her aunt had given her as a high school graduation gift — her only adornment besides the ring she always wore — a sparkly clutch, and a gray pashmina to stave off the chill October air.

She smoothed the lapel of Gregor's jacket. "Aren't we leaving a little too early to be fashionably late?"

"I'm supposed to meet Tomaž to discuss this new restaurant idea he has. He said he wanted five minutes before to give me the pitch."

"Do you think doing business with him is a good idea?" She tried to hide her distaste.

He knew her too well to miss it. "Why? He's very successful. Two of the busiest places on the river are his. The locals even brave the tourists to be seen in them."

"It's not that he isn't successful. I know he's your friend … he just comes off as shady." Damn it. She hadn't wanted to say it out loud.

"I'd hardly call him a friend, but I'm surprised at you. You and I are in no position to judge a man's personal life."

"No one I'm involved with has any delusions about my undying fidelity. You've been with Janez for two years and are head over heels in love, even if you can't shout it from the castle tower." She said it more testily than she had intended.

"Do you honestly think Tomaž's wife doesn't know that he's bedded every, well almost every, woman that works for him?" He looked at her like she was a child. He was the only person who could call her out on her bullshit and not make her want to kick him in the shins.

"Still. I'd call that shady. They work for him. It's asking for trouble." She leaned over to straighten the strap on her sandal. She slept around, but she kept that shit away from work, despite Vesna's teasing. Business was business, and anything else got complicated, fast.

"Look. I'll listen to the pitch—" He raised his hand when she started to interrupt him. "And. And I promise I'll talk to you before I make any decisions. In fact, why don't you just talk to him with me?"

She didn't relish spending any time with Tomaž, but this was the best offer she was going to get from Gregor. "I'll at least give you that." She could talk him out of it later if she saw legitimate reasons.

They walked in silence to the museum. It was just around the corner. A few people were milling around in French Revolution Square, in front of Križanke with its ivy-covered façade. It was one of Jo's favorite buildings in Ljubljana, especially in the fall, when the Virgina creeper that spilled down the front of the building turned crimson, setting off the green patina of the heavy bronze door with its raised cross.

Further down the square, close to the courtyard entrance to Križanke, Tomaž stood, flanked by two women. On one side was his business manager, petite, dark-haired Olga, dressed like she'd come as Stereotype: Repressed Librarian, right down to her heavy, dark-rimmed glasses and the pinched look on her face. On the other was his wife, Katarina, taller than Tomaž in her Louboutin stilettos. A mass of dark curls hung to her shoulders, and her flawlessly light-handed makeup played up her dark, upturned eyes. The fit of her black bandage dress belied the fact she'd had three daughters, the oldest of them the same age as Faron. Why the hell Tomaž needed to cheat was beyond Jo's understanding.

Gregor started the introductions, or rather, reintroductions. It was rare for Jo not to have met someone in his circles. "Olga, Katarina, you remember Jo Wiley?"

Olga shook hands and nodded curtly.

Katarina took her hand. "Yes," she said. "Our two eldest spend time at your teahouse with friends."

Jo nodded. "Yes, I know Veronika and Ivanka through Faron, my son. I don't think I've actually met your other daughter?" Jo couldn't remember her name.

"The baby is Ana. She is only 10. Ivanka speaks often of your cook, Frédéric, I believe. He helps her with her maths."

"Ah, yes. Our Fred is a man of many talents." Jo smiled.

Tomaž looked her up and down in a way that made her deeply uncomfortable. "I'm sure he is," he said, "and lucky to have you as his boss." He extended his hand to her. "Tomaž. But we have met?" He held her right hand in both of his warm, slightly damp ones. Dark and handsome, European artsy and expensively dressed, he was one of those charmers who looked attractive at a distance, but who had a personality that oozed over everything up close. She'd run into enough Tomažes in her twenties to peg them for sleazes at "hello." Maybe Katarina had been too young when she'd married him to see it. She certainly could have done better.

Jo extricated her hand. "We have, yes. A few times. At Gregor's New Year parties."

Tomaž nodded. "Yes. Of course."

Of course he remembered. A number of New Years ago, she had "accidentally" dumped a drink in his lap when he ran a hand up the back of her leg as she walked by. Jerk.

Gregor broke the tension before it built beyond her ability to be polite. "So, tell me about this idea of yours."

Tomaž startled almost imperceptibly, as if Gregor's voice had brought him back from a daydream. "Yes. The farm my parents owned near Tolmin is in some disrepair now. I hate to see it crumbling."

Gregor nodded and waited for Tomaž to continue. Jo loved to watch him work, especially with someone like Tomaž. Gregor never showed his hand and always insisted the other person speak first. They always found it flattering. Jo had seen how it gave Gregor the upper hand.

"I like the idea of these destination restaurants such as Fäviken." He stopped. "Miss Wiley, you must know of a Blackberry Farm in Tennessee. I believe that is where you are from?"

"I've read about it, but I've never been. On the rare occasions I go back, I spend my time in Chattanooga."

"Of course." Tomaž continued, addressing Gregor, "Given the popularity of these places, it would seem we could do well to turn my childhood home into such a destination. The setting is quite beautiful."

Gregor nodded. "It's worth looking into. But why are you trying to interest me?"

Leave it to Gregor to get right to the point. "Yes. Of course." It was Tomaž's turn to nod.

Jo was convinced ninety percent of Tomaž's vocabulary consisted of "of course."

He continued, "It would be a large undertaking. Renovation of the house and barn as a restaurant and inn and replanting the vegetable and herb gardens. Maybe bring in livestock … goats, chickens. This is more than the work for one person, or one person's money."

Gregor did not nod. "I see. I would need to look at the property and discuss it with my associates before making any kind of decision."

"Of course." Tomaž looked pointedly at Jo.

She cringed inside and started a tally of the times Tomaž said "of course" to distract herself from telling him what she thought he should do with his business idea.

"Olga can arrange for you to go out to the property. I'm traveling later this week to Fäviken. And I hope soon to visit the U.S. to see Blackberry Farm and Blue Hill at Stone Barns in New York." Tomaž looked again at Jo. "Perhaps, Miss Wiley, you can offer some recommendations for visiting Tennessee?"

She wouldn't embarrass Gregor by being rude. "I can email you a list or something."

"Of course. But I would like to see this teahouse of yours. Maybe I will come tomorrow to see you."

"We're closed on Sundays." She wanted to be sick. Tomaž was oilier than she remembered, and she had zero desire to spend one more second talking with him on the street, let alone to have him in her shop. Katarina and Olga had been silent through the whole conversation. Jo turned and looked up at Katarina. "Would you like to come on Monday instead? I can introduce you to Fred."

A flicker of annoyance flashed in Tomaž's face. Katarina seemed surprised, but she smiled. "I would enjoy that. Are you busy when you first open? We would hate to be a distraction."

Jo was relieved. "No. Things don't really pick up until late. Let's plan for four." If she couldn't find a solid reason to not go into business with Tomaž, she could at least cultivate an ally in his wife. Besides, Katarina seemed like she could use a friend.

More people had gathered at the entrance of the museum. They were looking at their watches and finishing cigarettes. Gregor placed his hand in the small of Jo's back and nudged her toward the museum. It was an unspoken signal between old friends that the conversation had ended.

Tomaž and his companions disappeared into one of the many corners of the museum after they all walked in together. There were several faces she knew, some government types and business people she'd met through Gregor. There were also a few artists and writers she'd known for years, either from the university or the shop. Lots of polite nods were exchanged across the crowded rooms, along with a few air kisses from some of Gregor's admirers.

The crowd murmured and buzzed around them. Glasses of champagne clinked on the trays carried by starched young servers. Gregor snagged two flutes from one and handed a glass to Jo. Over his shoulder, she caught the impression of a face that shouldn't be there, but she couldn't place it. She brushed the thought aside as the crowd began to hush and move into the interior courtyard of the museum. A small public address system crackled to life with the voice of the mayor of Ljubljana.

"*Dobrodošli in hvala lepa.* The city of Ljubljana and the City Museum appreciate your attendance and your support of what has been a very successful exhibit and festival of the ancient history of Ljubljana, Emona." He pronounced Ljubljana, *Loo-blana,* like a native to the city.

The crowd clapped politely. Jo bet dollars to donuts not ten people in the room had seen the exhibit at the museum before this evening. No one plays tourists in their own town, including her. The mayor said a few more perfunctory sentences about supporting tourism and preserving Ljubljana's past. There was more polite clapping. He seemed to be on board with brevity, and Jo was grateful.

"Thank you all again. Please enjoy the exhibit, the music, and the champagne."

In the corner of the courtyard a quartet began to play. For a moment it sounded like the theme from *M*A*S*H* floating on the evening air, but it resolved into a chamber piece she wasn't familiar with. Was this the song that had been stuck in her head all day? Where had it come from?

More waiters swooped through the few candlelit tables scattered about the courtyard, collecting empty flutes and replacing them with full ones.

She adjusted her shawl around her shoulders and looked up to see Helena standing in front of her with an amused grin, draped in a cream-colored gown that suggested a toga without looking like a costume. Her dark hair was shining in the candlelight, the edges of her bob brushing her jawline. In her expensive-looking heels, she towered over Jo, who stood a solid 5'7" flat-footed.

"I'm not surprised to find him here." Helena fluttered her hand in a wave at Gregor. "I am surprised to see you in something besides a Black Flag T-shirt."

"It does seem to surprise people I don't live in an apron and clogs." Jo smiled up into Helena's angular face.

"It suits you, this non-apron attire. It suits you quite well." Helena arched a perfectly drawn eyebrow, her signature gesture for I'd like to fuck you right now, no please or thank you about it. "What are you doing after this?" Then to Gregor, "You aren't dragging her off to some dreary after-party are you?"

Gregor smiled. "Maybe for a few minutes. Then she's all yours."

Helena laughed. "Not quite." She turned her gaze back to Jo.

"What did you have in mind?" Jo wasn't very good at playing coquette.

"Hm. Find me before you leave, and we can discuss." Helena ran her hand down Jo's arm, gently squeezing her fingers as she moved away to greet other friends.

Gregor chuckled when she'd gone. "Jo: always full of surprises."

"Are you surprised?" She had told him she was seeing a woman; she hadn't said who. He'd made it clear he wasn't interested in hearing about the fleeting ones.

"Not really. You're attractive and exotically American.

Helena's a collector. It makes perfect sense, just don't expect it to last."

"Spoken like a man of experience, but 'exotically American'? Really. Maybe 20 years ago, but Ljubljana is crawling with Americans now."

"You aren't a tourist. You live here. And I have known Helena a long time."

"Duly noted. And you don't need to worry. My heart's in no danger."

"Now that I do worry about." Gregor turned to her with a more serious look.

She sighed. "I'm perfectly happy. Things are as they should be."

"Things are as you think you want them. You've done an excellent job of leaving exactly no room for someone to fall in love with you or you with them."

"Exactly." She took a sip of her champagne. "Too dangerous." She didn't want the lecture. Besides, she could recite it for herself verbatim by now.

"Jo ... " He would have rolled his eyes if he weren't too proper for such a thing. "But I didn't invite you to lecture you." He motioned her off. "Go. Mingle. Do whatever."

"Yes, sir." She gave him a half-assed bowing salute, champagne glass in hand. "I think I'll go upstairs and actually look at the exhibit."

Several attendees were waiting for the elevator. The stairs would be quicker. Near the stairs, Jo noticed that a small, glass case labeled "From the Well" had drawn a handful of attendees. Olga and Katarina stood among them, admiring the items in the case. Olga was, at least. She seemed transfixed by the display. Katarina seemed uncharacteristically fidgety, as if she couldn't get away from the display fast enough. Jo couldn't tell if the look on her face was fear or revulsion.

Katarina succeeded in pulling Olga away, and they walked together back toward the courtyard. Jo stopped at the case to see what had so disconcerted Katarina.

It contained some Roman coins, a bone toothpick, a few potsherds, a small makeup or perfume container made of pottery, and a child's doll. Dated from the time of Emona, the pieces were carefully arranged on black museum velvet and neatly labeled with small white cards in both Slovenian and English. They'd all been uncovered during the excavation and preservation of the Roman well in the basement of the building. Maybe that doll was the thing that had unnerved Katarina. About half the height of a modern fashion doll, its individual pottery pieces were held together with wire to reconstruct what it must have looked like. It was finished with the kind of black and red glazes seen on Roman vases. Its worn face had been carved to reveal the lighter clay underneath, and the light gave a malevolent cast to its eyes.

It was not a doll she would have enjoyed as a child. Despite the simplicity of its etched-in face, the doll's eyes seemed to follow her as she walked around the case. Once she'd really seen it, Jo couldn't get away from it fast enough either.

She walked up the stairs behind two stocky men in suits discussing the EU's economic woes and was grateful not to be part of that conversation. She was very much interested in politics and the impact of globalization, but her opinion would probably not be welcome, and tonight she wanted to just enjoy the parade of Ljubljana's pretty people and the company of her "date," wherever he'd gotten to.

The conversation with Tomaž continued to bother her. He got under her skin, and she couldn't shake the feeling it was a very bad idea for Gregor to get into bed with him. Poor choice of words, but still. She didn't usually put much faith in hunches. When it came to business decisions, she preferred a logical balancing of pros and cons. Business this might be, but Gregor was family, and Tomaž nauseated her.

She strolled through the gallery distractedly, glancing at the dioramas and artifacts and reading the placards. After the first room, she was absorbed by the displays and read every card. A red carpet leading from room to room was emblazoned with the names of Roman gods and goddesses, an especially nice touch. Excellent lighting against a great deal of black drapery highlighted pieces of statues and vessels from every era of Ljubljana and told the story of a place tied to the river. A stone head of an ancient river god loomed in the last corner as she exited the exhibit.

A part of the head was missing at an angle toward the nose, but one stern eye looked out from the marble. It was part of a statue of Achelous, a river deity of Greece. Early Roman worshippers had brought him to their new outpost on the edges of the empire. The story of Achelous was presented in bold type over a washed-out, handwritten version of France Prešeren's nineteenth-century poem "The Water Man." She'd memorized part of the poem when she was learning Slovenian, mostly to impress Gregor, who knew by heart more poems, in both their languages, than she had ever read. The Water Man carried the woman who would dance with no one but him, the handsome stranger, into a whirlpool and was never seen again.

Gregor found her just as she got back to the bottom of the stairs. An hour had passed, and he was ready to stroll to the smaller gathering at the visitor's building and overlook at the Emona House excavation.

"Have you seen Helena?" Jo looked around him and over his shoulder at the thinning crowd.

"She went outside earlier. Maybe she's also going to the reception at the excavation."

They walked back out onto French Revolution Square. A few older guests and women wearing impractical shoes for walking were boarding a small bus.

Gregor looked down at her feet. "Are those walking shoes?"

"They are. Not quite as comfortable as boots, but walkable."

He offered her his arm. She took it and nestled up to him for warmth against the chill and the rising damp from the river. Vesna was her soul sister and partner in crime, but Gregor was the much cooler older brother she'd wanted when she was a child. He looked out for her but always took her seriously, even when she'd first arrived in Ljubljana. He later told her that he hadn't been sure what she was running from, but it had been clear she was running.

He had protected her in his way ever since that first night at the club. He was also the closest thing Faron had to a father. If not for Gregor, and more of his interventions than she would like to admit, she would not have been able to stay in Slovenia or have the life she had now. Like an older brother, though, he had a way of needling her in the places she'd prefer to keep private.

Gregor interrupted her thoughts. "What I said earlier, about worrying about you …"

"I know. It's because you care, and you want me to be happy. I appreciate it, but you know what the deal is."

"I don't believe Dušan was the only man in Slovenia, or even all of the world, you could love. You do know people meet on the internet all the time, right?"

"I know about internet dating. I'm not interested in an inbox full of dick pics." Jo nudged him. "It isn't just about Dušan. That hurt a lot, but not enough to put me off for life. I really just like being able to do what I want. Love is too complicated." How many times had they had this conversation? How many different ways could she tell him that she had enough people in her life?

"And you don't love Rok? Really? You've been fucking him for fifteen years, and you don't love him?"

"I love him like I love you, aside from the fucking part. It turns out that he is possibly even less inclined to fall in love than I am. Having a wife or girlfriend would definitely put a crimp in his vagabond lifestyle."

"Where is he these days?" Gregor adjusted his arm under her hand.

"He's in town, but he's on some celibacy kick to prepare for a pilgrimage to … somewhere. He told me. … Oh! To Nepal."

"So what do the two of you do if he's celibate? Play mahjong?

"No, chess mostly. And he's teaching me how to knit."

Gregor stopped. "Rok is teaching you how to knit?"

She looked up at him, miffed. "Yes. We are actually friends, per the whole 'friends with benefits' thing."

"I get that. I'm just trying to imagine that mountain goat knitting."

"You laugh, but he's quite talented. He made me a beautiful pair of socks."

"You never cease to amaze me."

She squeezed his arm, and they continued on. "Good. I'd hate it if you thought I was boring."

They walked on with a few others out to Mirje at the edge of the central district and into the residential area where the Emona house had been excavated in the 1960s. Along the way, they passed a community garden, one of the few left in the central city. It was too dark to see much, just enough light to make out the wired grape trellis near the shoulder-high brick wall that separated the garden from the sidewalk.

The entrance to the site was near a small block of flats and looked like the alleyway to someone's back garden. Gregor saw the small museum sign on the fence, or they would've missed it. Beyond, fairy lights were wrapped around the open gates and railing at the entrance as a signal to after-party-goers that they had arrived.

Another waiter met them inside the entrance with a tray of champagne flutes. Gregor took two and handed one to her.

He held up his glass to her. "I propose a toast. A small one, yes?"

She asked, "To what?"

"To continued happiness — whatever form that takes." He

looked her in the eyes, smiling, and they clinked their flutes. He took a sip then said, "Okay. Let's see who's here, and then you can go find Helena and abandon me."

She looked around for familiar faces and spotted Tomaž speaking with a tall, heavily built man in a tight-fitting suit. The stub of a ponytail and the full beard suggested he probably didn't live in suits, but he wore one well. He of the ponytail was talking with his hands, apparently describing something to Tomaž. Tomaž was nodding and making occasional asides to Katarina. She looked vague, maybe glazed by too much champagne.

Tomaž caught Jo looking at him. He waved, inviting her and Gregor to join them. She still had no desire to spend her evening with His Oiliness, but she did want to meet his friend. She took Gregor's wrist, and they merged into the small circle.

"Matjaž, I don't believe you've met Gregor or his lovely friend Miss Jo Wiley? She is the proprietress of the teashop on Zajčeva." Tomaž put his hand on her arm and turned her toward Matjaž. It was a possessive gesture, and it made her skin crawl.

Matjaž shook her hand. "It's a pleasure to meet you." His hands were large and warm and very calloused.

Definitely not a suit guy.

"I know your shop. I've passed it often, but I'm not much of a tea drinker."

"Oh, it isn't just mine. Gregor and I own it with another business partner. And we do offer things besides tea." She smiled up at him, trying not to play her whole hand with one glance. He wasn't classically handsome, but he had an appealing familiarity. His hazel eyes were flecked with gold, and deep laugh lines showed at the corners when he smiled back.

Damn.

"Tomaž was telling me about his idea for this destination restaurant in Tolmin. What are your thoughts?" Matjaž looked her in the eye.

She didn't want to speak her true mind in front of Tomaž, not yet anyway. Nor did she want to lie; besides, she wasn't particularly adept at it. "I think it's an intriguing idea, though I haven't seen the property. Tomaž would be the expert on such a high-end restaurant and its prospects. If you've seen the teahouse, you know we cater to a very different clientele."

Tomaž chimed in, "I imagine you do know business. Renegade Tea has been very successful. How long have you been open?"

"This year is ten years. I'm not the business person. I leave that to Gregor and Vesna. I sling tea and make fancy sandwiches."

"Jo, you sell yourself short." Gregor put his arm around her shoulders and pulled her into him. He knew she was uncomfortable and was enjoying it a bit. "You have an excellent palate and formidable culinary skills."

Her cheeks were flushed, and she felt embarrassed at the blush. "Thank you, Gregor, but I don't think my knife skills equate to Magnus Nilsson level cuisine and luxury fine dining. I am flattered though."

Tomaž laughed. "Whatever your skills are, Miss Wiley,

I'm looking forward to tasting your wares on Monday."

Gross. He was lewd and demeaning at the same time, calling her Miss like she was in her teens and talking about "tasting your wares." His wife didn't even blink. She must have developed immunity to her husband's smarm. But Matjaž looked uncomfortable.

Jo continued the fake-friendly act and made her voice sound pleasant. "Yes. I'm looking forward to seeing you and Katarina at the shop. I'll even turn the music down a bit."

Gregor squeezed her shoulders a little harder as a reminder to be nice. "Matjaž, what is your interest in a high-end restaurant?"

"I'm more interested in the idea of preserving and redesigning the farmhouse and barn. I own a firm that specializes in historic preservation and reconstruction." He produced two business cards from his suit pocket and handed one to Gregor and the other to Jo.

She held the cream-colored card out to read it but had trouble in the dim light. "And you live in Škofja Loka," she said, squinting.

"Yes. It would be nice to have a short commute for once. I've been on a project in the Veneto for the last year and a half."

"Would anyone else like another glass of champagne?" Gregor motioned to the nearest waiter with a full tray.

"None for me, thank you. I don't care for it." Katarina still looked a bit distracted, but her voice was firm.

Gregor passed a glass to Matjaž and Tomaž, who set their empties back on the tray. He took one for himself and gave one to Jo.

Last one, she decided. Or she wouldn't have walking-home legs, let alone shoes.

She noticed a little hush in the party chatter. Conversations around them seemed to be stopping, and then there was a silence so complete it made the hair stand up on the back of Jo's neck. A dropped glass shattered against the decking. She heard a wave of gasps making its way to her. The crowd was shifting to the railing that overlooked what was once the winter room of the house. She felt, more than heard, a whisper behind her ear. "Jolene, leave. Now."

Gregor got to the railing before she did and put a hand on her arm. "Don't look."

But it was too late.

Helena was sprawled out on the ancient black and white mosaic floor below them, partially hidden in the shadow of the canopy over the site. Her head was at an unnatural angle. Her eyes were wide with surprise, but there was no light in them or thought behind them. A cry caught in Jo's throat, and she turned her face into Gregor's chest to try to blot out the image of Helena lying there.

Matjaž came up behind them. "No. Helena? No. No. No." He climbed over the railing to reach her.

"You mustn't move her." A museum security guard tried to push between Jo and Gregor. "We need to call the police."

Several people pulled out cell phones at once.

Gregor took control of the situation. "Only one call needs to be made. Tomaž?"

Tomaž nodded. "Dialing now." His face had gone white.

Katarina stood next to him, her face still blank as it had been earlier. Olga appeared at her elbow, pinched-looking as before, but shaken.

Down on the ancient floor, Matjaž knelt and then sat back on his heels. He cradled Helena's head in his lap. He was rocking back and forth. "Call an ambulance. Please. Someone call an ambulance."

The man who had muscled past her clambered over the railing and joined Matjaž on the ruins. He leaned over to speak with him. "Do you know her? Was she your date?"

"She's my sister. We came together." Matjaž's words were halting, caught by the raw edge of emotion flooding him. Jo was in shock, and not just at the sight of Helena's twisted body. Matjaž was her brother? Jo really didn't know much about Helena. The time they'd spent together hadn't involved much talking.

She knew she was staring openly at Matjaž, but she couldn't stop herself. She was rooted where she stood. Her insides felt like ice. Gregor spoke soothingly to her in English and Slovenian, but his words didn't penetrate enough to mean anything. She sat as he told her to, her champagne glass forgotten and Matjaž's card clutched in her hand.

"The police are on their way. Would you like some water?" Gregor squatted down so he was eye level with her. He searched her face, waiting for a response.

"No. I'm fine." She wasn't fine. "I'm cold." Her teeth were chattering, and she couldn't make it stop.

He took his jacket off and draped it over her shoulders.

The weight and smell of it was comforting but didn't make her any warmer. The only clear thought was to do what the whispered voice had said, to run away from this horrible place with all these people milling around while Helena lay dead like a child's doll thrown down in a tantrum.

"Let's leave." She grabbed his hand.

"We can't leave yet. We have to wait."

No sooner had the words left his mouth than the first wave of police arrived. The sirens flooded out all other sound, and the lights bathed them all in alternating flashes of blue. One officer went down to the ruins. He checked Helena's pulse, but there was little doubt she was dead; there was no Helena in the unfocused stare. Jo was processing the events around her indiscriminately, as if her eyes and brain had been reduced to camera and film: everything came through with the same mix of urgency and detachment. Two other officers herded the crowd away from the deck back out into the parking area. One officer questioned Gregor but didn't make them leave. Paramedics arrived but didn't go down to Helena's body after the first officer answered their question with a grave nod.

Gregor spoke to a young paramedic closest to where Jo sat. "I'm sorry. Could you have a look at my friend? Something's not right."

The woman crouched down and looked into Jo's face. "Ma'am, can you tell me your name?"

"Jo. Jo Wiley."

"Okay, Jo. How are you feeling?"

"I'm cold."

The paramedic took both of Jo's limp hands in hers. "Your hands are like ice. I'd like to take you to the ambulance so we can warm you up a bit." She looked up at Gregor and nodded, then said, "I think she should go to the hospital. Might be shock. A doc can check her out and maybe give her a sedative. I'll check with the officer in charge to see if she can leave."

The paramedic disappeared. There were more police now. They were asking people their names. Two stood with Matjaž, still on the ruins of the winter room floor, asking their questions. His ponytail had come undone, and his hair was wild where he'd pushed his hands through it. Jo had to look away from the pain etched in his eyes and the grimace of his mouth. More officers cordoned off the place where Helena's body lay. The edges of everything — the people, the railing around the deck, her own hand — seemed to be lit in high contrast, like a Bergman film or one of Dušan's photographs.

The paramedic returned. "Ms. Wiley, let's go in the ambulance. Mister…?" She looked up at Gregor.

"Bregant."

"Mr. Bregant, the inspector in charge said we can take Ms. Wiley and you to the hospital. They'll have questions for both of you in the morning."

He nodded. "Jo, can you stand?"

She nodded and stood, then collapsed back onto the chair. Her legs were frozen, and she couldn't make them work. Gregor and the paramedic caught her and walked her between them to the ambulance.

The paramedic got Jo onto a gurney and layered a heat blanket over her with another blanket. She stayed with Jo, and Gregor rode up front with the driver to the hospital.

Someone else was in the ambulance with them. She looked around, but she couldn't see where. Her stomach sank. This was it. This was how it must have started for her mother.

When they arrived at the hospital, the receiving area was filled with people waiting for her. No one from the hospital or the ambulance crew seemed to notice or to care. Why wasn't anyone pushing them away? What could all those people possibly want from her?

CHAPTER 4

The longer Gustaf was there, the better he understood that the heart of the strangeness of this city was the river — the river of seven names. Its waters rose from and disappeared into the karst six times before bubbling up again in the marshes, where it became the brief but important Ljubljanica. Ten kilometers east of the capital, the murky river joined the glass-green Sava, found the Danube, and finally emptied into the Black Sea. It carried all the mundane debris and supernatural detritus of eastern Europe to be discarded in that basin, coloring the lives of those who lived along the way. There was a reason this was a part of the world that would never find peace.

Thousands of artifacts had been pulled from the depths of the Ljubljanica over the years by treasure hunters and professional archaeologists. More objects had been discovered in the marshes from which the river flowed. The most spectacular find was an ancient wooden wheel, the oldest ever discovered. Its renown fed the desire of unscrupulous fortune seekers, despite laws requiring diving and digging permits. It was impossible to trace everything. Many pieces disappeared into private collections, away from public view.

Archaeologists and amateurs speculated about the concentration of artifacts in the river. The prevailing theory held that the river had been a sacred boundary and a place to make sacrifices. That could explain the high quality and craftsmanship of the finds. For Gustaf, it also explained the power, both benevolent and malevolent, many of these artifacts carried. He had seen that nearly everything of supernatural origin in the city was connected in some way to the river.

The symbol of the city itself, the dragon, was also tied to the marshes. Jason and the Argonauts, after stealing the Golden Fleece from Colchis, followed the Danube to the Sava and then the Ljubljanica. The travelers overwintered in the marshes, where Jason encountered a dragon. He slew it, as the heroes of old were wont to do. The slain dragon became the symbol of the city, and Jason its first (brief) resident of note. The Argonauts disassembled their boats and carried them to the Adriatic to reassemble and complete the journey home. If Jason had known how his story would end, he might have stayed in the marsh.

After Jason's time, the Romans brought with them the cult of Achelous, a Greek river deity. It was Gustaf's belief that many of the recovered sacrificial artifacts had been placed in the keep of the river by those asking the god's favor or thanking him for safe passage. Achelous was a protector of the river and marshes, and unlike many other minor deities of the Greeks and their Roman echoes, he retained some power in the region. He appeared in works by the national poet as the Water Man, who steals beautiful but vain women to be his aquatic brides. A first-century stone head excavated from the Emona archeological layer was recognized as Achelous and put on public display.

As part of the preparations for the anniversary celebrations, the City Museum had embarked on a renovation in the basement of its building on Trg francoske revolucije. The work included preservation of an in-situ Roman well. Gustaf had hoped it would be only a minor disturbance. He now had reason to believe that was not the case.

He was obligated to report any activities at sites of interest to the Board, so he tried to sum up his thoughts in an email to Bettine. He had little doubt that Helena Belak's death was more than it appeared. His contact in the capital's police department had phoned him late to express the same thought. He heard the world weariness in her voice. She hadn't truly accepted the reality he dealt in, but each incident chipped away at her skepticism. She usually did a better job of hiding that.

It looked like a murder. In Ljubljana, where such things were rare, news of a murder would be plastered on newsstands and be blaring from every local radio and television show by morning. There would be no covering it up. He told his contact to treat it as she would any suspicious death, and he would handle the rest. With a yawn in her voice, she agreed and hung up.

He finished his message to Bettine and closed his computer. This would be a complicated business. The place, the players, and the timing all created an intricate web across the city, touching individuals he'd made diligent efforts to keep at a distance.

He stood and walked to the map to examine the blue flags

dotted across the neighborhoods of Ljubljana. He traced the line of the river to Trnovo, to a house near the church at the center of the district, and plucked a pin from the map. Helena Belak's name was printed in his cramped lettering on the flag. He twirled the pin between his thumb and index finger, then placed it in a silver dish on the nearest bookshelf with the pins of others who had crossed into what lay beyond this world.

CHAPTER 5

Jo came home to her empty apartment. Could it be only this morning that she'd rushed out with Milo, only hours ago that she'd put on silver sandals and gone to meet Gregor? It all felt like days, maybe years, ago.

She took her sandals off in the entryway and padded to the kitchen for a drink of water, faintly humming the tune that had been running through her head all day. It was the M*A*S*H theme, whose title, she recalled, was "Suicide is Painless." A terrible earworm after the night she'd had.

A layer of fine gray dust covered everything in her kitchen. Her bare footprints from the door had left a trail.

What the hell?

The plaster on the ceiling was smooth; the dust hadn't come from there.

She rinsed out a glass in the sink and filled it from the tap. She leaned against the counter, wondering why her usually pristine apartment looked like it had been vacant for years. The night's events had exhausted her, and she didn't need this on top of it.

She raised her glass for another sip, and through it she saw her father sitting on the futon. His clothes were sodden, and two tendrils of milfoil hung from his collar down the front of his shirt. His skin was gray and blue — blotchy, with abrasions on his cheekbones and brow.

She dropped the glass. It landed upright at her feet without spilling a drop of water.

Okay. This wasn't real. She was dreaming. Helena wasn't dead, and her drowned father certainly was not dripping Tennessee river water all over her floor.

"Hello, Jolene."

No, this was not real. She pinched herself hard on the top of her thigh but still couldn't force herself out of the dream.

So maybe she was awake. Or crazy.

Her father spoke again. "It's real, and it isn't. You are asleep though."

"You're dead. I saw you. I saw your body before they took you away. This is not happening." An edge of anger crept into her voice. If she was about to lose her shit, she would fight it all the way down.

"Jolene. Calm down. It is real, and I need to talk to you. I need to warn you."

"Warn me? She's already dead."

"It isn't about that woman. It's about you."

She shook her head, as if the dream was an image on an Etch-a-sketch, and she could smooth the fine silver dust again for a clean slate. "No. This is not happening. I'm sane, and I am not having a conversation with my dead father."

"Jolene, please listen."

"Stop calling me that. Nobody calls me that." She shook her head again.

"Okay. Jay. Please? Just listen to me. You are asleep, but this is not a dream. You don't have to be asleep. I just didn't want to scare you."

She stared at him.

"I'm not the only one who can talk to you."

"What does that even mean?"

He stood and took a few steps toward her.

"I don't understand what you're saying."

"Just be careful. There's something here, something dangerous."

"What are you saying?"

"I love you. I have to go."

"Wait! I don't understand."

He was gone. The futon and the floor were dry.

The glass at her feet shattered into a thousand pieces, spraying her with water and glinting shards.

She woke up bolt upright in bed.

Faron and Gregor appeared at the door of her bedroom and moved to either side of her. Gregor leaned down to push her hair off her forehead. Faron sat on the edge of the bed. "Mom? You okay there?"

It was still a jolt sometimes, how much he looked like his father. He had the same dark hair and the same build, broad-shouldered but slender, like a diver. Only his eyes, stormy blue like hers, gave him away as something other than a Dušan clone.

"Yeah. Just a bad dream." And a glimpse at her deepest fears. She took a deep breath.

Both men were staring at her now, worry etched between their eyebrows.

She looked at Faron and up at Gregor. "Is she really dead?"

Gregor nodded. "Murdered."

"Murdered? People don't get murdered in Ljubljana." Maybe she was still dreaming.

"Mom, someone broke her neck."

"How? With all those people there? No. She must have fallen from the deck or tripped down on the ruins."

Gregor looked down at her, frowning. "She didn't. The police want to talk to you this morning, as soon as you're up to it."

"This morning? What time is it?"

Faron pulled his phone out of his pocket and woke it up to confirm the time. "About ten."

"Fuck. I was supposed to let Igor in downstairs." She rummaged around for something to put on and tried to get up.

Gregor stopped her with his hands on her shoulders. "Already done. Vesna heard us come up last night."

She shook her head. "I don't remember that."

Faron laughed. "I'm not surprised, between the champagne

and the tranquilizer they gave you."

She bristled. "It's not funny." Nothing was funny this morning.

"Sorry. You're usually the queen of gallows humor." Faron took her hand again. "It's just not every day that you get to see your mom tanked — even if it's for a bad reason."

"Apology accepted. It's been a while since I've been this close to the gallows. And how did you get here, anyway?"

"Vesna texted me. She thought you might need me after she met you guys on the stairs."

Gregor said, "I tried to send him home, but he insisted. He slept on the futon, and I slept on Vesna's couch." He stepped to her armoire looking for a robe. "How did she get that thing into her flat?"

"No idea." She rubbed her eyes. "What's next?" She ran both her hands through her hair. Her fingers caught in a tangle of knots.

Faron stood. "Well, Gregor's going to take you to the police station, and I'm going to work. I can come back tonight if you want me to."

"Maybe? I'll text you." Jo tried to finger-comb the mess of her hair. "I need some coffee and a shower. I feel like shit."

"Trank hangover." Faron put one hand over his heart and emoted. "Mom, I'm shocked at your chemical use." He couldn't keep a straight face through the whole sentence.

She threw a pillow at him. "Go to work. I'll be fine. Or I won't, but he can handle it, I'm sure." She waved her hand in Gregor's direction.

"Yes, I can." Gregor offered her a red silk kimono. "Now to the shower with you. I'll make more coffee. Faron and I finished the first batch."

Faron leaned over to kiss his mother on the top of the head. Jo remembered the first time he'd done it, after a growth spurt when he was finally taller than she was. Faron waved from the bedroom door. "Love you. Text me, or I'll just come over and harass you."

"I will. I love you too," she called out to him before he closed the front door. The sound of him pounding down the wooden stairs two at a time reverberated through the wall.

She stood up to find she was wearing only underwear and a tank top.

"Um, did you or Faron undress me?"

Gregor backed out of the bedroom so she could pass him and head to the bathroom. "Actually, Vesna and I played Barbie with you while you were passed out. Vesna chose your ensemble."

"Thanks."

"Faron's right. You are pretty amusing when you're wasted, whatever the circumstances."

She glared at him. Losing control was right up there with rooms full of tarantulas and carloads of clowns on her list of lifetime phobias.

He turned her gently toward the bathroom. "Shower. Coffee. Clothes. Then I'll walk to the station with you."

She grabbed a towel from the back of the door, hung her robe in its place, and stepped up into the tiny bathroom. She would have preferred a soaking tub, but there wasn't room without sacrificing the little kitchen she had. Through the shower wall she could hear Gregor humming in the kitchen while he made coffee. It sounded like the theme from M*A*S*H. Her dad used to hum it all the time.

Maybe it was something else.

She turned off the water and reached over to grab her towel from the sink — the only spot in the bathroom that stayed dry when the shower was on. She rubbed the towel through her hair and over her body before wrapping her hair with it. She opened the bathroom door just enough to stick her arm out and grab her robe off the hook on the outside of the door. Gregor had seen her naked plenty of times over the years, but he was always a little embarrassed by her immodesty.

Covered and mostly dry, she joined him in the kitchen. He waved her to the table that served for dining and as her desk.

"Sit. I made you some oatmeal. I had to boil water for the coffee anyway."

She sat in the chair opposite the kitchen.

Gregor placed a blue pottery mug of milky coffee in front of her, then brought a red pottery bowl of oatmeal with a small pat of butter and splash of milk. He handed her a spoon, a heavy one, with U.S. Navy embossed on the handle. It was one of the few things she had that had belonged to her father; she'd packed it in her backpack when she'd left Chattanooga.

"Thank you. I feel like I've been a pain in the ass."

"You would have done exactly the same thing if it were me, or Vesna, or Faron, or a perfect stranger."

"Still." Jo stirred the butter and milk into her oatmeal. "Thank you." She took a bite. It all tasted like ashes in her mouth, but she swallowed it anyway. "I still can't wrap my head around this. Murdered? Helena. For god's sake, why?"

"I don't know." He sat down across from her. He held a mug, a gray one, in his hands. "But there's something you should know. Before you go to the police."

She put the spoon down. "That sounds ominous."

"I was trying to explain what happened to Faron when he got here last night. He wanted to know who'd died, and when I told him he blanched."

She pulled back in surprise. "Why? Does he know her?"

"Yes. Quite well." Gregor looked down into the depths of his coffee mug. It wasn't like him to be at a loss for words.

She froze. "How well?"

"They were sleeping together."

She choked on her coffee. He started to get up.

She put her hand up. "I'm fine." She coughed loudly. "Maybe some water, though, please."

He handed her his glass of water from the table. "Are you okay?"

"God, no. What the fuck? Did you tell him how I knew Helena?"

"No, but when I hesitated, he guessed."

She stood up. "Jesus."

"Apparently Helena's collecting was more extensive than I thought."

She put her hands on the back of the chair. "I think I'm going to be sick."

"I thought it would be better coming from me than the police if they know. Or from Faron even. He was mortified."

She flopped back into the chair. "I bet. Nothing like finding out you and your mom have the same taste in women."

He looked down into his coffee mug again.

"There's something else, isn't there?" He wasn't being cagey exactly, but there was something he wasn't telling her.

"Not really. It's just that maybe that's an answer to your question about why someone would kill her."

"Faron? He didn't even know."

"No, not Faron. But maybe there was someone else who wasn't happy to share her, or share with her."

She pushed the bowl of oatmeal away and stared at him. "I keep thinking about all those people at the hospital. I know something like this is sensational, but it seemed pretty awful to flood the place."

He seemed genuinely surprised. "What people?"

———

Jo was ushered into a small interview room furnished with four hard chairs and a table that held a heavy black recorder and a steaming cup of coffee. Her interviewer introduced herself as Investigator Marta Klančnik of the Homicide and Sexual Offense Division and motioned for her to sit, asking if she wanted something to drink.

"The coffee's fresh." Marta gestured toward her cup.

"Yes, please, with milk, if possible."

"I'll be right back." She left, closing the door behind her.

Jo inspected the room. Everything was gray. The walls. The chairs. The table. Everything except the recorder and Marta's bright orange paper cup filled with coffee. The room even smelled gray, like damp and old linoleum. The coffee barely registered against it. She wasn't claustrophobic, but the oppressive airlessness of the room would be a nightmare for someone who was. She looked at her hands.

Her nails were short and without polish. Long manicured nails didn't fly with restaurant work. Her cuticles looked a little beaten up. Everyone took turns washing dishes whenever they were between dishwashers, which seemed to be all the time. She didn't believe in asking anyone who worked for her to do something she wasn't willing to do herself. She twirled the wide silver band she wore on her right-hand ring finger. The small amethyst point set into it had been a gift from Faron for Mother's Day when he was about ten. A friend of Rok's who did silversmithing had set it for her. Unless she was working, she always wore it.

Marta returned with another orange cup filled with milky coffee. She sat it on the table in front of Jo before taking the chair opposite her. She laid her pen and notebook on the table, then opened the notebook, flipping to a blank page and folding all the used ones under. She did not pick up the pen again.

"I understand you were pretty upset last night. Are you okay to answer questions now?"

Jo nodded.

"Would you prefer to do the interview in English or Slovenian?"

"Slovenian's fine."

"Okay. If you feel there is something you might be better able to express in English, let me know. I can speak it fine, but we're required to have an interpreter present."

Marta turned on the recorder and stated her name, the time and that she and Jo were the only people in the room. "Please state your full name and address."

"Jolene Abigail Wiley. *Zajčeva ulica 2, stanovanje 4, Ljubljana.*"

"Mrs. Wiley, are you a Slovenian citizen?"

"Yes."

"How long have you lived in Slovenia?"

"Twenty-five years."

"Do you live with anyone at the stated address?"

"No."

"Do you have family in Slovenia?"

"Yes. My son."

"Please state his full name."

"Faron Črnigad Wiley."

"And his father?" Marta's pause hung in the air.

"Dušan Črnigad."

Marta looked up at her. "The Dušan Črnigad?"

"Yes."

"Oh." Marta paused and made a note. "Okay. Let's go through your evening."

"Gregor met me in the courtyard where I live."

"Gregor?"

"Sorry, Gregor Bregant."

"Is this the building where your business is as well?"

Someone spent the morning on Google. "Yes."

Marta looked up at her. "Then what?"

"We walked to the City Museum together. It takes maybe two or three minutes."

"What time was that?"

"About six forty-five. We went early to meet Tomaž, a friend of Gregor's, to talk about a business opportunity."

"Tomaž?"

"Tomaž Novak. He owns bars and clubs."

Marta nodded. "Yes. Mr. Novak is known to us." She scribbled another note in her pad.

"We met Tomaž in front of Križanke with his wife, Katarina, and Tomaž's business manager, Olga. I don't know her last name. We talked about a new restaurant possibility. He mentioned he was traveling to Sweden this week and to the U.S. soon, if that matters. We talked about going to look at the property with Olga. And we made arrangements for Tomaž and Katarina to meet me at the teahouse tomorrow to talk about Tennessee before they visit."

"That's where you're from?"

"Yes."

"Explains the accent."

She tried to smile politely. No matter how fluent she became in Slovenian, she couldn't shake her soft Southern twang.

"What time did you go into the museum?"

"About seven ten? Seven fifteen? I didn't look at my phone to check."

"What did you do then?"

"Gregor got champagne for us. And Helena came over to speak with me."

"Helena Belak? The deceased?"

"Yes."

"What did the two of you discuss?"

"We made plans to meet later before I left for the after-party." She found it harder to talk about than she had expected. Her throat tightened.

"Ms. Wiley, do you need a moment? Some water?"

"No. Thank you. I'm fine." She sat up straight in her chair.

"What were you and Ms. Belak planning to do?"

"She hadn't said. She only asked me to meet her."

"What did you think was going to happen?"

Jo shrugged. "I figured we would go to my place or hers."

"What was the nature of your relationship with Ms. Belak?"

"We were sleeping together."

Marta looked up at her again. She didn't look to be judging

her, only evaluating. "Did Mr. Bregant know about this?"

"Yes. Gregor and I are old friends."

"I see." She made another scribble in her notebook. "Were you aware of anyone else Ms. Belak was involved with?"

"Not last night. I mean, I knew she was sleeping with other people, but I didn't know who."

"But you know someone's name now?"

"Yes."

"And?" Marta looked up at her again, this time with anticipation.

This was awkward. "Like I said, I knew Helena had other partners. That didn't matter to me; we weren't romantically involved. I never asked her, and she never asked me." Involved. What a strange fucking word for it.

"But?"

"Last night Vesna called my son to come to my apartment because she was worried about me. Shock. Going to the hospital." Jo waved her hand dismissively.

"Vesna?"

"Sorry. Vesna Kos. My friend, neighbor, business partner with Gregor."

"And?"

"Gregor told Faron what happened, and it came out that Faron had been sleeping with Helena." She looked down at her hands, embarrassed. It sounded even worse telling it to a stranger. "I had no idea. Apparently Faron didn't either."

Marta was staring openly at her now. She'd laid her pen

down exactly parallel to the notepad. "You lead a very interesting life, Ms. Wiley. Are you involved with anyone else?"

"Is that relevant?" She really didn't feel the need to divulge anymore of her private life.

"This is a murder investigation. Everything is relevant."

"Yes."

"Yes, what, Ms. Wiley?"

"Yes I am involved with other people."

"Their names, please." She picked up her pen again. Jo had a flash of her numbering down the page like she was expecting a laundry list, but Marta just held her pen above the paper.

"Milo Rogel and Rok Zorko."

"And what is the nature of..."

Jo cut her off, irritated and embarrassed, and pissed off because she was embarrassed. Her life was being displayed and dissected, and she didn't much care for it. "Milo and I sleep together regularly. We occasionally go to the theater or to a restaurant together. Rok and I have known each other for fifteen years. He travels a lot, but we see each other when he is in town."

"How long have you been involved with..." she looked down at her notes, "Mr. Rogel?"

"A year, year and a half."

"Do Mr. Rogel and Mr. Zorko know about each other? About Helena?"

"Yes. I don't have secrets from people I sleep with about

other people I sleep with."

"They all know each other?"

"No. I mean each of them knows, knew, there were others, but I don't know if they all knew each other socially outside of fuck- … sleeping with me. Maybe they all go out and have beers and talk about me!" Her voice echoed in the emptiness of the room. She paused and said more quietly, "I prefer to keep the rest of my social life separate."

"I see."

"What does that mean?" The disdain in Jo's voice was unmistakable.

"Nothing. I just want a clear picture of what's going on. Was there any jealousy between you and any of your lovers?"

"Lovers? No. Everything was out in the open. I just told you that."

"With you. But with others?"

"What do you mean others?"

Marta looked her in the face again. "Since your lovers knew about each other, I'm assuming they may have other lovers as well."

"Yes. Well, not Rok. Not lately anyway."

Marta looked surprised. "You're sure about that?"

"Fairly. He's currently celibate to prepare for a pilgrimage to Nepal."

"But you still see each other?"

"Yes." Why was that so fucking strange to everyone? She wanted to leave.

"To do what, exactly?"

"Is that relevant?" Her volume crept up again.

"Ms. Wiley…" Marta looked at her, waiting.

Jo wondered if she practiced that patronizing look in front of a mirror. "We play chess. And he's teaching me to knit." She said it more to her lap than to Marta.

Marta laughed loudly. When she regained her composure, she apologized. "I'm really very sorry, it's just…"

"Why is that so funny?"

"It isn't." Marta tried and failed to straighten her face. "I mean, well, given everything you've just told me … Well, you didn't seem the knitting type."

Jo looked her in the face. She had moved past embarrassment and was simply pissed off. She said very quietly and clearly, "A girl needs a hobby."

"Yes." Marta laughed again, but more to herself. "Ms. Wiley, please tell me what happened after you spoke with Ms. Belak at the museum."

———

Jo met Gregor back out on the street in front of the precinct. "Jesus. That was awful." She ran her fingers through her hair.

It was the first time she'd wanted a cigarette in months.

"Twenty Questions about your sex life?" He brushed a stray strand off her face.

"More like 200. You?" The noise of the street was almost too much to bear after the tomb-like quiet of the station. She was grateful for the fresh fall air, though.

He nodded, grimacing. He wasn't exactly in the closet, but he didn't broadcast his private life to the world.

She took his hand. "Can I buy you a coffee? Sit for a second?"

"I would love to do something as normal as that, but I have a meeting this afternoon I can't get out of. Are you okay on your own?"

"Yeah. Some alone time might be a good thing." She didn't mean it, but it might be true. She hadn't even started to process that Helena was dead, and now there were all these other layers to sort through.

Gregor hugged her tightly and strode off toward the nearest taxi stand. He was one of the few men who could make a rumpled suit and morning stubble look fashionable at lunchtime.

She walked the few blocks back toward the river. The sky was a perfect, cloudless cobalt. The leaves were turning colors and falling, gilding the cobbles in shades of orange and gold.

She looked up to the castle perched at the top of the wooded hill below which Staro Mesto, the Old City, nestled. The beauty of central Ljubljana surprised her every time she saw it. Looking around was like immersing herself in a series of expertly illuminated dioramas. The changing light of seasons, even of a day, of a snowfall, of a rainshower; each shift of light transformed it like a set change. October days were her favorite though. The Baroque wedding cake of the central city was most perfect to her in the autumn, just before the dulling gray of the winter set in.

She found an open seat outside at Cacao. It was cool enough that the staff had put blankets over the backs of the seats and benches. She was dressed warmly enough not to need one. A server came to take her order.

"A café latte, please." Milky coffee after breakfast. So American, but she had worked hard to get to a place where she didn't much care what most people thought. And yet, a police officer doing her job had made her defensive.

The embankment was busy with *Ljubljančani* and *turiste*. She was thankful Cacao didn't have much of a crowd, at least outside, and she'd been able to get a seat next to the river. From where she sat, she could see up to the castle and down the river to the Three Bridges. No matter how bad things were, looking at the water soothed her. She could find herself almost trance-like watching the current.

She felt calmer, but she still ruminated on Inspector Marta's observations on her "interesting life." On how little that interesting life had let her get to know Helena, and now Helena was dead. Now she was murdered. The same inspector would be interviewing her son. She thought again about Helena's come-on at the museum and the lingering way she'd squeezed Jo's fingers as she'd turned away. That was the last time she would ever touch her. There was a last time. There had been a last time for her father. There would be for Faron, and Gregor and Vesna. She had never thought about savoring that.

"Jo?"

She looked up into Milo's concerned face. "I'm sorry. I didn't see you."

"Or hear me. I called your name several times."

"I was thinking."

"Are you okay? I heard you were at the Emona thing last night."

"Mostly okay. I just came from the police." She grimaced.

"I'm sure they have to question everyone who was there."

"Yes. And I knew the woman who was killed, Helena." She couldn't say murdered out loud again. She wiped her wet face with the back of her hand.

He sat down next to her. "You knew her well?" He ran his fingertips under her eye without mentioning her tears.

She smiled ruefully. "Depends on how you mean. Physically, I knew her about as well as you can know a person, but I didn't know her very well at all."

"I'm sorry." He put his hand on her thigh.

"I didn't reply to your text last night. I didn't see it until this morning. I'm so sorry." She put her hand over his.

"Jesus. I don't care about that. Last night must have been awful for you."

"Hm." She looked out at the river again as it flowed through the city, carrying only a standup paddle boarder in a wet suit and later, a river cruise boat half-filled with tourists. It seemed like she'd been more unnerved by losing her shit so spectacularly and winding up tranked at the hospital than she was upset by what happened to Helena. It was an awful feeling.

Had she actually felt something more for Helena? Did she know Milo any better than she'd known her?

He put his other hand over hers. "Do you want some

company tonight? I mean not … Just, I didn't know if maybe it would be better … to not be alone."

"Thank you. I think I do want to be alone tonight. I just—"

He interrupted her. "You don't need to explain."

"Thank you. Will you come tomorrow though?"

"Aren't you working? I mean, are you going to work tomorrow?"

"Yes. What else would I do? But I'm done at ten. Damijan agreed to train the new dishwasher and stay later."

"I'll see you at ten then." He started to stand to go.

"Make it ten thirty, so I can shower and peel off the smell of restaurant."

"Maybe I want to peel you?" She wasn't sure how he could make something kind of weird sound sexy, but he did.

She pretended to frown. "Yes, Napoleon. You can come at ten. I won't wash."

He kissed her on the cheek and disappeared into the foot traffic along the river.

She finished her coffee and tucked her napkin under the cup so it wouldn't blow away into the water. She left enough euro coins to cover the coffee and headed back across Prešeren Square to the teahouse to check on Igor, their new resident graffiti artist. He'd been setting up when she walked through the courtyard with Gregor that morning.

———

The front door of the shop was propped open, and two large fans pulled the heavy smell of aerosol spray paint into the courtyard. Every light was on inside the shop, and it was brighter than any customer had ever seen it. The floor, the bakery counter, and the tables were covered in drop cloths. A heavy piece was taped over the kitchen door to seal it. Igor paced on a stretch of low scaffolding along the right wall. She stood in the doorway and watched him deftly texture the waves with short bursts from a can of white spray paint.

He turned around to look toward the door. She guessed he'd sensed her standing there. He wore a full gas mask to combat the fumes, and he waved to indicate he'd come over. Jumping the two or so steps down from the scaffold, he motioned her outside and joined her in the courtyard. He was taller than she remembered.

"You shouldn't be in there without a mask."

"Well, hello to you too."

"Sorry. It's just that breathing that stuff is really bad for you." He shook the spray can in his hand.

"I'm sorry for being snippy. And thank you. For taking precautions. I hadn't even thought about the paint settling or anything." Or how much cleaning she'd have to do after all those cloths got taken up.

"I usually work outside where it's not much of an issue. I borrowed the drops and gear," he said, holding up the mask, "from a friend who does commercial painting."

"Will you be finished today?" She was surprised by how much he'd done already.

He laughed. "It isn't exactly oil painting."

"I know. I just thought you'd need more time."

"I usually complete a piece in one night, looking over my shoulder for police."

"There's that." She paused; he was scrutinizing her. "I should go and leave you to it. I just wanted to stop by to see how it was going. You can text me when you're done, and I'll come down."

He took her forearm, and the warmth of his hand reached her skin even through the heavy sweater. "I don't mean to intrude, but you seem distracted."

"I'm fine. I was at the Emona thing last night." Surely everyone in Ljubljana knew what had happened. Murders were exceedingly rare, and it had happened at such a rarefied gathering. The headline was plastered on every kiosk she'd passed.

"That must have been disturbing."

"Helena and I were … friends."

He looked at her with some surprise, though it was hard to tell with him. "I didn't realize you knew her." She thought he stressed "knew" slightly more than necessary.

"Apparently I run in some pretty interesting circles." She pushed her hand through her hair. Interesting, and much bigger and weirder circles than she'd ever thought.

"Helena's circle, as you say, was large."

His tone said that he, too, had been part of that circle. "Anyway. I'm going to go make myself some lunch. Can I bring you something?"

He shook his head. "I brought a sandwich."

"I'll be upstairs if you need me. And Vesna should be back

around four." She walked away backward as she spoke. He was a fine-looking man. She hoped Vesna wouldn't screw this one up.

He waved, and she turned around to take the stairs up to her apartment.

Tea. Sandwich. Nap, if she could close her eyes. It wouldn't be easy to turn off the hamster wheel churning her thoughts.

She opened her front door, keys jingling in her hand, and kicked her clogs off in the entryway. Gregor had tidied the kitchen while she'd gotten dressed that morning. His house was palatial compared with hers, but he understood that, in a small space, just a few dishes in the sink made the whole place seem a mess. She grabbed her blue mug from the drainboard and pulled a tin of chamomile tea down from the cupboard.

Humming softly, she busied herself making tea and a cheese sandwich thickly spread with the end of last year's apple chutney. Then she noticed what tune she was humming. It was the theme from *M*A*S*H*.

Why the fuck? She had Gregor to thank for the earworm. No, she had heard it last night too. At the hospital? No. Before, at the museum. That didn't make any sense. She must have heard it somewhere in the background before then, and it had lingered subliminally. To eradicate it, she sought and found a Leonard Cohen playlist on her phone. He was her constant companion in times of turmoil.

She gathered her tea and sandwich and curled up in the corner of the futon against the wall, listening to Leonard sing about the famous blue raincoat. She placed her tea on the wide windowsill that faced the courtyard and balanced her sandwich plate on her knees. She looked out the window while she ate, watching a neighbor's laundry blow gently on the line strung between the second-floor railings. The sun shone on one side of the courtyard, but the other side was already in deep shadow as the sun moved down from its zenith.

She was breaking her own rule by eating on the white-draped futon. Everything in the apartment was white, even the painted floorboards, and she was particular about only eating at the table. This was one time when comfort would triumph over self-imposed conformity. She finished her sandwich and set the plate on the windowsill between her mug and the orchid she was trying to get to bloom again. She checked her phone to make sure the ringer was on in case Igor texted, and set it next to her plate as well.

She was aware of some lingering grogginess from the sedative at the hospital, but every muscle in her body felt ready to run. That was unnerving, not least of all because it had long been her position that she'd run only if something were chasing her.

She slid down on the futon and balled up a throw pillow under her head. Now that she was trying to fall asleep, her mind began to race through a catalog of troubling thoughts: the morning's conversation with Gregor about Faron and Helena, the intrusive interview with Inspector Marta, the image of Helena's lifeless body on the mosaic floor, and of her wide-open eyes.

Deep breath in. Deep breath out. Rok had used the two phrases to talk her down off many an emotional ledge when Faron was younger and she'd been angrier. It wasn't working today. She tried instead to turn her mind to a happier image, punting up the river in the small boat Gregor kept tied up near his house. She concentrated on the surface of the calm water and the shadows of trees hanging over the banks. It finally worked, and she drifted off.

———

She bolted upright from a dead sleep. A noise in the apartment. It took a second to register: someone was at the table, and it wasn't anyone who had a key to her flat.

Helena sat there, calm as a cat in the sun, sipping tea out of Jo's gray mug. It was the mug Gregor had used and washed that morning. Helena's hair was disheveled, and her head tilted a bit to one side. She was wearing the toga-draped dress from the previous night; it was crumpled and soiled.

"Hello, Jo."

"Still asleep. I'm going to lie back down and dream of kittens or something."

"I'm afraid you are not asleep, kiddo." Helena sat the mug down, but it made no noise on the table.

"I am." She lay back down and squeezed her eyes shut like a child pretending to sleep.

Helena, or whatever was in her apartment looking like Helena, sat next to Jo on the futon. She laid her hand on Jo's thigh. Her hand was ice cold.

Jo moved as far away as she could, smack against the wall. "This is not fucking real."

"Calm down. It is weird, but I need to talk to you."

"Why do dead people keep telling me to calm the fuck

down?" Jo closed her eyes again and tried to breathe, but the intake of breath felt more like suffocating. She suddenly had a lot more empathy for her mother's habit of rocking and humming to herself when she was upset.

Helena lifted her hand to Jo's shoulder. Again she shivered.

She opened her eyes and looked at Helena. Her head was still wrong, but her eyes were soft, not wide open with terrified surprise.

"What do you want from me?" Whatever Helena was, Jo didn't want her in her apartment. At the same time, she didn't want her to be dead.

Helena repositioned herself on the couch. "I don't want anything from you. I knew I had to come to you, but I don't understand it."

Jo sat up, edging from freaked out into angry.

Helena said, "I need to tell you to be careful, but I didn't know that until I got here. There's something here in Ljubljana. Something new. No … Something awake. And it can find you the same way I did."

"What are you talking about? Of course you know where to find me. How many times have you been here?" She was forgetting that it wasn't actually Helena sitting on her futon. It was some kind of mental projection, some kind of ghost.

"I really don't know how to explain it. I didn't notice this about you when I was alive. But now that I'm, well, not alive, I can see it: you glow. You're all silvery. I knew where you were the instant I woke up at the morgue. And I knew you were in some kind of danger." Helena flopped back on the futon, stretching her arms out across the back.

"I … just … what exactly am I supposed to do with this information?" She couldn't sort out what was more incredible: what the Helena-thing said, or the fact that she was there, saying it.

"That, I don't know. But I feel enormously relieved having told you, and like I should probably go, though I'm not sure where exactly." She moved to get up.

"No. Wait." Jo grabbed Helena's forearm. It felt like a frozen pack of meat pulled out of the reach-in downstairs.

"I really should go."

"Since you're here. Why the fuck were you sleeping with Faron?"

"I take it you found out last night?"

"This morning actually. But why?"

"Why do people climb Triglav?"

"What does that mean?"

"Because they can, Jo. Because they can. Faron was a bit of fun, like you."

"I can't decide how grossed out I am right now."

"Don't be. Though I will say prowess seems to run in the family. He's quite impressive for someone so young."

"Stop, I am officially grossed out."

"Not sorry, dear. You asked."

"Not about … prowess. Anything else you need to unburden yourself of?" Jo leaned back against the wall. The thought crossed her mind that treating this like a conversation with a not-dead person might be a bad idea. Either she was having a hell of a dream or she was capable of serious sensory hallucinations.

"I really thought you'd ask me how I died." Helena plucked a pillow feather off Jo's skirt.

She flinched at the touch. "I thought this was my dream."

"Still not dreaming, dear. To answer my own question, though, I have no idea. I don't remember that part."

"Why did you want me to ask you?"

"Oh, to see if I could remember if someone else asked. I have no idea how this afterlife, death, whatever you want to call it, thing works." Helena stood up. "I really should go." She walked to the door.

Jo stared at her. She wanted to say how she was sorry she hadn't asked questions about her life, about her family, but she didn't. "You really don't remember anything?"

Helena stopped and turned back to her. "I remember seeing you at the museum and walking into the Emona house with a few people. I went down to look at the mosaic more closely while there were so few people there and no one seemed to be paying much attention. And I remember being surprised to find someone down there already." She tilted her head, which succeeded only in setting everything at even wronger angles where her neck and jaw were concerned. "I guess that person … No. I must have fallen. It was stupid to go down there."

"The police don't seem to think you fell."

Helena shrugged. "Doesn't matter much to me now. Dead is dead."

"That's funny, considering you are standing in my flat talking to me. Very unlike your average dead person."

"True. I think that might be more about you than me though, kiddo."

"Whatever."

Helena turned away again, then stopped. "There is actually one thing you can do for me. Would you tell my brother I'm okay, or at peace, or whatever you think might comfort him?"

Jo looked up at her. "How am I supposed to explain I have a message for him from beyond the grave?"

"I don't know, love. You're smart. You'll figure it out." Helena leaned over, kissed her on the cheek and brushed her icy hand over the top of Jo's head. "It really was fun, dear."

She was gone. She didn't walk through the door. She didn't fade. She just wasn't there.

Blasé in death. Leave it to Helena.

Jo's phone chimed with a text message. "It's Igor. I've finished if you'd like to come down to have a look."

She was a sucker for complete sentences in a text message. "I'll be right down."

Wait. Not asleep. This was bad.

Jo stood and ran her hands down her shirt and skirt to smooth them. She had her phone and went to the table to grab her keys. She picked up the gray pottery mug. It was full of cold tea.

Gregor just forgot it this morning.

She scooped up the keys, put her phone in her cardigan

pocket, and took the few steps to the door. She stepped into her clogs and then into the cool air on the landing.

Gregor hadn't made tea.

———

Igor was outside the shop folding drop cloths with Vesna when Jo crossed the courtyard. They looked to be working in companionable silence.

"*Živjo.*" Jo raised her hand to both of them.

Vesna ran toward her and threw her arms around her like they'd been apart for years. She let go and stepped back, holding Jo at arm's length. "I'm so glad you're here."

"Vee, I live here. Remember?" She was still shaken from the ghostly encounter upstairs.

Was that what it was? A ghost? Pretty fucking solid for a ghost. Maybe her mother's mental illness was hereditary. Maybe this was how it started, conversations with dead people.

Vesna's weirdly enthusiastic greeting felt equally wrong.

"I've been worried about you all day. Are you okay? I mean, how could you be? I felt so bad about taking off this morning, but Gregor and Faron said you'd be fine and I should go. I should've stayed, shouldn't I?" Vesna stopped to breathe.

Jo put her hand up. "Whoa. I'm fine. Or as fine as can be expected, I guess." Jo pulled her cardigan more tightly around herself. "Let's go look at this thing."

Vesna took her hand and dragged her into the shop, looking back like she thought Jo would break at any moment.

The shop reeked of spray paint but was stripped of the drop cloths and mostly back to normal except for the fans.

Vesna dropped Jo's hand and threw her arms wide. "Isn't it gorgeous?"

Jo nodded. It was better than she had imagined in their late-night scribblings. The mural took up most of the wall. As she had imagined, the water had the stylized illustration look of The Wave, but instead of the cartoony-tattoo boat of the sketch, Igor had continued the Hokusai style in his rendering of the ship and the burning crates of tea.

"Igor, it's perfect." She stood still to take in all the detail.

"I played with your idea a bit. I know you wanted something more—"

Jo cut him off. "My doodle was just an idea. This? This is amazing." She searched her pockets for her phone. "I should post it on our Instagram account."

Vesna stopped her. "Already done." She looked to Igor, "though he wouldn't let me post his picture with it."

"A man has to retain some mystery." He brushed off his hands on the front of his paint-flecked jeans. "Okay, ladies, I'm off. I'll leave the fans so you can run them some more tonight and tomorrow before you open."

"How will we get them back to you?" Vesna, ever practical, looked up at him.

"I'll come by to get them tomorrow afternoon." He held Vesna's gaze a few beats.

She blushed. "That works." It was adorable.

Vesna started again. "Oh. Oh. I have your money." She

patted the pockets of her perfectly pressed, lunch-with-mom pants and produced a folded stack of euro bills from her back pocket.

He took it from her with a nod. "Thank you. Both."

He picked up the stack of drop cloths with the respirator mask on top and headed out to Breg, where he'd pulled a truck up to load the scaffolding.

Jo still stood facing the newly transformed wall.

Vesna moved to stand beside her. "He really is good, isn't he?" She let out a little sigh.

"And good looking. And charming. He's interested, you know? In you."

Vesna laughed. "For once, I do know. He asked me to dinner. That seems too serious, so we're going to breakfast on Saturday."

"Nice. I'm glad you said yes."

"Why wouldn't I?" Vesna turned to look at her.

"Because you almost never do."

"There's that." Vesna shrugged and turned to look back at the clipper ship surrounded by burning tea.

Jo continued to look at the ship as well. "Vee, I think I might be losing my mind."

CHAPTER 6

A woman was dead, an artifact had been stolen from the museum the night of the murder, and Jolene Wiley was no longer dormant.

Gustaf watched her friends bring her, stumbling and babbling, up the stairs to her flat. Her aura, which had always been purple with brilliant red streaks, now gleamed with a silver shimmer, and a faint silver plume spiraled up from her head as far as he could see. It would grow stronger as whatever drugs or booze she had in her system wore off. She'd be a beacon to every dead person, and more, for miles.

Vesna Kos would notice it immediately and would undoubtedly go to her uncle. The Kos family's involvement was unavoidable, but Gustaf didn't welcome it. It had been Valter Kos, Vesna's father, whose insistence on religion over science was at the center of the tragedy Gustaf had first come to Slovenia to investigate.

Who would have thought the building of a simple, even ugly, carpark could be the source of so much anguish to so many? Then, as now, disturbing ancient soil proved to be the undoing of the unknowing. Believing that the earliest burials uncovered were consecrated graves, Valter Kos and his brother were content to leave the work of relocating them to local authorities and the Church.

The last grave excavated was that of what Mr. Stoker would have called a vampyr. It held the skeleton of a young girl arranged in a deviant pattern, with the head removed postmortem and placed between the feet, per other vampire burials discovered throughout central and eastern Europe.

Modernity had stripped away ancestral fear of vampires, leaving the general population with only a superficial pop-culture fascination. This burial was of interest only to the presiding archaeologists, hence no precautions were taken to preserve the bane. Thus, consistent with recorded folk traditions, once the remains were reinterred with the head at the top of the body, the undead girl had gone in search of kin on which to feed. The last of her particular lineage was Berta Horvat.

Miss Horvat kept company with Leo, the younger Kos brother. Not surprisingly, given the lack of vampiric activity in Slovenia for over a century, Valter Kos misinterpreted the signs. Condemning her for tempting his brother away from taking holy orders with the Jesuits, he declared Miss Horvat possessed and confined her in order to perform an exorcism. This made her easy prey for her vampiric ancestor, and she succumbed.

Miss Horvat's death was the result of ignorance, not of direct malice by the Kos family. Gustaf had spoken at length with Valter Kos and cautioned him about monitoring excavation work anywhere in central Ljubljana. Lingering misgivings led to his recommendation — no, his insistence —

that Bettine send Alessandro to Slovenia to keep close watch on the Kos family. But she said Trieste and Venice already kept Alessandro busy, and to be fair, that was true. And that was the reason Bettine had given Gustaf the assignment to the fledging country.

With Valter's death, Leo — now Brother Kos — had assumed the mantle of Witchfinder. As best Gustaf could tell, Brother Kos was a modern man, despite his faith. Unlike Valter, Brother Kos did not believe that every being of supernatural origin or ability was a demonic presence in need of execution.

That was small comfort. Gustaf still didn't completely trust the Kos family. He wasn't sure that delivering a vox de mortuis into their hands would be to anyone's best interest, especially Ms. Wiley's.

He couldn't help but think she was a magnet for those living behind the Veil. Rok Zorko, her friend (or lover, he was never certain) had been a puzzle for a long time. Zorko's aura was old, much older than his face. He looked about forty when Gustaf first encountered him and had not noticeably aged in the twenty years since then. Gustaf had not been able to find him in the registries; nevertheless, he suspected that Zorko was either an Immortal or a Long-Lived.

Through several requests for archives from India and Iceland, Gustaf pieced together some parts of Zorko's long life. He'd been known to the Observers in other times, under other names. In Reykjavik in the late 1890s, he was Arnbjörg Valdisson; he disappeared after the death of his much older wife. Alma Arunsdóttir, who had observed him, believed him to be more than a hundred years old at that time, and not of Icelandic origins.

Gustaf had also traced him to Kerala around 1940. Kadir Abassi had observed a Long-Lived named Michael Hale, a Secret Intelligence Service officer, in India on an unknown mission. The person Gustaf knew as Rok Zorko wore a heavy beard and had much longer hair than a military officer, but Zorko matched Hale's physical description, and his eyes were identical to the one photograph included in Abassi's files. Hale had left Kerala before the war ended, presumably to return to London. World War II provided excellent opportunities for many Long-Lived and true Immortals to go dark in the registries.

Gustaf had no idea why Valdisson chose Slovenia, or where he'd spent the decades after the war. He'd come to Ljubljana around 1990. As Zorko, he lived in Šiška, but he traveled a good deal, often on trips with Ms. Wiley that sometimes included her son. From visa requests, Gustaf knew the two of them had traveled to India, possibly even to Kerala. He had no reason to believe that Valdisson, now Zorko, interfered in politics or engaged in other activities the Observers had forbidden to the Long-Lived. But Gustaf had less trust in Zorko's kind than he had in witchfinders and demonhunters. Like some Observers, the Long-Lived developed a form of psychoscopy with people. He could only conclude that Zorko knew exactly what Ms. Wiley was. What he hadn't yet figured out was the purpose of Zorko's involvement with her.

Gustaf didn't want to admit it to himself, but he had developed a paternal sense toward Jo. He'd watched her son grow up, watched her take control of her life piece by piece. She'd built a family around her to replace the one she'd lost.

Gustaf had lost his own family, but unlike Ms. Wiley, he had never allowed anyone else back in. There was once a moment when he thought Bettine might become something more to him than a colleague, but that was out of the question now.

He didn't believe Ms. Wiley was capable of murder, but he had read the reports of her mother's unwinding. It was uncommon for Voices to enter the world as fragile as her mother had been. It was not uncommon for such people to be driven to insanity by the shades that haunted them. Gustaf hoped Jolene Wiley was made of sterner stuff than her mother.

He also hoped he was right about Leo Kos. If he was the fanatic his brother had been, Ms. Wiley was in danger from more directions than Gustaf could defend alone. Asking Bettine to come or to send an assistant would only jeopardize Ms. Wiley further. The Board generally moved quickly, without trial or recourse, to quarantine any perceived danger.

He needed to get to the heart of the matter. Investigator Klančnik hadn't been very forthcoming after her initial interviews, other than to report that Ms. Wiley led an interesting life. That much he had gathered on his own. To get more information from Investigator Klančnik, he would have to provide more information to her. He would have to share his instinct about everything, leading back to the museum and through it to the river. He could already picture the incredulity on her face.

CHAPTER 7

Vesna settled Jo into the overstuffed couch in her living room. She plumped pillows on either side and covered her lap with a crocheted throw.

"Sit there." She handed Jo a mug of tea.

Vesna's cat Cleopatra climbed up onto the back of the couch and gave Jo a gentle head-butt before clambering down into her lap to knead her thigh. Then Cleopatra stopped, looked up at Jo with doleful yellow eyes and curled up to sleep. Jo patted the cat's smooth orange fur while Antony, a handsome tuxedo cat, sat at her feet and stared at her — or rather, at the air above her head.

Maybe she shouldn't say anything more. Maybe she was just disoriented by the sudden awfulness of Helena's death, and maybe it would pass. But maybe she really was losing her shit. Vesna knew about her mom, and that might be enough to make her worry Jo was headed down the same path.

"So. Spill. What's going on with you? You look like you've seen a—"

Jo interrupted her. "Please don't say 'ghost.'" She sighed.

"Okay. Then what's wrong?"

"I did see a ghost. Or I dreamed one or two. I'm not sure. Anyway, I think this whole thing with Helena has me thrown for a loop." Jo picked up Cleopatra and snuggled her like a baby. She hadn't been in love with Helena, but in her way she cared for her. Helena was vibrant and alive. She'd made Jo feel that way too.

"What do you mean you don't know if you dreamed it?" Vesna reached out to rub Cleopatra's belly. The cat purred loudly.

"I mean that not an hour ago I was awake, sitting on the futon, while Helena drank tea at my table."

"Maybe it's the drugs they gave you last night?" Vesna looked hopeful and skeptical at the same time.

"No. I don't think so. I had a similar dream about my father, and he told me there would be others who'd know how to find me." Cleopatra wriggled her way out of Jo's arms and flounced off with her tail in the air. "But — it could just be the drugs, and how awful it was to see Helena like that." An image of Helena's head cocked at that impossible angle rose unbidden as she spoke, and her stomach clenched.

Vesna leaned in closer. "What did Helena say exactly?"

"She wasn't very exact, but she said she'd 'woken up' and known that she needed to speak with me. She said I'd been easy to find because now that she's dead, or as she put it, not alive, she sees I have some kind of silvery aura or something." Jo picked up her mug and took a sip of tea.

"Oh." Vesna's voice was quiet. She looked worried.

"I know. It's crazy, right?" She set the mug down.

Vesna looked down at her hands folded in her lap and paused for a long moment. She looked back up at Jo. "I don't think you're crazy or drugged, but I do think you need to see someone."

"What? Like a shrink?"

"No. Like a priest."

"Why?" She was confused. Vesna was about as religious as she was, which was about zero.

"I think they — these visions — might be demons." Vesna seemed surprised by the words coming out of her mouth. "Or something."

She stared at Vesna open-mouthed. "Are you serious?"

"Yes." Vesna sat up a little straighter, sounded more certain about what she had to say. "This could be something really bad, and I think you should see Brother Kos. He's my uncle, and he … knows about this kind of thing."

"Vee. I … just … It's not my thing." Jo sat up straight too.

"I know. But I think you should go. If nothing else, he'll be a good counselor — a disinterested third party — to help you deal with your grief." Vesna relaxed a little.

"I'm not sure how disinterested a priest is going to be when I tell him my female 'lover' was murdered and, oh, by the way, she was also schtupping my son." She punctuated that with a sarcastic laugh.

"What?" From the look in Vesna's eyes, this revelation was more astounding than the ghost story.

"I guess you weren't there when Faron and Gregor had their chat about it last night?"

"No. As soon as we got you to bed, Gregor shooed me off to my flat. I called Faron, and Gregor came over after Faron arrived." Vesna was stammering. "She was sleeping with Faron?"

"Gregor said she is, was, a collector. Apparently Faron and I were a set." Jo looked down at Antony, still at her feet staring at her. "According to Gregor, Faron was completely mortified. As you can imagine."

"That's just a bit too gross," Vesna said, hastening to add, "Not that either of you are gross. Just, well. Who does that?"

"Helena. Apparently."

————

Back in her own flat, Jo began to regret telling Vesna. The religiosity had surprised her. Was Vesna worried about both her sanity and her soul?

Maybe she was crazy. Maybe seeing a dead body snapped something. But it wasn't like she'd never seen a dead body before. Do crazy people suspect that they're crazy? Wasn't that what crazy people always asked themselves in movies?

She wanted to stop thinking, and there were only two ways she could get out of her own head. Well, three, if she counted sex, but she'd told Milo not to come over. Her alternatives were long aimless walks and manic-level cleaning binges. The flat was already pristine; too much clutter or dust in her place made her fidgety.

So she decided to clean the shop. Those drop cloths had protected everything from ambient paint spray, but they were probably dusty. She scooped up her keys, slid her feet back into her clogs, and headed back downstairs. The sun had just set, but it was already chilly in the stairwell. She went back to grab a jacket.

At the door to the shop, her cell buzzed in her sweater pocket. It was Faron.

"I thought you were going to text me?"

She fumbled with her phone, typing with one thumb while trying to open the door. "I'm sorry. Forgot."

"You OK? Want me to stay tonight?"

"No. I'm good. Cleaning in the shop."

"Maybe you should try a walk instead."

"Ha ha."

She got the door open, and the paint smell was still strong enough to change her mind about the cleaning.

She texted Faron again: "Maybe you're right. Meet for pizza later?"

"Sure. Trta?"

"Sounds good. 8? 8:30?"

"8:30. Zombie Church stuff."

"Gotcha."

Faron was involved in the Trans-Universal Zombie Church of the Blissful Ringing. They'd sprung up when the former prime minister referred to those opposing privatization as "a bunch of socialist zombies." Jo helped at their free food events, but Faron was more involved in the logistics. She was glad he had a fire in his belly about something.

She set off, planning to walk around Trnovo via the river. Then she'd head north, making a big box to come back along the edge of Tivoli, cutting back through the center and crossing the river to get to Trta. She didn't like walking through the park by herself after dark. She always felt safe in Ljubljana but didn't see much point in being careless. Despite these intentions, she walked straight toward the Roman house excavation.

It was after dark on Sunday, so of course the museum annex was closed. But the area was also cordoned off with blue and white police tape, and a guard had been posted. The uniformed officer at the gate wouldn't tell her anything.

For a few beats after the officer asked her to move along, she stood looking into the darkness beyond the locked gate. Maybe there was something she missed. This was where it started, where something had reached out from her past and flicked whatever switch was attached to the faulty wiring her mother had passed down to her. Again the image of Helena, her cream-colored dress twisted around her on the mosaic floor, her eyes open wide and empty, played behind Jo's eyes. In that moment she thought it would probably never stop.

The officer coughed. "Miss, please. You need to leave the area."

———

She walked back out onto the street, where the air seemed less dense, and backtracked to the river to sit awhile before meeting Faron. One of her favorite places in Ljubljana was the concrete steps down to the river on the university side. Despite not believing in much of anything, this felt like a holy place to her. The river was lined with willows for shade. After dark, the steps were full of teenagers and students smoking cigarettes, drinking beer, and occasionally making out.

Jo chose a spot where the concrete ended, away from a small group of people who looked about Faron's age. Ljubljana felt like a young city when university classes began in October. That vibrancy had pulled her in when she'd first arrived. Now it sometimes made her feel old, but it still made the city hum. For the most part, she didn't feel her age. She was wiser and more settled in her early forties than she would have imagined at eighteen, but she was nothing like what she'd thought fortysomethings were supposed to be. Most of the time that felt like a good thing.

A light crosswind blew over the current of the river, making hash marks on the surface. The dark water shimmered and sparkled under the street lighting. The breeze blew her hair around her face, and the long draping willow branches holding onto the last of their yellowed leaves rustled above her. The castle sat squat on the hill that dominated the opposite side of the river, ringed in up-lights to draw attention to its medieval lines. Voices of passersby drifted down from the street behind and above her, and voices from the opposite bank carried across the water. The chill from the concrete made her butt cold. She wished she'd grabbed a heavier jacket. The one she'd chosen wasn't enough to keep her warm when she stopped walking.

She started to get up to kill some time walking the opposite direction from the pizza restaurant when she heard her name.

She turned around, but she didn't see anyone. The students closest to her were leaned back, smoking cigarettes and looking out at the water. She turned to check behind the tree next to her, but nothing. Then she felt it, the same bone-numbing cold she'd felt when the Helena-thing had touched her.

"Jay." Her childhood nickname said with the soft Appalachian lilt and twang that was the voice that used to call her in to supper from the woods.

Her father sat next to her, wet and bruised as he'd been before, though the water dripping from his clothes didn't dampen hers. She didn't want to turn her head to see him fully. She didn't want to confirm her own loss of reality. He put his hand on top of her hand on the edge of the concrete step. It was cold, but not as cold as Helena's had been.

"Dad, I know you're not really here. I know this isn't really happening." Right. Then why the hell had she said that out loud?

"Jay, I know this is hard. But it is real. And I need you to listen to me."

"Okay, Make Believe Dad-thing."

"Jolene Abigail, don't be sarcastic. I've been trying to get your attention for a while."

Shit. That was real, all right. "I'm sorry. Let's say I do believe you. Can anyone else see you, or will they just think I'm a crazy person talking to myself?"

"They'll see a shadow, a shade of a person."

"So darkness is good for you?"

"I've been a shade for a long time, Jay. Helena could only make you see her because you were alone."

"What? Why?" Maybe she'd just hang out with people

all the time? The part of her that valued every moment of solitude revolted at that idea.

"It takes energy to manifest, even in the presence of someone like you. Newly dead don't have much control over that. Most of the time they don't even realize they're dead. They just get frustrated trying to talk to people and wind up slamming doors and breaking things."

"Poltergeist?"

"Kind of."

"So. Why are you here exactly? I mean how did you get to Ljubljana from East Tennessee?"

"That's harder to explain. Energy travels differently than mass is probably the best I can do."

"Okay. Next question. Why can I miraculously see dead people at forty-three when this has never happened to me before?"

"Short version is that everyone thought it skipped you."

"What skipped me?"

"The gift, the curse. Your mother's people have been able to speak with the dead for generations. The women anyway."

"No one mentioned this to me before."

"No. They wouldn't have. Jackie wanted to take you away then and there when they thought it skipped you, so you could have some sort of normal life."

"Is that why no one objected when she took me to live in Chattanooga after you … died?"

"Probably. But I'm guessing your mother wasn't in any

state to object anyway."

"No. She pretty much lost her shit."

"I know. And I'm sorry for that."

"Why are you sorry?" She turned to look him in the face for the first time. Despite the battering he'd taken in the river, the sorrow was obvious and deep.

"She couldn't see me. She was always a little too close to unhinged, and me drowning put her over the edge and interfered with the gift. Not being able to communicate with me just made it worse."

"Jesus. That's awful."

"Yes. I should have been a better steward for your mother."

"I don't understand."

"Wiley women with the gift marry a man who can be a stable provider and keep them grounded, though they always keep their family name. I didn't know what your mother could do until she was pregnant with you. I was young and foolish and not the best choice to be your mother's steward, but by then it was too late for your grandma to run me off." Her father looked out over the silent river.

"Jackie has failed to mention any of this."

"I'm not surprised."

"So why now? I mean, if it didn't skip me."

"I don't know. But I'm worried for you. You haven't had anyone to guide you."

"Isn't that why you're here?"

"I can't do much. I didn't have the gift."

"But you know about it and you were mom's steward, or whatever."

"It's not the same."

"Vesna wants me to go see her uncle who is a priest. She thinks you might be a demon."

"I'm not."

"I don't remember much from my few stints in vacation Bible school, but isn't that exactly what a demon would say?"

"Probably. Maybe you should go see him."

"Really? What if he wants to perform an exorcism in my apartment?"

"Yes, really. Go. Whatever this is, this presence, it's old and it's of this place. Maybe he'll know what it is and what to do."

She nodded. Helena said the same thing about a presence.

"You should call Jackie. And you should probably get married."

"I'll call her tomorrow. And no, I'm not getting married. I don't need a magical, mystical chaperone."

"It's not a chaperone. It's a sacred bond, Jay. It's a bane."

"No. That is some completely backwards nonsense."

"Surely one of those men—"

"Wait, how much of my life have you seen? What do you know?"

"Less than you're thinking, but enough to know you have a lot of people in your life."

"I really don't want to have this conversation with my

father, even if you are dead. I'll go see Brother Kos. I am not getting married. It's ridiculous and sexist."

"You need a guide, and a steward."

"Maybe it takes a village to be my steward."

"Jay …"

"I'm serious. You've already said I'm an outlier, not appearing to have this gift for forty-three years. I could be unusual in other ways."

"Go see the priest."

"I will." She turned to him again. "Question. How could Helena 'know' where I was after she died, and why did she say I was all silvery?"

"Only people who knew you in life can appear to you when they are dead. Initially anyway. They would only feel the need to come to you if they had unfinished business or died traumatically. People who can speak with the dead have an aura. Sensitive living people can sometimes see it. The dead with problems are drawn to it."

"All dead people? All dead people know where I am?"

"If they come across you, yes, they will recognize you. But only the dead with a connection to you are able to speak to you while your gift is new, or when you're young. I've always thought that was an impressive safety feature. I'm not sure how that will work with you. You're older, but you haven't developed your gift."

"This is still too much to absorb."

"I think you'll be able to absorb it, but you should be careful. I'm not so sure this is really something new with you. Maybe it was there all along, but you repressed it somehow. Other dead may be able to get to you already."

"Great. I can talk with my dead father and get haunted by people I know — and maybe people I don't know — and I still have to worry about my cheese sliding off my cracker because the first two things don't equal crazy by themselves."

"I said it is a gift or a curse."

"You did." She looked out over the river, so different than the one she'd grown up on. "Can you tell me what this thing is that I need to be worried about? This presence?" Not words she ever thought would fall out of her mouth.

"I don't know, Jay. I'm hardly all-seeing. It's powerful, and it's interested in you."

"How do you know that much?"

"I've been keeping my eye on you. I figured that was the reason for me sticking around this long."

"That's comforting. And creepy." She shifted her hand and laced her warm fingers through his cold ones.

He stood to leave. "I have to go."

Jo stood too. It was strange, looking her father in the eye. She remembered him as so tall. "Why? Can I just call you or summon you or something?"

"No. This was the reason I couldn't cross, I think. I had to stay so I could tell you what you can do. Now that you know, I feel it's time to go."

"Go where?"

"I don't know. There are still mysteries, Jolene. But I think it's somewhere good. I've wanted to go for a long time."

"That's why Helena left in such a hurry?"

"Maybe."

"She seemed quite blasé about being dead. But she wasn't one to have regrets in life either."

"Jay, I need to go. I love you. And please think about what I said."

"I will think about it. But I'm not making any promises on the getting-married thing. That scares me more than anything else you've said."

"Jolene."

"Sorry. I love you. I never thought I'd get to say that to you again."

"I know."

Jo hugged him. At first it was like hugging a statue in December. Then, for a brief moment, there was warmth between them, and it felt the way hugging him had when she was a child.

She sighed, and he was gone. No popping sound, no chill wind, nothing to signal that he had been there and now he was not.

Jo's phone buzzed in her pocket. It was a text from Faron. "Are you lost?"

He didn't need to be party to any of this. It wasn't something that affected the Wiley men. She texted him back. "I ran into an old friend."

CHAPTER 8

"How much do you really know about her?" Leo Kos shifted in his chair. It was unusual, to say the least, for his niece to call him. She'd made peace with who her father, his brother, had been. But she'd also washed her hands of it all.

"What do you mean? I've known her since I was twenty." The annoyance in Vesna's voice wasn't about the question.

"As you mentioned, but why now?" People were either born different or they were not. They didn't usually pick something up later, unless they were possessed or cursed.

"She was at the museum. The murder? When I saw her that night her aura was different." Vesna let out a heavy sigh.

He knew it. She could see auras, and she'd lied to him that morning at the cemetery when they buried his brother. No point in calling her out now that she'd confessed.

"How was it different?"

"Silver and part of it floats above her head."

"And you've never noticed this about your best friend before?" He scratched the stubble on his face and shifted again on the chair. The furniture in the Ljubljana rectory had not been made for people like him.

"No. Her aura has always been strong, purple with bright red flashes like lightning. But not silvered, and nothing like the flag that's waving over her head now."

"And you didn't tell her?"

Vesna paused a few beats. "No."

"And why, my dear niece, not?" He chuckled, mostly to himself.

"What am I supposed to say? 'I come from a long line of witchfinders who would have thrown holy water on you and burned you at the stake, but we're different now?' I doubt she would have found that very reassuring. She thinks she's about to join her mom in the madhouse." Vesna was quiet. He could feel her frustration. A world she wanted no part of was knocking down her door.

"What do you know about her mother?" Clairvoyants who weren't complete fakes generally came from a line of family seers. Both types tended to attract trouble.

"Not much. Her father died when she was little, and her mom lost it. Jo grew up with her aunt. I think her mom's been in and out of institutions. She hasn't seen or spoken to her in years."

"But she's still alive?" He stood and walked to the window.

"As far as I know. Why?"

"Not sure yet. Maybe it's inherited. I'll have to do some digging." He hated to call Lichtenberg, but it might be necessary. "Tell her to call me."

"I will, but you should know she's not about church, big or

small C." His niece hesitated. "And, she's, she's your type."

He bristled. "And what type would that be, Vesna?"

"Badly broken and mended. Fucking stubborn. Red flashes in her aura, just like Berta."

"That was a long time ago. I took my vows. You needn't worry about your witchy friend stealing me away from them."

He slid his phone back into his pocket and looked out onto the narrow, cobbled street. A pack of students on bikes whizzed through the passage and turned out of sight. A grandmother with a scarf tied over her gray curls waddled her way toward him, heavy shopping bags in each hand. Leo had not heard Berta's name in years. The mention of it made him feel more guilt than longing.

CHAPTER 9

She was sitting on the banks of the Little Tennessee River on a red picnic blanket, eating the last of her peanut butter and blackberry jam sandwich. Her baby cousin Michael slept in a bassinet next to her. Aunt Jackie was asleep, or reading a book, on a folding chaise lounge behind her. Mom and Dad were paddling around on the river in a canoe, just out of sight.

Jo felt the sun on her back. She felt the weight of her braids, warm and heavy and a little scratchy against her skin. Her mother had braided her hair that morning, with two fat green lengths of grosgrain ribbon, just because. Most days she just brushed the tangles out of Jo's hair, then gathered it up and held it in one hand while she snapped on an elastic band with two blue plastic beads to lock the ponytail into place. Making braids took more time and a lot more combing, but even when it pulled and hurt, Jo tried not to cry. It always seemed like a special day when her mother braided her hair.

She heard a voice, faint at first, then louder, and then it was her mother's voice. She heard her mother screaming, something about the canoe, something about John, where is

John? She saw her mother climbing up the bank with her wet sundress clinging to her skin, the dark circles of her nipples showing through the thin fabric. Aunt Jackie was jumping up to run to her, and her foot got caught in the chair as she stood and she toppled over onto the picnic blanket next to Jo. When she got up again with a rug burn on her cheek, she ran to her sister.

Aunt Jackie sat her sister on the edge of the picnic blanket. She shooed Jo off and picked up the bassinet to move the baby onto the grass. She pulled the blanket up around her sister Mary's shoulders and turned to Jo, putting her hands on either side of Jo's eight-year-old face.

"Run. Run to Mrs. Plemens's house and tell her to call the rescue squad."

Jo didn't stop to put her sandals on. Every stone and twig cut into her bare feet as she ran the quarter mile to the nearest house. She banged on Mrs. Plemens's door until she answered.

"Child. What are you …"

Everything came out in a rush, but Mrs. Plemens heard enough to pick up the heavy black phone and dial the rescue squad. It took an eternity for the dial to turn back after each number.

Why did an emergency number have so many nines in it?

By the time the rescue squad arrived, Mrs. Plemens had walked Jo back down to the river. Her mother was on the blanket, still and so quiet. Jo tried to look in her eyes, but they looked far away, in a place Jo didn't want to go. Mrs. Plemens pulled her away, holding her hand so tightly Jo thought her fingers might break, or melt together into one big finger. They all stood there for a long time. Aunt Jackie paced the riverbank calling out Jo's father's name. The rescue squad went out in two metal boats with outboard motors and zoomed up and down the banks.

Mr. Plemens arrived with his rifle and fired it over the river. Mrs. Plemens explained that it would make a body rise to the surface. Then one of the rescue squad volunteers started arguing with Mr. Plemens and told him to take his rifle and superstitions and go home.

The sun sank lower and lower. One rescue boat came slowly back up the river and beached near where Jo stood, her hand still squeezed by Mrs. Plemens. There was a lump in the boat, and the lump was covered with a faded blue tarpaulin. One of the men in the boat got out and went to Aunt Jackie to take her back to the boat. He lifted the edge of the tarp, and Aunt Jackie nodded, then turned her head away, crying.

Jo wiggled her hand out of Mrs. Plemens's grasp and was at the boat before anyone could stop her. She pulled up the tarp and saw her father's wet face. His lips were blue, and his skin was pale, despite the sun he'd gotten all summer. There was nothing of her father there in the motionless body. Jo didn't cry at first. Later in life she had concluded that she didn't cry then because, at eight, she was too young to process what death actually meant.

Her mother stood up and came to the boat to stand next to Jo. She started saying "John" over and over again, until she was screaming it at the top of her lungs. It was like she was trying to call her father back into his body from wherever he had gone. Jo was afraid then, and she started to cry. Aunt Jackie had Michael on her hip, and she pulled Jo in and held her close. Jo hid her face in the cotton of her aunt's sundress. Jackie's skin smelled like Coppertone, and the fabric of the dress carried the scent of the river from when she walked into the water calling her father's name.

A voice whispered in Jo's ear. "Don't let them in."

———

Jo woke up in her bed, in her apartment, in the middle of a city thousands of miles away from Tennessee and many years from that August day. Her face was wet with tears, and the scent of coconut oil lingered. She picked up her phone.

It was three o'clock in the morning in Ljubljana. In Chattanooga, Aunt Jackie would still be up. Jo found her aunt's name in her favorites list, tapped, and waited for her request to bounce off a satellite and connect to her aunt's phone.

Jackie answered on the second ring. "Jo? Are you okay? What time is it there?"

"It's early. I'm okay, but we really need to talk."

Jo relayed the events of the past two days. She included color commentary on the various stages of questioning her sanity. Jackie didn't say a word for the half hour it took Jo to tell the whole story.

"Are you still there?" Jo was sitting up in bed, leaning against the wall. She thought about turning on the lamp next to the bed but preferred the dark blue of night.

"I am so sorry."

"Dad said the same thing."

"I just never thought … I'm just so sorry."

"I appreciate that you were protecting me, and I appreciate everything you did. I'm past needing an apology though. I need some help. How do I turn this off?"

"Turn it off?"

"Yeah. If it suddenly turned on, there must be an off switch."

The line was silent for long enough for Jo to ask again if her aunt was still there.

"Jolene, honey, there's no off button."

Jo closed her eyes and tipped her head back to the wall behind her. She'd known that was what Jackie would say. She also knew this gift was the reason her mother had lost the plot. How many Wiley women had it taken? Why was it coming for her now?

"So I can't turn it off, then what do I need to do now? I don't want my apartment crawling with dead people." And I don't want to end up twisting my hair out in a Slovenian mental hospital. The image flashed through Jo's mind of her mother sitting in front of a puzzle with all of the pieces turned over to the blank side. That was the last time she'd seen her mother, and she'd been drugged into docility because she fought like a demon when anyone suggested she wasn't hearing real voices. At least some of that made sense now.

Jackie was speaking. "I think your friend and your father are right. I think you should go see this priest."

"What if he thinks I'm some kind of witch and wants to burn me at the stake in Mestni trg?"

"I can't imagine that will be his first reaction."

"You don't watch the news much, do you?"

"No. But he is your friend's family. I doubt she'd send you to him if she thought he was the Witchfinder General or something."

"True." Even if Vesna's question made her unsure which of them was reality-challenged.

"I can try to come next week. It'll take me a couple days to move money around and get a ticket."

"I don't think you need to come. We have all this modern technology at our fingertips. Surely we can do dead whisperer training via Skype?"

"Dead whisperer? Did you come up with that all by yourself?"

"Yes. Just now, with some help from my favorite TV trope. Sleep-deprived and nightmare-addled must be my happy creative place."

Jackie laughed. "At least you still have your sense of humor. You're probably going to need it. And you need some sleep. Go see this Brother Kos tomorrow if you can. If your father and this Helena person are showing up to warn you, it's probably serious."

"Thanks. It's not like I was worried already or anything."

"Women in our family have been doing this for a long time. You'll be fine. You just need some training and some protection."

"You aren't going to start in on the getting married thing, are you?"

"Am I married?"

"No. Why didn't I think to mention that to Dad?"

"Because he's still your father. He never knew what to think of me, so it probably wouldn't have done much good."

"Okay. I'm going to try to sleep. I've got work in the morning. Well, in a few hours. I'll try to sneak away for a bit this afternoon before we open. It'll be early for you."

"Maybe you should take tomorrow off."

"And do what?"

"Rest. Grieve." In her head Jo heard the unspoken "like a normal person."

"I really will go crazy if I sit up here all day doing nothing."

Jackie sighed heavily. "Your mother's illness isn't because of the gift."

"You'll excuse me if I find that hard to believe."

"I know you well enough to know you'll believe what you want, but I will tell you this. Mary was always fragile. She always danced too close to the edge. John's strong will was the last string that kept her from coming untethered."

"That's not very comforting."

"It should be. Honey, you're tied down like no one else I know."

Tied down did not fit at all with the image Jo had of herself. "Excuse me?"

"I'll let you figure that one out yourself. Get some sleep."

"I love you."

"I love you, too, Jolene."

Jo still missed dial tones. The sound of a dial tone rounded off a conversation more conclusively than nothing.

She set an alarm for eight and lay back down. She hugged a pillow and tried not to think about what Jackie had said. Tied down. Instead, she thought of Helena's brother. She wondered if sleep was eluding Matjaž too. She had a message to deliver. She stared out the window, wondering how her life had gotten so far outside the lines in such a short time. Her upstairs neighbor's laundry was still hanging on the line. The sheets were pale blue in the faint light that penetrated the interior of the courtyard. She watched them flutter until she finally fell asleep.

———

Interrupted sleep made Jo later than she would have liked, but she was still ahead of her usual schedule. She needed to set herself a challenge, a small one of the culinary kind — anything to keep from brooding on this mess. While she showered, she made a mental inventory of the shop's pantry and decided on twice-baked soufflés with custard cream as the day's chocolate item. She went over the recipe in her head while she dressed and put together a quick breakfast. She finished her coffee and two bites of toast and headed downstairs.

Bikini Kill blasted through the house speakers when Jo opened the door of the shop. Someone had beaten her to work. Maja was in the kitchen slicing bread for sandwiches. Jo was engulfed in the heady scent of vanilla.

"Someone's feeling her '90s this morning. Were you even

born yet?"

Maja raised an eyebrow and smirked. "Yes."

"Why are you here so early?" Jo put her apron on and glanced at the prep list Maja had put together. She peeked in the oven at the source of the vanilla fog that permeated the shop. Vanilla and candied shallot tartlets.

Maja looked up at her. "Why are you here at all? I assumed you'd take a day or two off. I thought it was just going to be me and Fred, and I wanted to get a jump on things."

"How'd you get in?" She really should have given Maja a key already.

"Vesna let me in when she went for her run."

"To answer your question, I'm here because I don't do the idle hands thing very well." And because alone in her apartment, she might wind up in another convo with Helena or her father. Her bandwidth for that was tapped.

"Makes sense, I guess. Menu look okay?" Maja pointed at the prep list with the tip of her bread knife.

"It does. Nice work. One change if you haven't already started. I was going to make twice-baked chocolate soufflés."

"Nope. Haven't started." Maja drew a line through the Nutella scones. "There's some candied orange peel, you could add that to the soufflés."

"Orange with chocolate is an abomination I refuse to perpetuate." Jo shuddered a little bit. The thought of that combination was the culinary equivalent of nails on a chalkboard.

"Didn't know you felt so strongly about it. We still need

another scone. Orange and something?"

Jo poked through the pantry and found a bag of dried cranberries. They were hard to get here, so Jackie always included some in her care packages, and they always found their way to the shop. "Let's do orange cranberry."

Maja nodded.

Jo assembled the ingredients for the soufflés and started the egg whites in the stand mixer. They would fall, but that was part of the plan. Before they went out, they'd get warmed again and topped with a pour of custard.

Just as she was getting them into the oven, she heard the bells on the door handle of the shop ring against the wooden door followed by a man's cough in the dining room. She poked her head out of the kitchen. Frédéric was there. "You're here early too."

"I didn't expect you to be here at all." Fred walked back and grabbed a clean apron out of the bag.

"Maja had the same idea. We should be able to crank out the prep list in no time, and then we can go over the menu for the catering gig next week." How much busy work could she generate today?

Frédéric nodded and scanned Maja's prep list. "Nice job."

Maja's blush reached the roots of her blue-dyed hair. Jo wasn't sure if Fred really was oblivious, or if Maja was just way below his too-young cutoff point. Either way, she hoped it wouldn't get in the way of their working together. Dishwashers were fairly easy to replace, her baker and cook were not.

Fred picked through the pantry and fridge to put together

his mise en place for a spicy lentil stew as the day's soup. Jo made a mental note to add mint tea to the day's tea specials.

She had another thought. "Maja, now that you're doing the bread baking and coming in early — I won't hold you to that — we should get you a key cut. You shouldn't have to wait on one of us."

Maja smiled up at Jo, who towered over her petite frame. "Yeah. I wanted to talk to you about picking up some extra hours. I'd like to quit the bar."

Jo was surprised. Maja made good money there, far more than they could pay her. "That's news. But yeah, let's talk about it. The new dishwasher starts tonight. Vesna and I can figure out a new schedule for next week."

Maja nodded. She bent her head back to the task at hand, cutting out orange-cranberry scones and humming along to Rancid's "Time Bomb."

At least something could go on normally or better in the midst of the other craziness that had beset her. Or not.

Smoke was pouring through the oven door.

Jo grabbed an oven mitt and pulled the tray of ramekins out of the oven. They had risen, liquefied, and burnt all over the tray in a sugary, acrid mess.

"Fuck." She looked around for a place to set them down. Nope. She carried the tray through the front of the house out to the courtyard and set it on the cobbles.

She leaned against the exterior wall, eyes closed. So maybe soufflés weren't the best idea. She opened her eyes and looked up into the balcony above her. Her elusive neighbor met her gaze, then turned back into the shadows.

Back inside, the smell of burnt egg and sugar blended with the odor of aerosol paint. She almost gagged. She propped the door open and pushed the big fan into the doorway. Maybe the air would clear enough to cover her mistake.

Frédéric stopped her halfway back to the kitchen with a plate and a cup of milky tea. "Sit."

"We need to finish." But she took the tea.

He set the plate on the nearest table and pulled out a chair. "We can finish. I've worked with you long enough to know you are a hazard to yourself and others in the kitchen when you're off your game."

She sat. "I thought I was holding it together better than that." She took a sip of tea. It was Fred's builders special, strong and toothache sweet.

Fred sat in the chair opposite her. "You know you don't have to do that, right?"

"But I do." She shook her head and took another sip. She couldn't tell him everything. How could he believe her when she didn't entirely believe it herself?

He stood up. "Suit yourself. You will anyway. At least finish the tea."

Her phone buzzed. The number came up unknown, but she answered.

"Ms. Wiley?"

"Yes, who is this?"

"Hello. This is Olga, Tomaž's business manager. He asked me to call to see if you would still be available to meet him at your teahouse today."

"Oh. Yeah. We're open. I'm here. Is it just him?"

"No, I think my— Katarina will be with him."

———

It was two thirty and the prep list was a line of marked through tasks. Jo and Maja split the dishes while Frédéric wrote out the chalkboard menus.

Jo put the scorched but clean sheet tray in the rack. "You can go if you want or you can have family meal here."

Maja dried her hands on her apron. "Can I take it to go? I might go talk to my boss now."

"Sure. I didn't realize it was that pressing. Everything okay?" Maja didn't like to talk much about herself. Jo knew she lived in a flat in Trnovo with a bunch of students and that she worked at one of Tomaž's bars on the river. Her parents had moved to Maribor, and she had a cat who left dead birds on her pillow. That was the sum total of the personal information Maya had shared in the year she'd been with them. Music and food were the only other things they talked about. The Fred thing Jo had figured out just by observing Maja's mooning over him while they worked.

Maja didn't dodge the question completely. "It's personal. I just kind of need a break from the two jobs thing."

"That's cool." Jo wanted to ask fifteen more questions but restrained herself. Maja's talent upped their game, and Jo was just glad she wanted to work with them more.

With her backpack slung over her shoulder, Maja took off. Her hair glowed neon when she walked through the shaft of sunlight penetrating the courtyard. Frédéric watched her leave.

He sighed heavily.

Jo nudged him. "What's that about?"

"I'm too old to deal with a schoolgirl's crush."

"She's hardly a schoolgirl. She's 24."

"Yes, and I'm 54. My daughter is older than her."

"True. I wasn't suggesting you pursue it. I just meant I don't think it will crush her dreams if you don't reciprocate. She's a tough cookie, our Maja."

"She is. But, you know as well as I that tough is often a façade."

"Also true. I've thought for a while that there was pain underneath all those tattoos."

Frédéric touched the sparrow on Jo's wrist. "You would know."

"Yeah. Well, I've had longer to shovel my shit than she has."

The deep, low tones of Frédéric's laugh filled the shop. "Well put."

She smacked the front of her apron with both hands, raising a puff of flour. "Let's eat and go over the catering menu." She needed something to do. She definitely wasn't ready to clue her employees into their boss's weirdness.

———

Jo was at the entrance of the courtyard balancing the chalkboard on the cobbles when Katarina and Tomaž arrived. Katarina was in a dark mood. Her jaw was set in a grim line, and Tomaž was deferential to her in a way Jo'd never seen.

Jo walked them inside and sat them at a table near the bakery counter where she could jump up to help in case she was needed. She probably wouldn't be. Damijan and Vesna would be there soon. Around opening time they got a few early people, usually curious tourists expecting older British ladies to pat them on the hand and call them "lovey." The students and regulars tended to come in after six and pack the place out around closing.

"What kind of tea would you all like? Today's pours are Darjeeling, Irish Breakfast, a white tea with jasmine, a green tea with toasted rice, and a Moroccan mint tisane." Jo smoothed the front of her apron. "If you don't want the same thing, I can do individual pots."

Tomaž looked at Katarina.

"I'd really like to try the white tea. I've never had it." Katarina looked up at her, unclenching her teeth, at least for a moment.

"Sure. And I thought I'd put together a sample plate of everything on the menu today so you can try what you like."

Tomaž looked relieved. "Wonderful."

"Be right back then." She started the tea in a large pot at the tea station and poked her head in the kitchen to speak to Frédéric. "Can you put together a sample plate? Tomaž and Katarina are here."

He nodded and pulled a plate off the rack above the work station.

She moved into the kitchen so she could whisper. "I think they must have had an argument before they got here. It's the first time I've seen Katarina anything but glazed or placid, and Tomaž is practically simpering."

"Maybe she's tired of his tomcatting."

"Maybe. But Jesus, why now?"

"Who knows. Maybe she thinks he wanted to meet you for more than sightseeing tips."

"As if." She mimicked gagging herself with two fingers. "Would you bring the plate out when it's ready? Katarina wants to meet you and thank you for helping Ivanka with her math."

"Give me a few minutes."

"Thanks." Jo returned to her tea as the timer went off.

She arranged the pot and three Japanese-style teacups on a tray with a honey server and a saucer of paper-thin lemon slices.

At the table, Tomaž murmured something that sounded apologetic. Katarina hissed back "She's barely older than your daughter." Jo approached and they both looked up at her with bright but rigid smiles.

"Thank you, Jo. It's very kind of you to see us while you're working."

Jo plastered on her best fake grin. "I'm always happy to talk about Tennessee." She sat down and poured them each a cup. "I'd recommend tasting it before you add anything. I think it's best on its own, but you might like to sweeten it."

Tomaž and Katarina tasted the tea and nodded their approval.

"It is quite light, but very lovely." Katarina turned the

teacup in her hand. "I've never seen these before."

"They're Japanese." Jo liked them but only used them for the white teas and fancier green ones. The cups were expensive and had a habit of disappearing.

Tomaž set his cup down and sat up very straight in his chair. "So, what should I see in Tennessee after my stay at Blackberry Farm?" Speaking in English, he said "farm" in the way Slovenians pronounced the "r" and "m" together, so it sounded like "farum."

"I'm most familiar with East Tennessee. It's a big state. It takes about eight hours to drive from Mountain City in the northeast corner to Memphis in the southwest one."

"I had no idea." Katarina looked surprised. If you drove nine hours from Ljubljana, you'd be in France.

"I think almost all the states except the teeny ones in New England are bigger than Slovenia. Anyway, Blackberry Farm is near Knoxville. I can send you a list of places to eat."

"Anything else?" Tomaž took a sip of his tea.

"The Smoky Mountains are close. If you're going soon, the autumn leaves will be beautiful." She thought about Chattanooga, about sitting with Jackie on her aunt's front porch overlooking the Tennessee, watching the leaf peeper boats creep up the river while she and Jackie drank their morning coffee.

"Do you miss it?"

Katarina's question pulled Jo out of her brief reverie. "Sometimes. But these mountains are home now." She gestured vaguely toward the snowy peaks that could be seen from the castle hill.

When Frédéric brought the sample plate out, Jo introduced him to Tomaž and Katarina. Katarina thanked him warmly for helping Ivanka survive her math classes and asked how he came to be so good with calculus. Frédéric just murmured a thank you and disappeared back into the kitchen.

It was a less than friendly departure, and Jo tried to cover. "He's busy finishing up a catering menu for a client to review."

Tomaž nodded distractedly. No big deal.

"It's nice to have an employee who is so dedicated to your business," Katarina said. She was looking more at Tomaž than Jo, but Jo agreed.

"Frédéric is very dedicated. I don't know what we'd do without him at this point." She held up the teapot to ask if either of her guests would like more tea.

Neither of them did. Tomaž looked more uncomfortable than he had when they arrived. He finished up the last of his tea, then put his hands on his thighs as if to stand.

"I guess we should be going. I'm sure you have things to do before the rush." He stood to help Katarina with her jacket before putting his on. "Thank you again for inviting us."

"Yes, thank you for inviting me," Katarina chimed in. "It was a pleasure to see your shop and to meet Frédéric. Ivanka will be pleased to know I met her maths tutor." Katarina smoothed the front of her jacket as Jo walked with the two of them to the door.

"I'm looking forward to your suggestions for places to eat in Tennessee." Tomaž stuck his hand out toward Jo. "Will you come with Gregor when he goes out to look at the farm?"

"If he asks me to." She didn't want to encourage Gregor in

this business deal, but she had promised that she'd discuss it with him. She would at least pretend to have an open mind about it.

"I hope he'll ask you. I will have Olga call him this evening to arrange it. I know you will influence his decision."

She didn't know what to say to that, so she just nodded. Tomaž strode out into the courtyard, but Katarina paused at the door.

"How do you do it?"

"How do I do what?"

"Whatever you want." She walked away without waiting for a response.

Inside, Jo went to the sound system that was set up behind the bakery counter and turned the music up. Joe Strummer's voice bounced around the room. Should he stay or should he go?

Frédéric came out of the kitchen drying his hands on his apron. "Gone?"

"Thankfully, yes." The shop felt lighter. Katarina's question puzzled her. Surely to god she did not think that Jo was one of Tomaž's conquests. The thought turned her stomach.

"You and Gregor know your business," he nodded at the door. "But those two are trouble."

"I agree with you about Tomaž. Katarina seems nice enough, though. Maybe a little sad." And jealous.

Frédéric shook his head. "Maybe, but they both make the hair on the back of my neck stand up."

She looked at the door where Tomaž and Katarina had

gone. "Well. I doubt there's much good that would come of Gregor getting involved with them financially. I trust Tomaž about as far as I could throw him."

"I don't know, if you were mad enough, I think you could probably hurl him a good meter or two."

She cocked her arm to make a muscle. There was a little bit of one. Her job was very physical, and there was a time when she had been queen of the mosh pits. They both laughed.

"Damijan should be here soon, and Tina, the new dishwasher, is supposed to arrive at five." She pulled out her phone and tapped it awake. It read 4:31. She slid the phone back into her skirt pocket and started to clear the table she'd shared with Tomaž and Katarina.

The bells on the front doorknob jangled again, and two of their regular afternoon customers came in. Janet and Evan were immigrant Brits who liked to get a taste of home at least once a week.

Evan stopped suddenly. "Jo, the mural! It's fantastic."

"I think so too. A local graffiti artist did it for us over the weekend. I apologize if it still smells like spray paint in here."

Janet laughed. "It adds to the authenticity." Their regular table happened to be the one she was busing. "Can we sit there?"

"Yes. Let me come back and wipe it off first." Jo balanced all the crockery on a tray back to the kitchen. She nudged Frédéric with her hip as she walked back out to the table, cloth in hand, "It begins."

"Bring it."

———

Even though it was a quick walk up to her flat, Jo pulled her jacket on. The temperature had plummeted after the sun went down, and the air was damp with promised rain. She checked with Damijan to see if there was anything else he needed. Fred was closing the kitchen station while Tina washed out the hotel pans. After ten until closing at midnight, the hot items ended, so Fred could leave, and only the remaining cold prep items were available.

She air-kissed Fred goodnight, waved at Vesna bent over more paperwork in the office, and headed out to the courtyard with a bag of trash for the receptacle down the street. She checked inside her jacket pocket for the card to open the lid. Her phone buzzed in her other pocket. It was Faron.

"You doing okay tonight? Need some company?"

"I'm good. A friend's coming over."

"Don't do anything I wouldn't do."

Cringe. Apparently she did exactly what he would do. Or who he would do. "Ha. Are you coming to the shop tomorrow?"

"Yep. Usual Tuesday crowd. We'll try to behave."

"Thanks. See you then."

"I love you, Mom."

"I love you too." Faron must still be worried about her. He was always sweet, but usually didn't check in so often.

Climbing up to the flat, she almost tripped over the bulk on the step before the first landing. "Jesus, Milo. You scared the shit out of me."

"Sorry. I should have come down when I saw you take the trash."

"It's fine." She didn't like being so skittish. She wouldn't get much done if she lived in dread of something jumping out from every shadow to confide its dead-person woes.

Milo put out his arm to indicate she should walk ahead.

She clomped up the steps in her heavy boots and started to unlock the door.

He wrapped his arms around her from behind and nuzzled his face into the back of her neck, kissing her silently with just parted lips. "Mmm. You smell of cinnamon." He kissed again. "And vanilla."

He knew exactly where to kiss her to bring every nerve ending to attention. It made it very difficult to open the door. Milo took the key ring out of her hand and turned her around to face him. He kissed her deeply on the mouth and took her hair down. She ran her hands up under his shirt onto his chest and moaned as he pressed into her.

He kissed her ear and caught her lobe and earring gently with his teeth. "God, woman. I have been distracted by the thought of you all day."

She moaned again. "We should really go inside."

He relented long enough to get the door open, accidentally mashing the button on the tiny LED flashlight she kept on the ring for when the stairwell light burned out. They were shedding clothes as the door closed, beginning with their shoes.

"Shower?" He whispered it as he kissed his way down her neck and across her collarbone.

"Bed first. I want a shower, but I think I want you more right now."

They kissed and undressed in the ten steps across the main room to the threshold of the bedroom. There was a step, which she stumbled against. He caught her and they both laughed and fell into bed together. He reached over to turn the lamp on next to the bed. "I want to see you."

She growled and flipped over on top of him.

She was glad her neighbors seemed to be heavy sleepers.

———

Milo was snoring softly. Jo got up, trying not to wake him. She needed to pee, and she still needed a shower. It was raining hard outside, and water drummed against the terra cotta shingles and echoed up to bounce off the courtyard walls. She walked naked to the bathroom and grabbed her towel off the back of the door. She started the shower to let it warm up while she used the toilet. Steam filled the tiny room, fogging the mirror. She stepped under the water with her head back to wet her hair, humming a few lines from "Time Bomb." Where had that come from?

She would have stood there for another ten minutes after rinsing off, but the water heater in the apartment was the size of a toaster. She turned off the tap and grabbed her towel from the sink to dry her arms and torso and legs. She paused to wipe a swath on the mirror with the edge of the towel so she could see to floss and brush her teeth, then bent over facing the sink to wrap her hair.

She straightened up and looked into the mirror and gasped when she saw behind her a delicate white face framed in neon blue hair.

Maja.

She turned; no one was behind her. The temperature in the bathroom had dropped, and she had gooseflesh up her arms. This was not good. Not good at all. She wrapped her robe around herself and tied it with trembling hands. Should she wake up Vesna, or Milo? Which would be willing to follow her out into the city at one in the morning? More importantly, which of them would require the least explanation?

She shoved her feet into her clogs and dashed across to Vesna's apartment. When the bell didn't work, she knocked quietly. Nothing but a loud meow from behind the door. She was about to knock again when the door opened. Vesna looked concerned.

"What's wrong?"

"What makes you think something's wrong?"

"I don't know, because you're half-dressed and knocking on my door in the middle of the night?" Vesna looked over Jo's head. "Wait. Did you see Helena again?"

"No." She hesitated to say it out loud; that would make it real, or at least closer to real. "I think I saw Maja."

Vesna's eyes widened. "Are you sure?"

"Blue hair."

Vesna nodded. "What do you want to do?"

"Go to her apartment and check on her." Adrenaline ebbing, Jo was feeling the cold.

"Now?"

"Yes. Either she's there and fine, or she's not and something bad has happened." Or Jo was just batshit. That was definitely a possibility.

"Okay. Give me five minutes." Vesna nodded and closed the door.

———

Jo opened the wardrobe as slowly as she could, but the door creaked anyway. She pulled out some jeans and a sweater and closed it again. Milo stirred, then sat up and turned the light on.

"Where are you going?"

"Out. I need … I need to check on something downstairs."

"Now?"

She nodded and pulled the sweater over her head. Vesna knocked on the door.

He cocked his head at her. "Are you expecting someone?"

"Vesna." She pulled her hair back and wound the elastic from her wrist around the ponytail.

He got up and walked past her to answer the door. Naked. "Jesus, Milo. Put some clothes on first."

He scooped his jeans off the futon and stepped into them commando. Vesna came through the door before he got them up.

Usually her friend would have been embarrassed, but she picked up the first T-shirt she saw on the futon and threw it at him. "Jesus, Milo. Put some clothes on."

Milo laughed. "You two have known each other a long time." He pulled the T-shirt over his head. "Now, which one of you is going to tell me what the hell is going on?"

Vesna looked at Jo and then launched into a completely boldfaced lie. "I had this awful dream that something had happened to Maja. And I know I won't be able to sleep unless I go check on her. I didn't want to go alone, so I woke up Jo."

"Does Maja not have a phone?" Milo looked at Vesna and back at Jo. Clearly he thought they were smarter than that.

"I tried calling. No answer." Vesna shoved her phone in her pocket. Jo knew she hadn't made that part up.

"If you two are determined, I'm going with you." He picked up his sweater from the floor and pulled it on over the T-shirt.

"You really don't need to do that." Jo walked past him to stand next to Vesna inside the door.

"Yes. I do. Remember? I'm not supposed to be here if you're not here?"

Jo rolled her eyes. It was impossible to argue that point, given how many times she'd thrown it at him.

———

The three of them walked through the quiet streets to Trnovo, Milo grousing at the cold and rain and at the ridiculousness of going to check on a grown woman in the middle of the night. He might have been less miserable if he'd had a raincoat.

"Seriously, Vesna, how bad was this dream?" He shoved his hands deeper into the pockets of his jeans and bowed his head against the drizzle.

She shook her head like she was trying to shake away the memory of the dream. "Just terrible."

When they got to the apartment building, Jo realized she had no idea which flat was Maja's. Vesna signed the paychecks, so she led them up to the first floor. Milo and Vesna stood shoulder to shoulder behind Jo, and she knocked.

Nothing.

She knocked again louder.

The door to the next apartment opened. An elderly man poked his head out the door. "What do you want? Those girls are never home."

Vesna stepped toward him. "You haven't seen them all day?"

"Am I their keeper?" He slammed the door, and Jo could hear him stomping back through his flat.

"I guess it's no picnic living in a building full of students." Milo shrugged. "Can we all go back to bed now?" He rubbed his hands together and shoved them back into his pockets.

"Let's stop by the blue bar and see if she's at work." Jo walked between them and headed back down the stairs. She could practically hear Milo rolling his eyes at her.

"The blue bar?" His question trailed after her.

"Spotlight," Vesna said. "Maja's second job. Jo can never remember the name of it."

They walked back to the old town and crossed the river at the Shoemaker's Bridge. Jo looked out over the water. Even in the dark, it looked like chocolate milk rushing under their feet. There was no calming force in the churned-up depths, but something was there, and that something made her feel like the river was watching her.

"Hey, Jo. Let's get on with it." Milo nudged her with his shoulder.

She walked on, unable to shake the sense of something sentient in the river, waiting.

The blue bar was closed. She'd forgotten that on weeknights they were only open until one. Should've gone there first.

"Look. She's probably at some club and can't hear her phone, or it's dead." Milo put his arm around Vesna's shoulders and squeezed her. "You can tell her in the morning how worried you were."

Jo peered into the darkened bar. Maybe Milo was right.

Maybe it had been some other random shade trying to get in touch with her. Shit, if she were Maja's age, she'd probably be out at a club too.

"You're probably right." She turned and walked past her friends. A flashing image of the muddy river rising up over the embankment to carry her away stopped her before she stepped onto the bridge. Great. Now she was hearing voices and seeing anthropomorphic rivers.

———

Jo and Milo sat in silence on the futon after Vesna left. Her head was churning. Questions about Maja tumbled through her mind along with prayers to whoever, or whatever, might be listening, that the pale face framed in wet, blue hair peering from her mirror was something she'd imagined.

When Milo stood and offered her his hand, she took it and he led her back to the bedroom.

He pulled her into a bear hug at the foot of the bed and rested his chin on the top of her head. "You're a little crazy, you know that, right?"

She stiffened.

He laughed and pulled back to look her in the face. "I'm just kidding. Are you okay?"

"I guess. Maybe worried a bit."

"Because of Vesna's dream? Is she a prophet or something?"

She wouldn't wish any of this bizarre paranormal crap on her worst enemy, let alone her best friend.

"I think maybe you should have taken some time off. You don't have to always be the tough-as-nails punk chick, you know."

She pulled back and looked him in the face. "Is that how you see me?"

"Why do I feel like that's a trick question?" He hugged her back to him and put his chin back on the top of her head. "When I first met you, yes. I know better now. You've got a soft center like the rest of us mortals."

His heart raced in his chest under her cheek.

"Let's get some sleep." He untangled from her and undressed on the opposite side of the bed.

Sleep was the last thing she wanted. It was the closest thing to being alone. She slid next to him under the duvet and wrapped her leg over his hips and her arm across his chest, settling herself under his arm. She brushed the backs of her nails down his stomach to just below his navel.

"I don't think I can possibly sleep." She felt a pang of guilt at using him for the distraction of sex.

He lifted his head to look at her. "Really, now?"

"Mmm." She moved her leg and ran her hand down his body, digging her nails in lightly on the inside of his thigh.

He moaned in response. He turned on his side to face her, then gently pushed her flat onto her back and slid his slender body between her legs. He kissed down across her belly, teasing her.

He whispered softly against her skin, "How do you still smell like cookies?"

———

She woke to a small brown bird twittering at her window. She thought she saw a long blue hair in its beak, material for the nest it had started on the deep sill outside. She stood up and crouched at the window to examine the bird more closely.

It was only thread, but that didn't make her feel less guilty.

She'd spent the dark hours fucking Milo's brains out. How had Maja spent the dark hours? Had they still been hers to spend? She resisted the thought that Maja could be dead. What could've happened to her? Who could want to hurt her? And what duty did Jo have to the dead who came to her?

Jesus, she really needed to talk to Jackie.

Milo had stirred when she'd gotten up, then settled back into sleep. He looked completely at peace curled around the warm spot in the bed where she had been.

Would she ever be able to sleep like that again?

She walked to the armoire to get a robe. The silk was cold as it settled around her. She tied the belt and padded softly into the kitchen to make coffee as quietly as possible.

No visitors, please. She needed some caffeine first.

———

Milo got up. She must have made more noise than she thought.

He walked up behind her as she was pushing the plunger down in the French press, and he untied her robe. He turned her to face him, pressing her ass into the countertop behind her. "You were even more amazing than usual last night."

She tied her robe back together and kissed him chastely on the cheek.

He looked disappointed. "Not up for an encore this morning?"

"You …" She laid her hand on his chest. "You are always a temptation. Especially rubbed up against me all naked." She kissed him squarely on the mouth to soften the blow. "But I'm way too deep into my head this morning to be much fun." She ducked under his arm and turned to get mugs from the cupboard.

He didn't push. He retreated to the bedroom and came back wearing another of her robes, a deep blue silk one patterned with images of white paper cranes. He looked better in it than she did. She handed him a cup of coffee and brought the milk and sugar to the table.

"Toast?"

"Sure. Do you still have some of that apple butter stuff?" She made tons of it for the shop but kept her own stash squirreled away in the flat, and she'd happily passed her addiction on to Milo.

She assembled a stack of toasted bread and all the accompaniments, carried the tray to the table and sat down opposite Milo. She slathered a piece of toast with butter and lifted it to take a bite. Her teeth were halfway through the toast when he thoroughly ruined her morning.

"Jo, you know I'm not actually seeing anyone else."

She completed the bite and looked up at him. "What?" she said around a mouthful of toast.

"I'm in love with you."

A gulp of coffee helped the toast go down. She set down her mug and stared at him. He was still speaking.

"I know you don't believe in love—"

She interrupted him. "I do believe in love. I know it exists. I just … It's not my thing."

"I know."

She smiled sadly at him. Her heart was breaking a little. "I care for you. As more than a friend … I mean last night … What we have … It's important to me." Shit. The words she had to say would be worse for him if he really did love her.

He tried to help her finish her thought. "But you can't give me what you think I want."

She sighed heavily. "What do you want?"

"More mornings like this. More nights like last night. Well, minus roaming around in the rain in the middle of the night."

He chuckled.

"I can give you that." She smiled at him and looked down into her coffee cup. She was pretty fond of those things too. She waited for him to speak again.

"And everything else. And for all that not to change you."

She cocked her head at him. Already she was more changed than he could possibly know.

"The Jo that I am completely, stupidly in love with exists because you don't belong to anyone else but you."

"What about this woman you've been seeing?"

"I made her up. I was afraid you'd get spooked if you thought I was only seeing you."

She looked down into her coffee again as if some universal truth about the capriciousness of human hearts might be floating around with the milk. Milo knew her better than she'd thought. "I want to say I'm sorry, but that sounds incredibly cheap somehow."

"I'm not telling you to make you feel guilty."

"Why are you telling me?"

"Because last night while I was sitting on your stairs watching you take the trash out, I was thinking about telling you I couldn't see you anymore. You would've chalked it up to me falling for my imaginary girlfriend and never been the wiser."

"But?"

"But then there you are, smelling like a bakery, willing to entertain your friend's crazy goose chase, and I thought I could be willing to be with you on your terms."

"And this morning?"

"It's not enough." He didn't look away. There was a whole speech he wasn't making, but she could see it in his face. "We're friends who fuck. That's great but, I …" He looked down, then back up at her, resolved. "I want more than that. I want a life with you."

Her heart was breaking for him. There was no way she could continue with him now. It would be monumentally unfair to trail him on, letting him think she would change.

She stood up and walked to his side of the table and pulled him up. She led him back to the bedroom. He stopped her and looked into her face with a question etched on his.

"For goodbye," she said.

CHAPTER 10

Jo wasn't thrilled to be alone in the apartment after Milo left, but Leonard singing "Hallelujah" at the top of her speakers' range might be enough to keep at bay anything that had a message for her. She wanted to shower and get dressed and out onto the cobblestones of Ljubljana, out into the world of living, breathing people. People who mostly didn't know her, and who wouldn't be in love with her if they did. She needed to see Vesna. She needed to go to church, apparently. Then she needed to Skype Jackie.

She stood in the shower until the water was cold. She could still feel Milo's warm hands and mouth on her skin. She would miss him, but ending it was best for both of them. She didn't want to be a source of pain to him, didn't want to invite feelings of resentment on his part and guilt on hers that pity sex was all she could give him. Maybe those lonely housewives in science fiction novels with their android lovers were onto something. Maybe robot sex was too gross to think about. Maybe she just needed to take a break from other people.

Leonard had moved on to "Who by Fire" by the time she

stepped out of the bathroom. She'd always thought the song should start with "who by water." Drowning was infinitely more terrifying to her than burning. Either way, the last thing she needed at this moment was a rundown of all the ways people she loved could die. Skipped. "First We Take Manhattan" made a better background for toweling her hair and layering on her shield of clothing for the day. She was halfway into a black ballet dress when Vesna's usual three light knocks sounded at the door.

She pushed her arms and head through and walked to the door still pulling the dress down over her thick black tights. It wasn't Vesna at the door.

Gregor stood on the stone flags of the landing, with a pale gray scarf casually wrapped around his neck and shoulders and a corduroy jacket that looked cat-belly soft. The smallest worry line marred the skin between his dark brows. "Are you alone?"

She laughed. "Yes. You probably won't need to ask me that for awhile, given recent events." She motioned him in.

"I can't stay." He stood in the entryway. "I just wanted to stop by and make sure you're doing okay."

"You didn't have to come all the way down here. You could've called."

"I know but I was worried about you. I woke up feeling guilty for not checking on you yesterday."

"I'm fine. Or as fine as can be expected." Should she tell him about the dead whisperer thing? "I worked yesterday, and Milo and Faron and Vesna have been keeping me company." Not to mention my dead father, Helena's ghost, and maybe an apparition of Maja.

"Okay. I've got a meeting for lunch and then I'm free for the afternoon. Are you working?"

"No. Enforced day off per Vesna, but I have errands." She needed to find Maja, and she needed to see a priest.

"Smart of her, and of you, for listening to her."

"Did you stop in downstairs?"

"Yes. Vesna and Frédéric are doing prep."

"Vesna's doing prep?"

"Maja hasn't shown up yet."

Her heart sank into her stomach.

"Are you listening to Leonard Cohen?" In the background "Suzanne" was offering tea and oranges.

"Yes."

"Are you really okay? What did you mean I won't have to ask if you're alone?"

"Milo and I just ended things."

Gregor closed the door behind him and slid his shoes off. He sat on the futon and pulled her down by her wrist to sit by him. "What happened?"

Recounting the morning's events was going to earn her another lecture on love, but she told him anyway, because they were friends, and because it might put him off the scent of what had really shaken the foundations of her world. At least for another day or two.

Gregor had a way of listening that made her feel like she was the only person in the entire world of interest to him.

She told him about her morning, minus a blow-by-blow of the farewell sex. She did not mention the real reason she'd taken off to Trnovo in the middle of the night.

He ran his hand over the top of her hair and followed it to the very ends where it was still a little damp. "I'm sorry. You've had a bad week." No lecture.

"That would be putting it mildly." Jo put her head on Gregor's shoulder. He and Vesna and Faron were the solid center of her personal universe. In the midst of the hip-check craziness that had descended on her, they were the reason she wasn't curled up under a table eating pudding with her fingers.

When Jackie said Jo had more than one thread tethering her, that's what she'd meant.

Gregor put an arm around her shoulders. "You were going out, weren't you?"

"Yes. The errands."

"I'll walk you down." He leaned back on the futon, and she got up to finish putting herself together.

"I'm guessing by the scarf it's cold this morning?" She wound her own scarf around her head.

"Hm, and wet." He gestured toward the wet umbrella leaning against the wall, holding his phone in both hands as he typed a reply to a text. He looked up at her. "Ready?"

She nodded. She had to steel herself before going downstairs to face whatever news that might be waiting. But staying in the flat alone was not a tempting prospect. Out looked like the lesser weirdness, if not the lesser evil.

———

Gregor kissed her goodbye and disappeared through the courtyard door onto Zajčeva. Jo went into the shop and poked her head into the cramped kitchen. Frédéric was busily frosting burnt butter cupcakes with warm ganache. Vesna looked at the prep list with a frown but leapt up when she saw Jo in the door. She flung her arms around her, nearly knocking her down in surprise.

"Vee, what the hell?"

"I'm just worried about you. Are you doing okay this morning?" And then very softly with her mom face on, "Anything else happen?"

"Not what I think you mean, but yes. Milo and I ended things."

"That snake! How dare he break up with you!"

"Whoa. Cool your jets. He did not break up with me, if you want to call it that. It was a mutual agreement." She wasn't entirely sure that was true. She suspected Milo would've let things linger a little longer if she'd let it.

"Oh." Vesna didn't much look like she believed her either. "On a completely different note. No Maja?" It didn't take a search to see she wasn't there.

"No." Vesna stepped further away from Fred. "It's not good."

"No, it isn't."

Jo was still clinging to her last shred of denial. "I'll stay and help—"

"No, you won't. I already messaged Damijan and asked him to come in early." Vesna motioned her out of the kitchen.

Out of Frédéric's earshot, Vesna stopped. "You need to go see Uncle Leo. Now."

"No. If I'm not going to help you open the shop, I'm going to go look for Maja."

"Maybe Milo was right, and she's just sleeping one off this morning?"

"Do you honestly believe that?"

"I want to."

So did Jo. But she had also not believed in corporeal dead people hanging out in her apartment.

She started to speak, but Vesna cut her off again. "I messaged Leo when I got up."

"What did you tell him? That your batshit best friend was coming by to chat about her in-depth convos with the dead?"

"Not in so many words. He's a good guy though. He'll meet you at the cathedral."

"Text me if Maja comes in or you hear from her." Vesna nodded and sent her marching.

Out on the cobbles, Jo took a deep breath. She looked up through the open square of the courtyard to the leaden sky. She pulled her coat tighter around her and walked out onto the embankment and along the river to Tromostovje, the Triple Bridge. There was less foot traffic than usual. Even so, people were making their way to and fro between Mestni trg and Prešeren Square. A green Kavalir car hummed by her and crossed over the center bridge. She wondered what Richard Scarry would have made of the old city traffic of fancy golf carts, bicycles, and pedestrians? Would he have drawn a little cartoon Jo with a Halloween ghost wafting beside her and a label that said Dead Whisperer?

She passed the copy of the Robba Fountain, boarded up for the season, and continued down to the cream-colored cathedral of Saint Nicholas. Its dome and belfries shaded the street, and like every cathedral she'd ever seen, she felt small and fleeting beside it. She stood at the sundial on the south side of the building and looked at the inscription. She didn't know Latin, but Gregor had told her many years ago that Nescitis diem neque horam translated roughly to "you don't know the day or hour."

The hour of what? Of death? Of Jesus's return? The thought pulled on a deep childhood memory from the few Sunday mornings she'd been dragged to church. The mystery of death had taken center stage in her life, become a far more constant companion than she liked. The idea pricked her thoughts as she reached the heavy bronze door that was really a high-relief sculpture of a line of churchmen wearing tea cozy hats. She wrapped her hand around the bright polished handle where hundreds of hands kept the patina from settling, and she pulled.

The church was quiet except for the riot of decoration shouting from every nook and cranny of the walls and ceiling.

Gilded and ornate, it was not much to her taste despite its being well known. Whatever gods were hers, Jo was certain they preferred moss and trees and open fields.

There was one other person in the church. A man sat in the first pew. He was maybe in his fifties, and his dark head was bowed in what she assumed was prayer. She walked to the front of the church and sat in the pew across the aisle from him.

He looked up. It was impossible to sneak up on anyone in there, especially in clogs. The smallest sound echoed off every carved and blinged inch of the place. He looked over at her, and in one fluid motion of black cloth he stood and walked to stand in front of her. He extended his hand and spoke to her in British-accented English.

"You must be Jo."

She stood and extended her hand. "I have to say, Brother Kos, you aren't what I expected."

"Not gray-faced and angry-eyebrowed?"

"Something like that."

"Vesna's father, my brother, was fifteen years older."

She had to look up at him. Maybe he was an ex-basketball player? He had Vesna's dark eyes and her same smile. "Is there somewhere less shiny and more private we can talk?"

He laughed, an open clear laugh that cinched her affection for him. "Yes. I know you sell tea, but do you drink coffee?"

"Enthusiastically."

"We can go to the rectory. I make a serviceable cup of Turkish coffee."

She followed him out of the cathedral and back out onto the pedestrian street as gray as the sky and the day. He put his hands deep inside his cassock and walked briskly, with her in his wake trying to keep up with his long strides.

———

The inside of the rectory was plain and worn but cozy. The scent of incense from the church had followed them, or maybe it lived there in the couch and curtains. She wondered if Brother Kos could still smell it after so many years. Some days she could still smell the butter and sugar and spice of her work. Sometimes she forgot until someone else reminded her she smelled of baking. Usually Milo.

But not anymore.

She reined her thoughts back to the task at hand as she settled into the rectory couch. "Brother Kos, do you live here?"

He came back to the sitting room from the kitchen. He'd taken off the heavy cassock and stood tree-tall in his Roman-collared shirt and black pants. "No, but I am friends with the Father and stay here when I am in Ljubljana. Cream and sugar?"

"Cream only please, or just milk if you have it."

"Milk it is." He walked back to the kitchen out of her sight. His footsteps echoed away from her, and there was a hiss of gas as a stove burner lit.

The sitting room had a large window of old, imperfect glass. It had started to rain with gusto since they'd come in, and water droplets were combining into rivers that raced each other to the windowsill. Beyond the rain spatter, terra cotta roofs radiated out from the center of town. They were the brightest thing in the wet fall day. She hoped Maja was out there sleeping off a night of after-work drinks.

Brother Kos returned with two steaming cups of coffee. She took the cup he offered her and settled back into the couch.

She was happy to have the warm mug to wrap her cold hands around. He sat opposite her on the couch and stretched his legs out into the sitting room.

"Vesna didn't give me much detail about why you were coming, only that it was personal and urgent."

Damn. She was really hoping Vesna had explained things to him. It sounded crazier every time she spoke the words out loud. Best to be blunt. "I can talk to dead people."

She hadn't been exactly sure what she expected, but his complete lack of reaction had definitely not been it.

"Brother Kos, did you hear what I said?"

"Jo, please call me Leo. And, yes, I heard you."

"Okay, Leo. Um…"

"Vesna would not have sent you to me if it hadn't been something out of the ordinary."

"Out of the ordinary? I thought it was more like batshit crazy."

"I don't think you are mentally ill. You have a gift. Must be a new one." He took a sip of coffee.

She sat her cup down. Maybe she should run. Maybe he was crazier than she was.

He must have sensed her fight or flight response kick in. "I didn't handle that very well. Let's start over. Tell me what's happened, then I'll explain my lack of surprise."

She relaxed a little and started with Helena's body at the reception. Once she started, it tumbled out faster and with more detail than she'd shared with Jackie, even Maja's face in the mirror, even the sex, even Milo's departure.

Leo leaned closer to her. He didn't interrupt.

"And Aunt Jackie agreed I should come to see you, and she and I are supposed to Skype and discuss what I need to do to protect myself or develop my gift or whatever." Jo leaned back into the couch and pulled her legs up underneath her. She was drained and relieved that Brother Kos, Leo, hadn't made the sign of the cross at her with his fingers or splashed her with holy water.

"How are you holding up?"

"Strangely well most of the time. I'm guessing that's when I am in denial." She shrugged. "And then I have moments where I think this must be what it's like to spiral into madness."

"That's a healthy response. Nothing prepared you for this."

"You can say that again." She wrapped her arms around her legs.

"Are you cold?"

"Yes."

He got up and disappeared into another room. He came back with a throw and draped it over her legs. He sat back down and turned to her and started to speak.

She stopped him. "Sorry. But am I not going to get some sermon on my highly immoral lifestyle or something?"

"No. You aren't Catholic, so you needn't live by our rules."

"I have to say that's a refreshing attitude, but I'm a little shocked."

"We're not all narrow-minded Bible-thumpers."

"Guess my prejudice is showing."

"You're hardly the first."

"Still. I apologize."

"Thank you, but it's unnecessary. The Church doesn't do very well in the PR department sometimes."

"Sorry. You said you'd explain why you were so nonchalant about my revelation."

"The supernatural is my area of expertise. Actually, it's our family's area of expertise."

That was news. "Wait. What? Vesna?"

"Well, no. She's knowledgeable, but she chose not to go into the 'family business,' as it were."

"But. She never said. I mean. Fuck … oops. Sorry."

He laughed and shook his head to indicate her apology was again unnecessary.

"What exactly is the family business?" Jo sat up and picked up her coffee again.

"This place is old. Much older than Ljubljana. Older than Emona. Older than the bits and pieces of past civilizations that bubble up in the marshes. With that long history comes layers of beliefs and lives and all the endless possibilities on the edges of most people's day to day reality."

"Okay."

"Someone has to keep an eye on all those things that would most likely tear through the veneer of civilization we all maintain. My family has been doing that for a very long time."

"You're like, what, the ghost sheriff?"

"Not quite so formal. And ghosts are the least of worries." He laughed. "But, like your family, we have a purpose and a job to do."

"And I, with my dead whisperer superpower, just happen to be best friends with a scion of the mighty supernatural watchdogs of Slovenia?"

"People are drawn together for many reasons." He leaned back on the couch.

"I know, 'everything happens for reason.' Blah blah blah." She flung her hand out sarcastically.

He bolted back up. "No. Everything does not happen for a reason. The universe we see, and don't see, is chaos. Our jobs are to stand on the edge of that and try to keep it at bay for as long as possible."

She was duly chastised. "I didn't mean to…"

"It's just important that you don't cling to this fantasy of predestination or resigning to our fates. Everything you do has an impact, Jo, especially now."

The responsibility of what all of this meant settled onto her like a lead blanket. She'd thought it was something happening around her. Leo made it seem more like it was happening because of her.

She sighed and sat up straight on the couch, her legs still covered by the throw some parishioner must have knitted a long time ago. "So what's next?"

"I think you should talk to your Aunt Jackie and learn what you can about how the Wileys have dealt with this particular gift. And I think you should go to the police and report Maja as a missing person."

"Maybe she just didn't show up to work."

"Don't fool yourself. You are clearly smarter than that."

"I'm not sure how that conversation is going to go." She could already guess the look she'd get if she spoke to Investigator Klančnik again. She was pretty sure the woman already thought she was some kind of reprobate. "Anything else?"

"I think we should keep in touch."

"Dead whisperer confession?"

"You can call it that, but I believe we can be of use to each other, and it's good to have someone you can confide in who … understands."

"There's that." She stood up. "I should let you get on with your day. I'm going to check in at the shop to confirm Maja never showed or called. Then it looks like I'm going to the police."

He stood and looked down into her face. "I'd like to offer you a blessing."

"Brother … Leo. I don't believe."

"You do believe in something. It's all the same magic, just dressed in different clothes."

She nodded her acceptance.

He put his hand on the back of her head and bowed his. Jo closed her eyes. He spoke in Latin, finishing with "amen."

"What did you say?"

"I asked God to walk with you and keep his Guardians near."

"Thank you." She hugged him on impulse.

He hugged her back, warmly. She relaxed into him, a little too easily, and pulled back when she remembered herself. Leo released her and held her by the shoulders out from him. "Please be careful. It is not the dead you need to be afraid of. They have no physical power over the living."

She nodded.

"The dead are usually only concerned with their own fears and problems. Here." He stepped away and rummaged through a small drawer in the table he'd set the coffee tray on. She expected a crucifix, but he produced a highly polished stone. "Take this." He dropped it into her open palm.

It was cool and smooth in her hand. "What is it?"

"It's a rock, Jo."

They both laughed.

"I know it's a rock, but why take it?"

"It's from a holy well near one of the Mithras shrines. It won't stop evil, but it'll let you know it's close."

"Why is it so smooth?"

"It's been carried in many pockets."

She slid it into her own pocket. "Thank you, again. For the coffee, for listening, for…"

"For making you feel like maybe you aren't batshit?" He smiled at her.

"Exactly that." She gave him another quick hug and stood on her toes to kiss him on the cheek.

CHAPTER 11

Leo closed the door behind Jo. He didn't have his niece's gift to see auras, but he didn't need it. Jo was powerful. It came off her in waves, like the scent of vanilla off her hair when she'd embraced him. Vesna was probably right about her being his type, as well, but that wasn't a thought he wanted to linger over.

A conversation with Lichtenberg was in order. He lived in Jo and Vesna's building. He'd assumed it had been to keep an eye on Vesna, and therefore on him, but maybe he knew about Jo and her family all along. He and his organization had endless archives, or so Leo's father had said.

He moved to the window and watched her walk up the street. Her head covered by the black hood of her raincoat, she looked as much a monk as he did in his cassock. He suspected she could handle herself. That wasn't the root of his worry for her. She turned a corner and disappeared into the rain.

He sat down on the chair and picked up the battered phone on the end table. He held the receiver on his shoulder with his head while he looked for Lichtenberg's number in his mobile phone contacts. He figured Lichtenberg knew how to get in touch with him, but he had no desire to make it easier for him by calling from his personal phone.

He punched the numbers in and waited to leave a message. He got the man himself instead.

"Brother Kos, I've been expecting a call from you."

No point in being politic then. "Have you always known what she was?"

"Yes and no."

Leo waited for him to continue.

"I, we, knew about her family lineage. She would only have been of interest if she'd borne a female child, otherwise she was an anomaly."

Few people had Lichtenberg's ability to irritate the shit of him. His voice, his wordiness, his very existence, was damn near insufferable. His uncharitable thoughts would be another thing to discuss at confession.

"I saw her, that first night. Her au- … Something had changed. She is a *vox de mortuis*. If I'm not mistaken, she's an especially unusual one and therefore potentially very dangerous."

Lichtenberg was baiting him. He wanted him to spew the medieval garbage his father and his brother had believed about people like Jo, who, admittedly, they would have labeled a witch. "I would think her ability makes her an asset. Especially if this gift is rare."

"It is quite rare. The assumption was it would die out with her mother and aunt. Have you spoken with her?"

"Yes. Just now." He had no intention of volunteering anything else.

"Did she tell you her mother is unstable?"

Leo paused. He knew Lichtenberg knew more than he would ever tell him, and he had no desire to betray Jo's trust.

Lichtenberg continued after his pause. "She isn't Catholic. Your conversation wasn't under the seal of the confession."

"It wasn't." He gritted his teeth to avoid saying something he would regret.

Lichtenberg sighed. "She is unstable, her mother. Ms. Wiley may have inherited that trait as well. Whether or not Ms. Wiley knows it, she is both in danger and a danger. Without any kind of training, she is unlikely to be able to control her ability. I would appreciate your being circumspect about that, especially given your desire to protect others from harm."

Leo hung up the phone. He was past the point of tolerating Lichtenberg's condescension. His presence in Ljubljana was a reminder of his family's failure to save Berta, and she, in turn, of his own failures. He would not fail his niece's trust in him to protect her friend. He would protect Jo from Lichtenberg and his cronies. If it came to it, he would protect her from himself.

CHAPTER 12

The rain changed to the kind of heavy mist an umbrella was no use against. Jo stood on the embankment in front of the blue bar. "Spotlight" was splashed across the front door in a nearly indecipherable font. At night the place was bathed in neon blue light. The hue didn't exactly bring out the best in most people's complexions, and Jo had never liked the place, but it was where Maja worked. Had worked? If she really had quit yesterday. They weren't open yet, but a young man stood behind the reflective black granite bar polishing glasses with a towel. She should have gone straight to the police station, but she wanted to confirm something first. She knocked.

The man turned and waved her away. She knocked again, harder.

He put the bar towel down and came to the door. He turned the lock and opened the steel and glass panel just enough to stick his face out and tell her to go away because they weren't open yet.

Before he could close the door, she stuck her clog inside. "Look. I know you're closed. I'm looking for someone, Maja

Demšar. Do you know her?"

"Yeah. She didn't work last night. I haven't seen her today." He tapped the end of her clog with his own shoe to push her foot out and closed the door in her face without another word.

She resisted the urge to bang on the door with her fist. No point in taking out her fear and frustration on some douche-y barkeep who didn't give two shits. She started back toward the police station. It was raining again, and she put her head down and pulled her raincoat hood up in a vain attempt to keep her face dry. She plotted the rest of her day as she walked, trying to keep her spirits from sinking along with her heart. She knew Leo was right. She'd known last night that Maja was dead. It didn't make sense though. What could have possibly happened to her? Helena and Maja. There was no way this wasn't all connected. With Helena's death she'd suddenly become a lamplight to the dead. They'd both come to her. Were they dead because of her?

She stopped in a doorway to pull out her phone and text Vesna. "Did Maja show?"

Jo waited for a reply. "Called multiple times. No answer."

She returned her phone to her pocket and leaned against the door behind her. She took a deep breath and an emotional inventory. Fear. Grief. Loneliness. Anger. Anger was good. Anger would get her through the next hour. Everything else could wait.

The rain slowed, and she stepped back out into it, her shoulders squared. She walked up through Prešeren Square, past the Union Hotel, and on to the police station. She had no idea what she was going to say when she got there, but someone should be looking for Maja's body and the police had more resources for that kind of thing than she did.

She told the sour-faced woman behind the glass partition at the front desk that she wanted to speak with Marta about a missing person. The woman hrumphed in response and picked up the phone next to her.

"Investigator Klančnik is with someone." She emphasized Marta's title to remind Jo she had been terribly familiar. "She asked for you to wait in the lobby."

"Do you know how long it will be?"

"No." She slid the glass closed with an unmistakable finality. Jo sat on the nearest molded plastic chair. The lip of the orange seat bit into her thighs. She figured on a long wait and tried to make herself comfortable without success. Her phone vibrated in her pocket. She was going to ignore it but thought better of it on the off chance it was an apologetic Maja.

It was instead an apologetic Vesna. "Hey. I know I said you should take the day off. But Miha called to ask if he could bring a tour through around five."

Vesna's brother was a tour guide and occasionally brought groups to the teahouse at the end of a tour. It meant an hour or two of madness but usually brought in good money, which was nice as the tourist season ended. The tea shop was business as usual, even if everything else was upside down.

"Where're they from?" Country of origin usually gave an idea of what to prepare for.

"China."

"Oh." No English or Slovene speakers and typically only one

or two translators. Orders took forever, with the result that those who ordered first were ready to leave before the last orders were in. It was a pretty sweet juxtaposition though: Chinese pensioners rocking out to the Ramones and eating cucumber sandwiches.

"I'm with the police," she told Vesna. "Be there as soon as I'm done."

She'd rather be at the shop. Shit, she'd rather be cleaning the underside of the range than here. This. All this. The dead whisperer thing, Helena's death, Maja's death: if she was being honest with herself, it was more the stuff of fever dreams than her waking life. How had any of the Wiley women stayed sane when absolutely none of this made any sense?

She tapped the email app icon just as Marta emerged from the warrens of the police station to collect her.

"Ms. Wiley, I'm glad you came. I have a few more questions."

"Okay, but can we discuss something else first?"

Marta tilted her head just enough for Jo to notice. "Sure."

"Privately?"

Marta motioned her through the metal door and into an interview room. They sat, and Marta moved to start the recorder.

"Can this part not be recorded please?"

"If it's in regard to Ms. Belak's murder, I need to record it."

"It isn't. At least I don't think so."

Marta clasped her hands together on the table and leaned toward Jo. Jo's instinct was to move back but she didn't. "I think something may have happened to Maja, our baker."

"Why would you think that?"

"She didn't show for work today and didn't call."

"How old is Miss…?"

"Demšar. She's 24, about 5'2", slight build, bright blue hair, brown eyes."

"She's 24? How long has she been missing? Sure she's not just flaking off work?"

"She left the teashop a little early yesterday afternoon to go and quit her other job. We had discussed bringing her on full time. It's just not like her. And … there's something else."

"What?" Marta looked up at her, her expression inscrutable.

"I had this … I saw … I have a terrible feeling about it. Like a premonition."

Marta looked hard at Jo. "What kind of premonition?"

"Just a really bad feeling." If she told a police officer she could talk to dead people and had seen Maja in her apartment, she would be hauled off to Polje.

"Ms. Wiley, I can't file a missing person's report just because you have a bad feeling."

"Someone should be looking for her."

"I will send someone around for a welfare check."

"That's not very helpful."

"That's all I've got." She flipped the recorder on. "I need to ask you a couple more things about the night Ms. Belak was killed."

———

Jo left the police station hoping her anger would warm her against the weather and the cold that had settled around her heart.

She pulled the hood of her raincoat up and walked as quickly as she could without taking a tumble on the rain-slick grates and access covers in the pavement. A solid bulk of person ran into her, or she ran into it.

"Oprostite." Jo looked up into Rok's face.

"My Jo." He slid both his cold hands into her hood on either side of her face and kissed her hello.

"Mm, you've been quiet." She had missed him.

He pulled her into the nearest doorway, out of the rain. "Deciding on this trip. To go or not. I am feeling this is not the right time."

"I have recently learned it's best to listen to your hunches."

He smiled at her. "I hope because of a good thing." He studied her face for a moment. "Are you not working?"

"Not today. Vesna decided I needed a day off."

"You don't seem to be enjoying this day off."

"Just a lot going on. Did you hear about the murder?"

"I saw papers at a kiosk." Rok was the least plugged-in person she knew. No TV, no smart phone, no cell phone period. He had a phone at home but no answering machine.

"I was there. I knew her."

"That is more than enough to be sad."

"And now our baker has disappeared."

"Maybe she decided to have an adventure." Rok was known to disappear himself.

"I hope so." She wasn't very hopeful. Her conversation with Marta had made it all a little too real. But what had happened? Where was her body?

"Such a mother. She will be fine." He pulled her into a one-armed hug in the cramped doorway. He was the same height as she was, but built like a rugby player. He was maybe a little thicker around the middle now than when she'd first met him, but his wiry hair was still jet black. She could feel his body heat through his slicker and his heavy sweater. "We should go somewhere warm." He let her go and ran his hand down his face to brush off the mist that clung to his beard and eyebrows. "And dry."

"I'm heading to the shop." She needed to talk to Vesna. She needed to figure out what to do next.

"All criteria are met." He put his arm around her waist, and they walked on, heads down against the rain.

Vesna met them at the door. It was almost three o'clock. Where had the day gone?

"Maja?" It was for confirmation more than anything. Vesna shook her head.

Jo's stomach growled loudly enough for Vesna and Rok to hear.

"You need to eat." Vesna looked down at the chalk sign in her hand. "Lentil soup? Rok?"

He nodded in agreement. Vesna set the board near the door and went back to the kitchen. Jo peeled off her wet coat and hung it on a row of pegs near the door. Rok followed suit and sat at the nearest table. The shop was empty besides them. She was hungry, but since her conversation with Marta, she was feeling every minute tick by. She should be out looking. She couldn't wait for Marta to send someone out to Maja's apartment. She needed to go now. She started to reach for her coat again.

"The ship. It is Igor's work, no?" Rok was gesturing at the newly painted wall.

"Yes. He did it on Sunday. We needed a change."

"It's a good change."

Vesna came back with two bowls of lentil soup and a plate of cheese scones. "Sit, Jo. You still have to eat."

Jo sat next to Rok. Vesna was not to be argued with when she was in full-on mom mode. And Jo really did need to eat.

Vesna sat down opposite her as she put the soup on the table in front of them. "How did it go at the police station?"

Jo swallowed the spoonful of hot soup she'd just put in her mouth. "They asked me how well I knew Tomaž."

Vesna snorted. "Well enough to know he's a snake."

"That's pretty much what I said, that he wasn't one of my favorite people."

Rok laughed. "Sad for him. No soup."

Jo smiled, relieved that she had walked smack into Rok. His unshakable calm had rubbed off on her over the years, but it was good to have him there as reinforcement. Another tether. Her insides were twisted, but Fred's lentil soup had its own soothing powers. She needed something else to focus on for a few minutes.

Vesna popped up from the table. "I'm going to help Frédéric finish up a couple things in the kitchen."

Jo and Rok finished their soup and scones in silence. Rok took her bowl and stacked it inside his to carry back to the dish sink. Jo followed with the plate holding a lonely uneaten scone. They stood in the doorway to the kitchen. Vesna took the dishes from them.

"What's the plan?" Jo addressed both Vesna and Frédéric, but Frédéric answered.

"Simple menu today. I figured we'd be slow with the rain. The tourists may be all we get."

"Hm. Faron said his crew would be in tonight. But I'm guessing you're right about anyone else." Jo looked out the front window. It was dark, and the rain was blowing against the window in waves. "Vee, it might be worth checking in with Miha. That doesn't look like tour weather at all."

Vesna went into the office to excavate her phone from a pile of paperwork. She came back quickly. "He's already messaged me. No tour. Maybe tomorrow if the rain lets up."

Rok put his arm around her waist. "You can go back to taking the day off."

Vesna nodded. "Yes. Take her out of here. We'll be fine."

Jo was relieved and disappointed. She really wasn't in the mood to be "on" and play host, but they could always use the business. However, now she could go back to Maja's apartment. Surely one of her roomies had to be home.

Rok tightened his arm around her waist. "Where to?"

They walked back to get their coats. Hers was cold and

wet, but it still beat getting pummeled with rain. "Rok, where were you going when I ran into you? Do you have stuff you need to do?"

"I must have been looking for you."

She wrapped her scarf back around her neck, tucking it into her raincoat. "Were you serious about not having anything to do?"

"Yes. You have the look of trouble in your eyes." He squinted at her.

"Would you go to Maja's with me? I want to check on her."

"In this?" He turned to look at the rain coming down now in sheets.

"I'll go by myself." She held out the keys to her flat on her palm. "I'll be right back."

Rok curled her fingers back over the keys. "I'll go with you."

They both put their hoods up and headed out into the rain. Moving from doorway to doorway, bent to protect their faces, it took them about twenty minutes to get to her flat. They stood on the damp landing. She knocked on the peeling gray door. She hoped it was the right one; everything looked a little different in daylight. A blonde waif of a woman opened the door.

"Does Maja live here?"

The woman looked up at Jo with eyes the color of a swimming pool. She was stoned out of her mind. "Not now."

"What do you mean 'not now'?"

"She must still be at work. She isn't here and living, being, whatever."

Jo rolled her eyes. Shaking her silly wouldn't get better information, but she wanted to do it anyway.

The woman-child looked past Jo to Rok, who stood back from the door. "Do you want to buy some pot?"

Rok shook his head and pointed to Jo.

The woman looked back to Jo, slowly. "Do you want to buy some pot?"

"No! I want to talk to Maja."

"She must still be at work."

Jo pulled the door closed in frustration. She did not want to be responsible for throttling a baked waif.

———

Rok beat her twice at chess. Jo couldn't concentrate enough to be much of an opponent. She made them a pot of tea because she wanted something warm to hold in her hands. Even with the radiators on, the apartment was chilly. The two of them sat on the futon, Jo with her back against the wall and her legs stretched out on the futon over Rok's lap. They drank their tea. Rok rested his warm cup on her shin.

She should still be looking, but Rok had convinced her it really was raining too hard to be out. The sheets and buckets had turned into a torrential downpour. The river was swollen and churning, and walking along it on the way to Maja's, she had gotten the creeps again. There was something in there.

She broke the silence. Usually she was happy just to be with him, but her thoughts had started leading her places she did not want to go. "So why are you thinking this isn't the time to go to Nepal?"

"Not a clear reason. It's been many years since I have spent all the seasons in a year in Ljubljana. Or anywhere."

"I'm glad you're here." She meant it. She'd never felt afraid in her apartment in the time she'd lived there, but now the place felt almost alien to her. Everything she touched or saw seemed to trigger a memory, a dream, or a visit. It was quieter with her old friend.

He sat his mug on the windowsill behind them and rubbed his calloused hands over her shins. "I am too."

She laid her head back against the wall and closed her eyes and tried to think only of the moment they were in. She tried to be in her body; things had gotten awfully crowded in her head.

"I can stay. If you don't want to be alone."

"I'm sure you have things to do."

"I have time for you."

"Would you then?" Jo opened her eyes and looked at him. "We can go hang out downstairs with Faron and his crew for a bit."

"It would be good to see him."

Rok doted on Faron. He didn't have any children, and it was important for him to pass his knowledge on to others. They hiked together in places she would never go. When Faron was ten they'd climbed Triglav, the Slovenian rite of passage. From where she sat she could see the picture of the two of them at the top.

"I should put clothes on." She had traded her damp clothes

for a robe when they'd come up. "I don't think Vesna would appreciate me coming down like this."

———

Downstairs, Faron and his crew, which included Tomaž and Katarina's daughters Ivanka and Veronika, were sharing a couple pots of tea at two tables pushed together. No one else was in the shop. Faron jumped up when he saw Jo and hugged her tightly.

"You doing okay? Vesna said she was a little worried about you."

"I'm good. Vesna made me take the day off."

"So why are you here?"

Vesna came out of the kitchen at the sound of the door. She was drying her hands on her apron. "Yes. Why are you here?"

"It's more fun than my apartment?" Jo cocked her head at Vesna. "What are you up to?"

"Washing dishes. I sent Tina and Damijan home."

Jo hated to cut people's hours, but Vesna was more business-minded than she was.

"Ah. Makes sense." Jo took Vesna's hand. "Can we talk a second, in the office?"

"Let's."

Jo moved the hamper of towels and dirty aprons so she could close the door. "You might have given me a little heads-up about your uncle."

"I think he's pretty serious about his vows."

"That is not what I meant." He was attractive, but despite Vesna's teasing that wasn't the only reason she existed. "I meant the 'family business' business. Why did you never tell me?"

Vesna looked at her, her eyes narrowed slightly. "Why didn't you tell Gregor you can talk to dead people?"

"Because I'm pretty sure he'll think I'm crazy. Oh ... point taken. But I was worried you'd think I was crazy, too, and I told you what was going on with me."

"I guess I wanted you to talk to Uncle Leo to make sure you weren't."

"Thanks."

"There's more weird stuff in this world than people know." Vesna let out a tired sigh.

Jo put her hand in her pocket and wrapped her fingers around the stone Leo gave her. "I'm figuring that out." Jo sat on the desk. "I, we, should be out there, looking for her."

Vesna leaned against the wall. "I wouldn't even know where to start beyond where you've already been. And besides, I think we'd drown."

Jo shivered. "There's got to be something we can do."

Vesna stood back up. "Have you tried contacting Maja? I mean, I don't know how this works or anything."

"I have no idea. So far they've only shown up when I've been alone, or mostly alone." Jo looked down at her hands and twisted her ring. She had already asked Rok to stay. As much as she wanted to confirm what had happened to Maja, she wasn't sure about taking a step that would confirm what she was becoming. Or already was.

"You okay?"

Jo nodded.

Vesna pulled her into a hug and then held her at arm's length, her hands soft on Jo's shoulders. "I'm so sorry this has happened to you."

"Me, too. But sorrier for Helena and Maja. What the fuck is going on?"

"I don't know. But we'll get to the bottom of it. But promise me—"

"Promise you what?" She felt like she was making more promises than she could ever possibly keep.

"Promise me you will take care of yourself. Please do what Uncle Leo tells you to do. He knows what he's doing, and he said he'd look after you."

Jo bristled at the idea of needing to be taken care of like she was a child or like she was her mother, but Vesna had a point. She didn't know what the hell she was doing, not really. Somehow the dead could become solid in her presence. She could see and talk to them, and none of them had come to her with good news. And someone, or some thing, if that was possible, seemed to be targeting people close to her. It was hard not to believe she and her newly minted superpower were at the center of it.

"I'll listen to him, I promise, but I'm not going to sit here or upstairs and twiddle my thumbs. I don't want anyone else to get hurt, especially if this is because of me and what I can do."

Vesna nodded. "I get that. You, we, don't know what we're

dealing with. But you aren't alone."

"I know that." Every person tethered to her could be in danger. Looking into Vesna's concerned face, she'd never felt more alone in her life.

———

In the dining room, Rok was telling Faron and his friends about traveling in Tibet when he'd gone to climb K2. Maybe they could go on a trip together when all this was over. It had been a while since the three of them, or even just she and Rok, had taken off somewhere.

Jo stood in the doorway and watched her son watch Rok. It was hard to believe Faron was twenty. Most Slovenia kids lived with their parents, but when he started at the university, he'd insisted on making the very un-Slovenian move into student housing. The tiny apartment had been part of it, but she suspected he also wanted some room to figure himself out. The single-mom thing had often had a "two of us against the world" quality, and now he needed to find his own way.

As she watched, Ivanka put her hand in Faron's lap, and he threaded his fingers through hers. She was a little sad because he hadn't told her he was dating anyone, and a lot worried because it was Tomaž's daughter.

CHAPTER 13

The rain on the terra cotta roofing tiles kept Gustaf awake. If sleep was going to elude him, there were better ways he could spend the dark hours than staring at the crack spidering across the ceiling. He made a cup of chamomile tea, hoping the rain would let up and he could get some sleep.

Something had been stolen from the museum the night of Helena Belak's murder. His contact at the museum was evasive about what exactly was taken. All Gustaf knew was that during the upheaval when Helena's body was found at the Emona house, an item or items had gone missing from the exhibit of Roman era artifacts. The case that housed the stolen property had not been smashed; it was simply empty. Gustaf had little doubt that the theft was connected to the murder, and that both events were somehow connected to Jolene Wiley.

He didn't believe in coincidences.

He stood in his room, tea forgotten. He'd added a pin with a dated red flag to the map. Light from the lamps placed around the room converged where he stood. He repositioned two of the lamps to focus on the map of pins. He stared more closely at the cluster of blue flags marking his own building. It hadn't been necessary to include one for himself: Observers weren't considered supernatural, though they existed to protect the secret of the Veil. Gustaf had a pin for himself because unlike most of his colleagues, he could see auras.

Jolene Wiley's aura had always been peculiar, even when she was believed to be dormant. A purple bordering on indigo radiated from her. It was the color of powerful visionaries. Lightning bolts of crimson and burgundy danced within this purple halo, indicating a deep connection to the earth. Wiley was different than most Voices he had seen or read about. He was angry at himself for not realizing sooner what that meant.

Her uniqueness made him suspicious of every other blue-pin individual who had crossed her path. If he could see how different she was, so could they. He doubted the benevolence of anyone around that kind of power. He wondered what people or beings were out there that he didn't have represented on his map.

He sat at his desk and pushed open his laptop. Bettine needed to know what was going on at the museum, and he needed to get the Board's permission to approach Wiley. Bettine must be told there was another active Voice, and that — unlike her mother or aunt — Jolene Wiley was most likely a Portal. It was doubtful that her family had trained her at all, and he was certain they hadn't told her about this possibility.

His message sent, he went to his kitchenette for a glass of water. He leaned against the counter and downed it in one long drink. His computer chimed with an incoming email.

He had long suspected Bettine didn't sleep, that she was more than she appeared, but keeping his own secret forced him to keep hers. Her reply email at three in the morning did not prove his theory, but it fit in with the mounting evidence.

Gustaf,

I trust your evaluation of the situation. Please approach Ms. Wiley, but do it cautiously. Whatever else you know about her, don't forget that she is descended from an unstable line of Voices.

I am concerned over the theft at the museum. The murder indicates that the artifact stolen is a Vessel. If that is the case, and you are correct about Ms. Wiley also being a Portal, things are even more serious. Under no circumstances should she be in the presence of a possessed person or other supernatural beings.

You have reported Vesna Kos as a seer of auras. I know you have deep grievances with the Kos family, but you must enlist their help. Ms. Kos can assist you in finding the possessed, and if a demonic being has indeed escaped, her uncle will be valuable in returning it to its Vessel.

I doubt Ms. Kos knows that revenge demons are masked by the auras of those they possess. The aggrieved are easy marks for a revenge demon, and their auras are often dark and murky. Start with those who may have been at the museum or Roman house who have such auras and are friendly with Ms. Wiley.

I expect daily updates regarding this situation.

Regards, B.D.

He closed the lid of his laptop and leaned back in the desk chair. The matter had become more complicated. It had crossed his mind that the artifact could be a Vessel. If a demonic being had sensed a Portal near, it may have taken the opportunity to find a host willing to release it.

No demon had been successful in permanently crossing into the waking world in his lifetime. The chaos and destruction the last one released still reverberated through the politics and psychology of the human population. Those who spoke about the evils of the Second World War had no idea what humanity had really been up against.

CHAPTER 14

Jo woke up in a puddle on her bed. Water dripped from the rafters above onto the duvet. It dripped down the wall opposite the window, behind the framed photos of the Smoky Mountains wrapped in autumn mists. She nudged Rok, barely rousing until he woke enough to realize that the duvet was sodden. He jumped from the bed with a mumbled, "What the fuck?" and with heavy-lidded, concerned eyes, he looked at Jo in the night's blue gloom. "You okay?"

"Just wet. Mattress is probably ruined."

"Maybe." He pulled the duvet off and stripped the bed while Jo went to the kitchen to get some bowls and pans for the ceiling drips.

She gathered up the few towels she had and went back to the bedroom. Rok had stood the mattress up next to the window and the electric radiator. It felt pretty dry, but just in case. The two of them placed the bowls strategically and rolled the towels into bright blue snakes to lay out along the trim on the floor.

A crack of thunder on the heels of a lightning flash made her jump. Rok took her wrist and turned her cold palm up to cover it with his warm one. He didn't say anything. He never needed to. His touch had the power to calm her heartbeat.

"We can open the futon out." She doubted she could fall back to sleep, but that didn't mean he wouldn't.

He nodded. She let his hand drop and turned to the wardrobe for a clean sheet and dry blankets. He went into the main room and pulled the futon out and flipped the back down to make a double bed. They put the linens on and climbed in together. She curled up next to him and put her head on his chest. Looking up through the window, she could see a patch of midnight sky between the angle of the terra cotta roofs. A curtain of silver rain fell from it, illuminated white every few seconds by another lightning flash. She wanted to fall back to sleep but was mesmerized by the rain and beset by thoughts of how and when they would find Maja.

It was unnerving, this water infiltrating her flat. She had a ridiculous thought of walking down to the river and screaming at it to leave her the fuck alone, as if the river could possibly have a hand in what was going on.

Rok's chest rose and fell in a regular rhythm under her head and hand. She envied him the ability to drift right back to sleep. If it was the sleep of the just, not the dead, what did that make her?

———

Jo woke up early, if she had ever really fallen asleep. She extricated herself from the tangle of limbs Rok became in his sleep and crept into the bedroom to see if the mattress was okay. The walls had dried, and the leaks had stopped. She ran her hands up and down the mattress. It seemed dry. She muscled it back onto the bed, then sat on the edge looking out the window into the courtyard. The rain had stopped, and the sky was turning a light shade of pre-dawn blue. Her bird neighbor was snuggled in its nest, its face hidden under its wing. She got up to close the door, sat back on the bed, and picked up her phone. Aunt Jackie would still be up six time zones behind, but her phone was dead.

Remembering to charge it was not her strong suit. She sat looking at the window, thinking about Maja, gazing somewhere into the middle distance. The chorus from "Time Bomb" drifted through her thoughts.

Someone sat next to her on the edge of the bed. The door hadn't opened, and Rok was still snoring in the main room. She turned to look.

Maja was wet and dripping, though the bed and the floor remained dry. She was looking out the window. She had a choker of red and blue bruises around her neck that Jo had not seen in the mirror. She spoke before Jo had a chance.

"I'm sorry if I scared you. I should've guessed you'd be surprised to see me in your bathroom. I wasn't thinking very straight."

"I was definitely surprised."

"Eh. I probably would've been too. I'm just glad you didn't deck me or something."

"Not sure ghost punching is approved dead whisperer conduct."

"Is that what you are? A dead whisperer?" Maja looked at Jo. Her eyes were clear, but there was sadness in the set of the corners.

"It's a recently acquired title. Helena's death seems to have awakened my family's gift."

"Not much of a gift."

"I'm not sure yet. You okay?" That was a stupid question.

"Aside from being dead? Yeah. It's surprisingly peaceful. I don't really want anything and nothing really matters anymore."

"Then why are you here?"

"That is strange. I woke up in water and at first I panicked, but I wasn't cold and didn't feel wet. I climbed onto the bank, but my body was still in the river, tangled in the ties of one of those party boats down where the river cruises turn around. Honestly, my first thought was that I should have worn blue lipstick to match my hair."

Jo huffed a small laugh. Clearly she wasn't the only one who survived on gallows humor.

"I looked up the river bank back toward the central city, and there was this kind of silvery thread above the roof lines. I knew it was you and that I needed to get to you and tell you what happened."

"And I gasped at you."

"Shit, I know I didn't handle that very well. Sneaking up on you in the bathroom in the middle of the night. By the way, damn. Milo. The man is hot."

"What happened?"

"I left like I said, to go quit at Spotlight. I wanted to talk to my boss, but he wasn't there. Tomaž was."

"Oh my god, did he hurt you?"

"No, he fucked me on the desk."

"You were sleeping with Tomaž?" This was not where she thought this conversation would go.

"Yeah. I know it was stupid. He is kind of slimy, but I seem to like them older."

"You had a crush on Frédéric. He would have been a better choice than that snake."

"You knew?"

"I'm pretty sure everyone knew."

"Even Fred?"

Jo put her hand on Maja's cold arm. "He didn't want to hurt your feelings, but he thought he was too old for you."

"He's pretty smart."

"Then what?" How was she this calm? Maybe she'd come to some level of acceptance. Maybe she'd fallen completely and utterly down the rabbit hole.

"His wife opened the door while Tomaž and I were going at it. She was pissed, and she came at him like a tiger, all claws and hissing. She didn't even acknowledge I was there. I picked up my shit and left as fast as I could."

"That explains their behavior when they came by here."

Maja shrugged. "I walked around for a long time. Had a beer or three with a friend in Metelkova. I was walking home along the river, and it was raining pretty hard. Someone came out of the shadows at me and started choking me. I ended up in the river. It was moving fast, and I don't swim. I don't remember drowning, though."

Jo coughed in a poor attempt to hide the tightness in her throat. "Then you woke up in the water and came looking for me."

"Pretty much."

"What were you doing all day yesterday?"

"I thought if you could see me, maybe one of my roommates might be able to. Mira was home but high as a fucking kite. She could hear me, maybe? She kept asking God why She was so angry at her. I left and kind of waited for you to be alone."

"Sorry. I was being a chicken and was in some denial. I really didn't want you to be dead. Your roommate is a space cadet. I met her when I went looking for you."

"Thanks. It's not as bad as I imagined."

"Don't you feel like you need to go somewhere? My da- … others have had this real urge to leave, to go to whatever it is that's next."

"No. No white light. No door. No nothing. I was hoping maybe it was going to be like Valhalla or something, but instead my afterlife seems to be stalking you, boss lady."

Jo laughed again. "I'm not sure what that means. I have someone I can ask though."

"Cool."

"What are you going to do in the meantime?"

"I definitely don't want to hang out in your apartment while you go at it with that hairy guy."

"Wait, I thought you liked them old?"

"Old, yeah, but grizzled? Not so much. He's a fucking bear."

"Whatever. While you're out exploring dead Ljubljana, I'll try to get the police on finding your body so we can tell your family." That would be another fun conversation with Marta, or, rather, Investigator Klančnik.

"Can I come back tonight?"

"Yes."

Maja was gone as silently as she'd arrived. Her departure didn't even disturb the gauzy curtains.

Jo watched the brown bird wake up and fluff its feathers against the cold, readying itself for the possibilities a bird's day held. And Maja. Twenty-four, a handful of years older than Faron, and all her possibilities were all gone. At a certain point in her brief life, she had come to work at the teahouse. She'd chosen the line that crossed Jo's path, and that led to her abrupt end. This had to stop. Jo had to stop it.

She plugged in her phone and waited until it woke up.

"Hey. Isn't it the middle of the night there?" Jackie sounded wide awake.

"No, it's about five a.m. I'm glad you're still up. I need some immediate advice."

"More weirdness?"

"Um. More dead people."

"Someone else you know?" An edge of worry crept into Jackie's voice and broadcast across the connection.

"Maja, who worked at the teahouse for me."

"Jolene!"

"What? I didn't kill her."

"That's not what I meant. I'm coming over there." Jo could hear papers shuffling in the background.

"I don't think that's necessary."

"Well, I think it is. Michael is going to come stay at the house with the dogs. I fly out Friday night."

"I'm guessing that means you bought your ticket already?" Jo sighed. She wanted Jackie's hand to hold, yet she really didn't want to involve anyone else she cared about.

"Yes. And I booked a hotel room. I love you, but staying in that dinky apartment of yours is like being trapped in a dog crate."

Jo laughed. "I love you too."

"Anyway, what's this immediate advice?"

"Two things really. You said there were some things I needed to do to protect the flat from unwanted visitors?"

"When you didn't Skype me, I sent you an email with some stuff you can do. Don't you check your mail?"

"Not religiously."

"What's the other thing?"

"What does it mean when a ghost or spirit or whatever you call them doesn't feel the need to leave or move on?"

"Shade. I call them shades. And, um … Oh."

"Good 'oh' or bad 'oh'?"

"Mm. Neutral 'oh.' Who are we talking about?"

Jo paused. She realized just how little she knew about how all this worked. What if she'd already done something really bad? "Maja. She said she knew she had to get to me but that she had no desire or sense that she needed to go anywhere else."

"It may mean that she's your spirit guide."

"I get one of those? Why couldn't it have been Dad?"

"It's not usually someone that close to you. Helps to keep emotion from clouding your judgment, or theirs. At least that has always been my best guess as to why. Is Maja kind of feisty and irreverent?"

"She has blue hair and is covered in tattoos."

"I take that as a yes. If she's accepted death and was drawn to you, it means she has work to do."

"Okay. Is there protocol for this? I wasn't exactly ready to have someone looking over my shoulder all the time."

"I don't think she can actually do that. There's usually a signal she's near. A song you sing or hum."

"Damn it!"

"What?"

"I think I know why that damn Rancid song has been stuck in my head for two days." That was probably why she'd kept hearing the *M*A*S*H* theme song too.

"Could be worse. Could have been the chicken dance song."

"That would be evil."

"You'd be surprised."

"At this point, I doubt it. Who's your guide, and what terrible song are you stuck with?"

"I've had a few over the years. Currently, it's a woman named Betty that I used to play Bunco with occasionally. She's a mess."

"And the song?"

"Promise you won't laugh?"

"Absolutely not."

" 'Edelweiss.' "

Jo laughed. "Guess you're regretting that Sound of Music obsession right about now."

Jackie laughed too. "Right about always. Okay, kiddo. I do actually need to get to sleep. Check your mail. Do those things this morning. Promise?"

"I promise. See you on Saturday. Oh, are you flying into Ljubljana?"

"No, too expensive. Venice, then a GoOpti shuttle to the train station."

"Cool. Send me your itinerary, and I'll meet you at the station."

Jo touched the red receiver button on the screen and then pulled up her email. What nineteenth century dead whisperer could have guessed their progeny would wind up halfway around the world holding a supercomputer in her hand learning to set wards to protect herself and her apartment from bad shades. She scrolled through Jackie's email. Most of it was doable with the stuff she had in the apartment. She didn't have a porch, so she didn't need to worry about painting it "haint" blue.

Rok knocked softly at the door, then opened it.

"Why'd you knock, silly?"

"You were talking."

Jo gestured with the phone. "To my aunt."

"All is well?"

"Pretty much."

"The mattress is dry?" Rok ran his hand over his beard and blinked. He seemed a little more awake.

"I think so. I'll leave it unmade today, just in case. Hungry?"

"I could eat."

She stood and walked to the armoire to pull out a robe. It was the one Milo had worn the morning before; it still smelled of him. She started to put it back, but she didn't have the emotional reserves to be sentimental about it. Rok stood still in the doorway instead of letting her pass. Standing on the step made her a few inches taller than he. He stepped back, and she stepped down so they were eye to eye. He put his warm, calloused hands on both sides of her face.

He looked her hard in the face. "There's something you are not saying that you need to say."

"Breakfast first. I don't think I can make it through the whole story without caffeine and protein."

He laughed and kissed her chastely on the mouth. He tasted of morning breath. "Okay." He moved aside to let her pass.

He showered while she made eggs and toast and coffee as

strong as she could stand it.

They sat opposite each other at her dining desk. She thought about how many interactions, conversations, and revelations this configuration had been witness to, especially in the past few days. Maybe she needed to set a ward on it too. "How superstitious are you?"

Rok seemed genuinely surprised by her question. "Not very. I accept there are many things I don't know of or that there isn't an explanation for yet."

"I can talk to dead people."

"Is this new?"

"That's it? 'Is this new?'" It was her turn to be surprised.

"What? I believe you."

She stared at him, openmouthed. "Really?"

"You don't lie well. Or make up things."

She set her mug down with a thunk and leaned back into her chair, still staring.

He leaned across the table and took her wrists and pulled her back to him, almost nose to nose. "My Jo, I am not interested in uninteresting people."

"I know."

He continued to hold her wrists, gently. "Do you? I wonder. I do not think you know your own power." He let go, but Jo didn't move away.

"Will you help me?"

"If I can."

"I need to protect myself. Protect the flat. I have a list from

Jackie."

"Why does your aunt know of such things?"

"It's probably best if I start at the beginning. With Helena."

———

Their coffee was cold. Rok stood and motioned for her to stand. He wrapped her in a rib-crushing hug. "You are strong. This is a heavy burden."

She could barely breathe out. He was taking the whole thing remarkably well. Maybe a little too well. Maybe there was something he needed to say that he wasn't saying.

God, she hated this thing. It made her doubt herself and her friends. She was not going to let it beat her down.

He let her go. "This list?"

She retrieved her phone from the bedroom and showed him the list. She started pulling things from the kitchen cabinets and then went back to the bedroom to get a carved wooden box from the wardrobe. She ran her hands over the deep grooves depicting a flowering dogwood branch. Her grandfather had made it for her when she was in high school. To keep her treasures in, he had said.

Together she and Rok ran lines of salt along the windowsills and the threshold outside the front and only door. She had six kinds of salt, but she decided on salt from Piran because it was local-ish. She tied bells around the inside knob of the front door. The only bells she had were on an old Indian anklet Rok had bought her in a market in Delhi. They made a witch bottle to Jackie's specifications, using needles she'd raided from her travel kit and salt and herbs from the spice rack, and placed it in the easternmost point of the apartment, which they established using the compass on her phone. Finally they burned some rubbed sage in a ramekin and walked around the edges of the apartment fanning the smoke with a sketch book to cleanse the space. Rubbed sage probably wasn't the kind Jackie meant, but it would have to do. Rok chanted a prayer he'd learned in his travels and set the ramekin in the sink to let the sage burn out.

"We have done our best." He dusted his hands together. "Do you think Maja will still be able to get in?"

"I think all this is for — haints? — that want to hurt you." The word was new to him. Jo explained that "haints" wasn't exactly proper English.

"If she can't get in, maybe she isn't the guide."

"True." Jo flounced to the edge of the still-open futon and threw herself back against it. The silk of her robe fluttered and settled around her. She was calmed by the quirky rituals and relieved that now four people, well, four living ones, knew her secret — and none of them thought she had lost her mind. Maybe that said more about them than her, but she would take it at face value. Faron, she decided, still should not be told. She wouldn't endanger her son by drawing him into this mess. Nor was she ready to tell Gregor. He would worry and try to fix something that couldn't be fixed, and his efforts to help would only put him in harm's way.

She looked up through the window. The sliver of sky above the terra cotta roofline was fully blue. She pulled her phone out of the robe pocket to check the time. Rok took the phone from her and set it on the table. He lay down next to her and propped on his elbow so his face was over hers. His dark eyes were soft and hungry. "It's been a long time."

"It has." She touched his face, cupping his bearded jaw in her hand. "But what about Nepal?"

"Nepal can wait. Maybe I need to be here."

CHAPTER 15

Jo was late to work. It was getting to be a habit, but it was worth it this morning. Sex with Rok was the tether she had needed. He kissed her goodbye at the door to the teahouse and headed off into Ljubljana to do whatever it was he did when they weren't together. She was relieved that he was putting off Nepal. It wouldn't hurt to have him here until this was all resolved.

In the cramped kitchen, Frédéric was already deep into the prep list. Vesna was in the office leafing through the papers, but she had her hair up and an apron on.

"Sorry I'm late, guys." Before Jo could announce that she was going out to look for Maja, Vesna stood up.

"I think we all need to talk."

Frédéric laid his knife down on the cutting board where he'd been removing the crusts of deviled egg salad sandwiches. The look on his face was inscrutable, but Jo knew he was worried about Maja. Vesna stepped out of the office and waved them both out of the kitchen. There wasn't any music playing. The bells on the front door rang. The sound reminded her of the anklet she and Rok had hung on the door upstairs.

Faron and Gregor were hanging their coats by the door as she walked into the main room. Jo looked to Vesna, whose face was stern and set. Her in-charge mom face.

"What the hell? Why are they here?" She had decided against telling Faron and Gregor anything about the dead whisperer thing. And she needed to get to the party boat dock.

"Maja's been missing for two days. We need to make some decisions." Vesna's delivery was matter of fact.

Jo sat at one of the bigger tables, her stomach knotting and re-knotting with every shallow breath.

Faron sat down next to her. "Mom, are you okay?"

"Yes and no." Jo sighed. "Vesna, can we at least have some tea for this?"

Frédéric turned back toward the tea station and got a pot started before returning to the table. He sat down next to Gregor, who sat across from her. "Okay. What is all this about?"

Jo folded her hands in her lap and looked down at them. She twisted the amethyst ring around her finger. Best to face the music. "I think Maja is dead."

She wasn't sure who was responsible for the cursing or the sharp intakes of breath, but Gregor spoke first. "How can you possibly believe that?"

Jo looked up. His face was not amused. "Because..."

Vesna sat on Jo's other side and covered Jo's cold hands with her warm one. "Jo's had a rough week. Since I sprung this on her, maybe I should start."

Jo listened intently as Vesna recounted Jo's trip to the police station and her efforts to find Maja. She told them about Maja leaving to quit her other job and that they hadn't heard anything from her since.

Faron was shaking his head. "You aren't joking?"

"No." Jo and Vesna said it in stereo.

Gregor hadn't said anything. He was just staring at the two of them. Frédéric got up to get the tea and came back with cups and a pot of English builders tea strong enough to stand a spoon in. The warm cup in her hands felt like the only real thing in the room.

"I know it sounds crazy. But I think we need to prepare ourselves for the worst." Jo looked at the men, trying to will them to believe her even though the evidence she could give them was flimsy at best.

Gregor leaned in closer to her. "I just … I don't want to believe what you've said is true. But I know you too well to think you're overreacting."

Jo nodded.

Frédéric coughed. "What do we do now?"

Faron started to speak but was interrupted by a heavy knock on the front door. Investigator Marta Klančnik and a uniformed officer were standing in the courtyard. Vesna went to the door and let them in.

Marta looked over Vesna's shoulder to the seated group. "Family meeting?"

"Something like that." Vesna gestured for them both to come in.

"You should probably sit back down. I'm afraid I'm not here with good news." Marta and the officer followed Vesna back to the table. When Vesna had taken her seat, Marta let out a long breath. "I am here to inform you that Maja Demšar's body was found this morning in the Ljubljana river."

They all looked at each other and back to Marta.

Marta surveyed their faces. "You don't seem surprised by this news."

"I told you I had a bad feeling. I knew she didn't just take off." Jo hoped she sounded appropriately respectful. What was the penalty for kicking an investigator in the shins?

"It seems you were correct." Marta looked to Vesna and Frédéric. "I have some questions for the three of you."

Vesna stood. "I should make a sign for the door."

Jo and Frédéric nodded. Marta stared at Vesna, who took off her apron and draped it over her chair.

"We can't open today. A member of our staff, our family, has died."

Faron and Gregor spoke at the same time. Gregor asked, "Do you want me to stay?" and Faron asked, "What can I do?"

Jo squeezed Faron's hand. "Yes, please stay, both of you. I don't know what you can do but I'm glad you're here."

———

Marta started her interview with Frédéric. Vesna, Faron, and Jo went into the kitchen to wrap and refrigerate what Frédéric and Vesna had accomplished, hoping some could be saved for whenever they reopened. Gregor went to the office and closed the door to make a phone call.

"Why didn't you say something sooner?" Faron had turned from the sink where he was washing knives and cutting boards.

"I didn't want to be right. I was hoping she'd just show up." Jo sighed. Maja had just shown up, but not as she would have liked.

"But you talked to Vesna about it. No offense, Vesna."

"None taken." Vesna body-bagged the egg salad sandwiches with some damp paper towels to keep them from drying out.

"Vesna's not my kid whom I'm sworn to protect from all harm, or something like that." Jo ruffled Faron's hair in exactly the way she knew irritated him most.

He snorted at her and went back to washing dishes.

Frédéric appeared in the door to the kitchen. "Vesna, she'd like to speak with you next."

Vesna handed him the double wrapped plate of sandwiches and nodded her head toward the reach-in. "I'll leave these with you."

The three of them finished in the kitchen and then stood looking at each other. Jo wondered if they should stay there or go sit in the dining room.

Vesna came back quickly. "Jo, it's all you."

Jo took her apron off and hung it on the office door. She walked out to the table where Marta sat reading over her notes and tapping her pen on the table. The officer who'd come with her was outside talking on his cell phone.

Marta looked up as Jo approached the table. "I'm guessing

you'd like me to apologize for not taking you more seriously at the station?"

"No. You were doing your job, and I imagine a murder takes precedence over anything else." Jo sat and leaned back in the wooden chair, her hands in her lap. She tried not to clench them. It didn't matter if Marta believed her or not. Maja was already dead.

"It does. But now it looks like there are two murders."

"What makes you believe there were two murders?" Jo tried to sound surprised.

"People generally don't strangle themselves."

"Do you know what happened?"

"I should be asking the questions here. When did you last see Miss Demšar?"

"I told you all this at the station." Jo clenched her hands anyway.

"Tell me again."

Jo recounted the last conversation she'd had with Maja the day she disappeared.

"Do you know if she did go straight to Spotlight?"

"Spotlight? Oh. I think so. She hadn't mentioned doing anything else."

"Did you know that she worked for Tomaž Novak?"

"I knew he owned the bar where she worked."

"You've made it pretty clear you don't like him." Marta looked at her notebook again while she waited for Jo to respond.

"I guess. He's sleazy where women are concerned. And I don't trust someone who treats people, anyone, not just women, with such disrespect."

"Did you know he was sleeping with Helena Belak?" Marta looked her in the face now.

Jo sputtered. "No."

"Really?"

"No. I had no idea. I mean I guess I'm surprised. Helena seemed to have better taste than that."

Marta smirked. "And you wouldn't want you and your son to be lumped in with someone you dislike so much?"

"That's not exactly what I meant, but, yeah, I guess so."

"Would you mind telling me again how you 'knew' something had happened to Miss Demšar?"

"I told you, I had a premonition, a really bad feeling. It just wasn't like her to not show up for work. She had seemed relieved to be quitting at the blue bar and excited about being here full time."

"You went to her apartment to check on her."

"I did. I'm kinda surprised her roommate remembered. She was wasted."

"She did. She also told me that God told her Maja was dead."

"Interesting."

"Did you tell her that?" Marta's expression was set at poker face: level master.

"No. Do I look like god? I asked her if she'd seen Maja. She said she wasn't there, or that she wasn't living there."

"Wasn't living there?"

"I don't know. She was really high."

"Did you have someone with you?"

"Yes, my friend Rok."

"Did he speak to her?"

"Not really. She asked him if he wanted to buy pot, and he said no."

"Where were you the night she disappeared?"

"Here until about ten, then upstairs in my apartment the rest of the night." She didn't see any reason to tell her she'd dragged Milo and Vesna through the rain to look for Maja. She doubted Vesna would have shared that either.

"Alone?" Marta arched her eyebrow when she asked.

"No. With Milo."

"I guess you don't spend many nights alone."

In the interest of ending the interview before she succumbed to the desire to kick a member of law enforcement in the shins, Jo shrugged the comment off.

Marta closed her notebook and looked at her with an expression Jo couldn't quite place. "Ms. Wiley, I know there is something you are not telling me."

Jo didn't say anything but she didn't look away from Marta's scrutiny.

"When I find out what it is, I can't promise that it won't be bad for you."

"I can promise I have told you all that I can." She was a bad liar, but what she said wasn't exactly untrue. She had told all she could without Marta thinking she'd lost her marbles.

"I don't think I need to tell you that you shouldn't leave Ljubljana." Marta stood and gathered her jacket from the chair.

"Am I a suspect?" She couldn't possibly think Jo had killed Helena. There had been too many witnesses at the museum. And what reason could she have for killing Maja? She'd gone to the police station to report Maja missing. Yet it was clear that Marta didn't believe or trust her.

"Not yet." Jo stood.

Marta didn't speak to her again. She walked out the door into the courtyard, startling the officer on the phone. She said something to him Jo couldn't hear, and the two of them disappeared through the doorway to the street.

———

Jo sat at the table farthest from the door. Vesna had her going through old catering menus to see if there was anything they could throw away. It was mostly mindless but did require her to think about whether the items had been well-received and if they would make them again.

She found the menu for the party they had catered where she met Helena. Helena had been playfully flirting with her. She had completely missed it, but Helena took her witty comebacks as flirting back and followed her into the small kitchen. She'd maneuvered Jo against a countertop and run her hand down her bare arm. She felt the electricity again in thinking about it.

Who else had been at that party? Faron had helped them out serving. Is that when Helena had started her collecting? Tomaž was also there with someone who wasn't Katarina. Had that really only been August? Of course Helena and Tomaž knew each other. She seemed to know everyone, and Tomaž made it his business to be "familiar" with the glitterati. Why had that not occurred to her before? And Tomaž was at the museum and the after party. And Maja…

Jesus. Maybe Tomaž killed them both. Had that oily fucker worked up from sleazeball to serial killer? That seemed really unlikely. Maybe he was just covering his tracks, or maybe Katarina had threatened to leave him.

Gregor came out of the kitchen. His shoulders were tight, and his eyes were tired. He set his phone on the table on top of the stack of papers Jo had ignored while she pieced together Tomaž's dastardliness. She looked at the bright screen at the end of a series of text messages with Tomaž. Services for Helena were going to be the next day at her brother's house in Škofja Loka.

Jo looked up at Gregor. "Did he say anything else?"

"Only that Matjaž wanted you and me there. He said he was sorry to hear about Maja and that she had been a good employee."

"That fucker."

"Jo, I know you don't like him, but…"

"He's just… Do you think he could have killed her? And Helena?"

"Tomaž is a lot of things, some of them particularly unpleasant, but I really don't see him as a murderer. I doubt he'd have the stomach for it. And what could he possibly have against Maja?"

"I detest him." She wanted to tell him what she knew about Maja and Tomaž, but then she'd also have to tell him how she knew.

"That doesn't make him capable of killing someone."

"Even to keep his wife from leaving him?"

"You could be on to something there." Gregor sat in the chair next to her and leaned back, crossing his ankles under the table. "All of 'his' money is actually her money. Her family has bankrolled most of his ventures."

"That sounds like a motive."

Gregor sat up and leaned closer to her. "No."

"No, what?"

"No. You are not going to turn into Nancy Drew on this."

"Of course not. Why would you think that?" She shuffled the papers in front of her.

"Because you have that look, like you're plotting something."

"I'm not plotting anything. I'm just wondering who could possibly kill two people I know in less than a week. It's weird. And awful. And maddening."

"It is. But I don't know if I believe Maja's murder has anything to do with Helena."

"How can you not?" She left out the part about both women being directly connected to her.

He looked at her, his concern clear. "I'm less worried they are connected to each other and more worried they are connected to you, but I can't for the life of me think of any reason for it."

She started to tell him. She wanted to, but telling him would compound his worry, not lessen it. She nodded and took his hand. She needed to change the subject. "Thank you."

"For what?"

"For listening earlier and believing me."

"Of course I believed you. Just promise me you won't get any more involved in this than you already are."

"I promise." She didn't cross her fingers under the table, but she might as well have.

CHAPTER 16

Lichtenberg called Leo that morning when he learned of the second murder. Vesna had beaten him to it by a half hour. She had done her best to remain calm and factual, but Leo heard the slimmest edge of panic in her voice. She didn't say it, but she feared for her friend's life. He wasn't afraid for Jo yet, but he was concerned. An old and malevolent thing had been awakened; of that, he had no doubt. And for that supernatural entity, Jo would be a beacon without a shade.

A faint knock on the door signaled the arrival of Leo's unwelcome guest. He crossed the small chamber to the door.

Lichtenberg stepped into Leo's space. It took everything Leo had not to push Lichtenberg back out the open door and slam it on him.

"How do you live here?" Lichtenberg ran a hand over the top of his head where he'd grazed it stooping through the door.

"The monastery wasn't built in a time of giants." Leo motioned for his guest to sit in the straight-backed chair next to the low table he used as a nightstand. He sat on the edge of his bunk.

"I have many concerns. Some I am certain you share."

Leo nodded.

"Jolene Wiley is a Portal. She is untrained. Surely you can extrapolate the rest." Lichtenberg's stare bore through him.

"A Portal?" That was not the news he expected. He didn't think they still existed. He really wasn't sure he'd believed they ever had existed. Vesna was right to be concerned for her life. "Does she know?"

"No. I have received permission to approach her to explain the danger." He leaned back against the chair and crossed his arms over his chest.

Leo stood and walked to the cabinet next to the door. "I think it would be better if I told her."

Lichtenberg laughed. "And what do you know of Portals?"

"It isn't what I know of Portals; it's what I know of her." He crossed back to where Lichtenberg sat and looked down into the man's face. Everything about him was tidy and clean, but he still looked like a dust mote. His hair, his skin, his suit, even his eyes: everything about him was a shade of the same gray, the gray of the sky on a particularly shitty day.

"She doesn't distrust me. To her, I am the funny little neighbor." Lichtenberg's gaze never wavered as he looked up into Leo's face. "No. I will tell her."

Leo didn't argue. He picked his battles. Lichtenberg's next announcement would be that for her "protection," he wanted to take Jo into custody. Leo would go to the mat to prevent that. As his father had said, the Board had a way of disappearing anyone deemed a threat. He would not let that happen to her.

Lichtenberg continued. "I am concerned for her well-being. There are others, other supernatural beings, who may want to use Ms. Wiley's powers for their purposes. Do you know of Rok Zorko, the Long-Lived?"

"Only what Vesna has mentioned in passing. He is a friend of Jo's. I didn't realize he was different." The Long-Lived were of little interest to Leo's family as long as they kept to themselves.

"He is very old, and I find his interest in Ms. Wiley troubling, especially given the current circumstances." Lichtenberg looked down at his hands in his lap.

Lichtenberg cared for her. Despite all his smug, asinine behavior, he cared what happened to Jo. The revelation was stunning. Leo never thought the man capable of human emotion.

"She has known him a long time. I doubt his interest is nefarious. They are friends, and, according to Vesna, he is one of the few people Jo has told about her new gift."

Lichtenberg looked up at him. What looked like disbelief flitted across his face. "I hope you are right."

"Tell her if you must." If he was going to build a truce with Lichtenberg, it was his turn to give. "The item stolen was a Roman doll made of clay. My friend at the museum said she was glad the thing was gone. It gave everyone there the creeps."

Lichtenberg's eyes narrowed. "How long have you known?"

"Since last night."

He relaxed again. "It is as I thought, then. Poppets and dolls were commonly used as Vessels."

"And what do you believe was in that vessel?"

"A demonic being. Most likely a revenge demon. Our modern sense of justice is external to ourselves, which makes us especially receptive to the false power they offer."

Leo let out a long, slow breath. He had only encountered one demon in his life, and it had taken three Witchfinders to re-imprison it. He had been nine, and the sound the demon made in defeat haunted him still.

His face must have betrayed his thoughts.

"Yes. It is as bad as that." Lichtenberg patted the bed. The gesture was condescending, but Leo sat down opposite his still repugnant but slightly less unwelcome guest. "Do you know who was possessed?"

"No. I had hoped your niece could help us locate them, but a revenge demon's aura is masked by its host's."

Leo didn't show how surprised he was that Lichtenberg knew about Vesna's ability to see auras. "What other way can we find the demon?"

"It will have to reveal itself. And its host has to be someone who was at the museum the night of the murder."

"That's most of Ljubljana's elite."

"Yes. But it also must be someone who knew both Helena and Maja."

"It narrows it down, but not by much. Helena knew everyone, and Maja worked at some fancy bar on the river."

"That is true, but it won't be a mere acquaintance. It will be someone closer, most likely someone also connected to Ms. Wiley. Ms. Belak was her lover. Ms. Demšar worked for her."

Lichtenberg's distaste for Helena was clear, and he made no attempt to mask it when he said her name.

"I'll ask Vesna."

"Do. And please let me know what you learn." Lichtenberg stood to leave.

Leo let him cross almost to the door before he stood to let him out. There was something Lichtenberg wasn't telling him. He could feel it in the air that crackled with animosity between them.

Lichtenberg turned back. "Brother Kos, I know you and your family have little reason to like me, and the incident that brought us together gave me no cause to feel anything but distrust of you and your brother. I didn't look for a reason to mend this relationship, but I see we have been presented with one. Jolene Wiley is something that has not been in the world for a very long time. We are both charged with protecting her and protecting others from her. Success in that endeavor will come much more easily if we are united in our work."

Leo took the extended olive branch, if only for Jo's sake. "I agree. Shall we divide the tasks?"

"Yes. I will explain the situation to Ms. Wiley. You seem to have a more receptive source at the museum. Will you try to find the doll?"

Leo nodded. He opened the door. Lichtenberg extended his hand, and Leo took it. It was a handshake not of friends, but of reluctant business partners. For now, that would have to be enough. Leo hoped it would be enough to prevent an unfettered revenge demon from wreaking havoc in the world.

CHAPTER 17

Jo sat silently in the passenger seat of Gregor's car looking out the window at the flat open fields in the valley surrounding Ljubljana. The apple trees tucked into the neat gardens of the occasional house were heavy with fruit under a clear blue sky. In the distance, the mountains rose up from the valley floor, blues and greens giving way to white-dusted peaks. She'd lived in this place for almost twenty-five years, and its beauty still caught her off guard. Years ago she'd been to Škofja Loka a handful of times to take photographs for a project for university. It was one of the best-preserved walled cities in the country. The oldest part nestled against the river, and the old, but not quite as old, part sat across the watery divide. Both parts were equally charming, as the butter-yellow plaster houses all over Slovenia always were. Škofja Loka always struck Jo as an especially good place to hole up.

Gregor paused the car briefly before entering a roundabout. He continued to look out the windshield but spoke to her. "You seem far away."

"Not so very far. Thinking about how pretty this place is.

Trying to remember the last time I've been to Škofja Loka. It seems like I hardly leave the city anymore."

"We all have our orbits. It's just that when you leave town, you generally leave the country."

She laughed. "True."

"Something more though?"

There was, but she wouldn't share it with him. Not yet anyway. "Maybe." She smoothed the fabric of her dress across her thighs and looked out the window. Her reflection flickered back at her in the glass as they passed a high row of dark vegetation along the side of the road. There was no denying how tired she looked.

"I miss her." She missed both Helena and Maja, but today was the day for mourning Helena. "Helena."

"Of course you do."

"I didn't expect to. Not like this."

He nodded. This was his way of keeping her talking when she was starting to pull back into her own thoughts.

She resettled in the seat to look at him as she spoke. "We spent time together. Not a lot … well, maybe …" There was that weekend in September when they didn't leave Helena's apartment for two days. "But we didn't talk. Not about anything important."

"That sounds like Helena. But honestly, it sounds like you too."

"What does that mean?" She bristled, surprised at how much his words stung.

"I didn't mean to offend you. But you have a very developed

system of ramparts in place to keep yourself from getting too close to people other than the handful you've trusted with the key to the portcullis."

"That doesn't mean I don't want to get to know people."

"That's not what I said. You talk about books and art and music and politics, but you don't talk about personal things."

"I do. Milo had met you, and he knew about Aunt Jackie and—"

"Demographic information. Did you tell him about Faron's father?"

"Why would I do that?"

"I think I've made my point."

She pulled herself up in the seat and glared at him. "I don't see how."

He kept his eyes on the road. "Why did you and Milo, someone you knew intimately for almost a year and a half, never discuss your only child's father?"

"It never came up."

"Really? Milo seems more curious than that."

"He might have asked..." She twisted her hands in the fabric of her skirt.

He had the sense not to say anything along the lines of "See" or "I told you so." His being right was even more irritating because he was always above rubbing it in.

"Still. I didn't even know Helena had a brother."

"Did you ask her?"

"No."

"Did she ask about your family?"

"No. Not even Faron, whom she apparently knew quite well." The terrain had changed into low rolling hills. They were close.

"I wouldn't beat yourself up too much. You might not let many people in, but the people you do, you're fierce about." He put his free hand over hers.

"Thanks."

"Now. Where is Matjaž's house?"

Jo pulled up the map on her phone and played navigator.

It was what she had expected, a traditional Slovenian house with enlarged windows and a wraparound deck that gave it a modern feel.

As they entered the driveway, a young man dressed in a white shirt and black vest under a lightweight ski jacket held out his palm to stop them. Gregor rolled down his window.

"Do you mind parking in the grass next to that blue car? I can park for you." His twentysomething face was marked with the indignity of teenage acne.

"I don't mind, thank you." Gregor pulled slowly onto the grass as the young man stepped away from the car. "Are you ready for this?"

"As ready as I am going to be."

Death had once been an abstraction, a word, useful in referring to a vague projection of her own life's end or to the abruptly specific conclusion of her father's. Death was now a daily companion — quite literally, if Jackie was right about Maja's new job as her spirit guide. The thought of it made her laugh.

"I'm guessing you're okay then."

"I don't know if I'm okay or not, but I think I will be." She opened the door and stepped into the grass outside the car. It wasn't wet, but the sod under the blades was still soft from the recent rains.

Gregor stepped around the car and met her at the corner. He offered his arm and wrapped his warm hand around hers as she took it.

"Your hands are like ice." He squeezed her fingers.

"Maybe I should have brought gloves. I just didn't think it was that cold."

"It isn't. Are you sure you're up for this?"

"Because my hands are cold? Yes. I'll be fine."

She looked to the top of the stairs to the entrance to the house on the second level. Matjaž stood there. He was dressed in the same suit he'd worn the night of the murder; it was probably the only one he owned. He looked as quirkily attractive as before, but grief made him less animated as he greeted the mourners ahead of them.

She watched her footing climbing the stairs, holding her dress up to keep from stepping on the hem. Matjaž's relieved face greeted her at the top. That look of relief at her presence was puzzling.

He took her hand as she stepped onto the deck. "I'm so glad you could come."

There it was. Her stomach fluttered, and she could feel every hair on her body stand at rapt attention.

"I cared for your sister. And I … there aren't words to express my sorrow at your loss." She looked away from his face, to his tie, to the decking, to their hands still locked together by his grip. His familiarity made it impossible to separate her feelings for the loss of Helena from her attraction to him.

"She cared for you as well." He held her hand for another moment before letting go to shake hands with Gregor.

She waited while the two men exchanged greetings. Clearly, Helena had mentioned her to him. What had she said?

She and Gregor walked inside to join the others and to greet an elderly woman who sat ramrod straight in a polished wheelchair just inside the door. She introduced herself to the people ahead of Jo and Gregor as Mrs. Belak, Helena and Matjaž's mother. Jo offered her hand, and Mrs. Belak held it in both of hers.

"You must be Jo. You are not what I expected."

"Yes. Jo Wiley." So this was where Helena and Matjaž got those green and amber eyes. "I'm sorry, ma'am. What was it you expected?"

"I expected you to be beautiful, given Matjaž's description."

She guppied in response to that. Nothing quite like a verbal slap from your dead fuck-buddy's mom to put you off your game.

Gregor introduced himself to Mrs. Belak, giving Jo sufficient cover to collect herself and suppress a reply inappropriate for the setting and occasion. He ushered her to the next group of people standing silently in a circle a few more feet into the dark, paneled room. The group included Igor. And Tomaž and Katarina. Jo considered going back to chat with the charming Mrs. Belak.

Katarina extended her hand. "It's good to see you again. Well, despite the circumstances." Her expression was tight, as the circumstances warranted.

Jo took her hand and nodded stiffly. Her phone vibrated against her thigh. She put her hand in her pocket to quiet it, then realized that it wasn't her phone. It was Leo's stone, and it was buzzing like a handful of bees. Could that be the way it warned her evil was near? Maybe she had been right about Tomaž.

"It's been a difficult week for all of us. First Helena and then Maja." Gregor put his arm around Jo's shoulders and pulled her to him in a reassuring side hug.

"Of course." Tomaž nodded. He looked like he'd been pulled backward through a knothole. His shirt was wrinkled, and there were dark shadows under his bloodshot eyes. She caught herself staring at him.

"Gregor, I think I need some air. I'm gonna…" Jo tapped his arm and gestured back to the door.

But Matjaž stepped inside, closing the door behind him. "It looks like everyone is here. Mother and I have a few words we'd like to say, and then we'll try to honor Helena's wishes the best we can."

Thwarted in her bid to escape, Jo faded back into the room and found a big window to stare out of. She could see the walls of the old town in the distance, and she imagined throwing Tomaž into the river that ran between.

Mrs. Belak cleared her throat as gracefully as one could. "Helena, my daughter, was a creature of her own making.

I often asked myself if there had not been a mix-up at the hospital that sent me home with some other person's headstrong offspring. The fact that she looked exactly like her asinine father indicated otherwise. It was her wish that we not have a funeral for her, but rather a party for her friends and what family she could stand. I am sure that means I am here only by Matjaž's grace. In any case, it is a surprise to see that her friends were not all degenerates. Matjaž, I'm sure, will have more pleasant things to say about all of you, and about her." She waved a dismissive hand toward Matjaž, whose face had gone ashen, and she straightened the blanket across her lap.

Jo had not looked directly in Mrs. Belak's face the whole time she was talking, but now their gazes met. Mrs. Belak's expression was difficult to parse, but overall it came off as equal parts disgust and intrigue at Jo's continued presence. Jo had no idea what she'd done to provoke such rudeness, but never had she wanted so badly to pinch an old woman. Those were not pleasing thoughts.

Matjaž pulled at his tie and moved deeper into the room in front of the windows. His face was hidden in shadow as the late afternoon light filtered through the glass behind him.

"Yes … um … At our father's funeral many years ago, Helena made me promise that if she died first, I would do everything in my power to avoid, in her words, a dreary send-off. A party, she said, would be a better way to mark the end of her life. I'm sure she had no idea how difficult that would be given the circumstances." He paused and looked down briefly before continuing. "Given the circumstances of her death." His voice cracked with the unmistakable strain of trying not to cry in a public setting.

Another woman stepped forward to stand next to him and took his hand. She looked so much like Helena she had to be a cousin.

"Thank you all for coming and, whether you knew it or not, helping us to honor Helena's life in the way she would have wished."

The Helena look-alike stepped farther into the room and clasped her hands together in front of herself. "There's champagne and food. Please enjoy yourselves and tell each other your best stories about Helena. She will be deeply missed."

At her word a trio of black-tie servers emerged from the kitchen door behind Jo and dispersed into the crowd of thirty or so in the living room bearing trays of champagne flutes filled with rosé champagne, Helena's favorite.

———

Jo took advantage of the distraction to duck outside. She still had her coat on, and she rooted around in her pockets uselessly for the forgotten gloves as she crossed to the railing of the deck. Even at this distance, she could hear the Sora course over the spillway below the wall of the old city. She took a deep breath and closed her eyes, trying to find the peace this place could offer.

Footsteps on the deck brought her back to the moment. Matjaž stood next to her looking out at the distant castle hill above the walls of the town. "I'm sorry about my mother. Polona, my cousin, said you had a tense interaction with her when you arrived ... then she was kind of an ass to everyone after that."

She shrugged. "I know what mothers can be like sometimes."

"I'm afraid with Mother, it's all the time. At least since my father died. He must have been the softening force. She wasn't always like that."

"I'm sorry." Jo turned to look at him. His eyes were shadowed with loss of sleep or just simple grief. Either his suit was making him itch or he was nervous speaking to her.

"Don't be sorry. It is what it is. I came out here to check on you."

"I'm fine. I just needed some air. We're supposed to be here for you today." She resisted the urge to rub his arm or take his hand or touch him in some way that was too familiar.

"And you. I know you were seeing her. I didn't put it together until later. She never told me your family name, just that you were American."

"I didn't realize she thought enough of that to discuss it with anyone. I mean, she was seeing other people too." She cringed a little. "Not that anything's wrong with that. I mean, I'm hardly …"

"No. I know what you meant. Helena was never one for romance or attachment. I think you were a puzzle to her."

"She didn't know the half of it. I'm a puzzle to myself these days." Jo sighed and leaned into the railing.

"For whatever it's worth to you, she was also intrigued by you." He turned to face her, leaning against the railing.

"It means something." Tears caught her by surprise, but she kept her composure on his account.

"I should get back inside. Don't stay out here too long." He turned to walk away.

She turned and caught the edge of his jacket sleeve. "Matjaž, wait. Helena's okay, you know."

"What?" He stiffened. "I'm sorry. I don't believe in all that 'better place' nonsense."

"That's not what I meant. I don't know what happens after exactly, either, but I know she's okay." She must sound crazy. "I mean. I can feel it, that she's … not at peace, exactly, but …"

"If that comforts you, I'm glad for you, but my sister was murdered. She was violently removed from her life, and I can't believe she'd be okay with that." He walked away from her and back inside.

Fuck. That went well. Jo looked up. "Sorry, Helena."

"I don't think she can actually hear you." Maja was standing on the grass below the deck, near where Matjaž had been standing. "You blew that."

"Thanks." Jo turned facing the railing again so no one inside could see her talking to herself. "How long have you been there?"

"Long enough."

"Suppose we work out a signal, so I know you're here or if you need to talk to me or something. Now. Would you like to explain your obsession with Rancid to me?"

CHAPTER 18

Jo was a Portal. That fact explained a great deal; it also presented a new array of questions and uncertainties for Jo. She knew so little of her own family's lore, and nothing at all of the lore of Voices and Portals. If discovering this gift of speaking and interacting with the dead caused her to doubt her sanity, what would she make of her second, more dangerous, gift? Leo would honor his word to Lichtenberg, despite his misgivings. But he felt compelled to check on Jo.

He stood in front of Vesna's door. Vesna opened it before he knocked.

"Your aura was drifting under the door."

"Is that even possible?" He chuckled at the absurdity of a shadow he couldn't see announcing his arrival.

"Not with everyone. Your aura, I don't know, sticks out farther than most people's. It kind of billows and ebbs."

"What color is it?"

"Do you really want to know?" The sitting area she led him to was nearly filled by a couch that must have been born in the flat. Leo had to admire his niece's ability to find something to cram into every space in the room. "Not if it's bad."

"It isn't bad."

He nodded.

"Orange and red." His niece held his gaze a few beats, then looked away.

Although he couldn't see the colors that swirled around people, he knew what they meant. Orange was the color of physical power, but also of addiction or desire. It was the color of someone who wrestled with an inner demon. Red meant that, for now, he was winning.

She motioned for him to sit. "You asked me."

"I did. We can't hide from ourselves. It appears I can't hide from you either."

"Is it really something to hide?" She sat in a chair nestled against the end of the couch. An orange cat jumped into the chair behind her.

"I took vows."

"You chose to."

"It wasn't as simple as that, but I didn't refuse."

"And now there is Jo. I haven't seen the two of you together, but I can only imagine."

"I'd prefer not to discuss it. She is in a great deal of danger, and my personal struggles are the least of your worries — or hers."

"It's something more than talking to dead people?"

"Yes. Your friend is a Portal."

Vesna flinched, though most would have missed it. She

was made of stern stuff. She raised her eyebrows and waited for him to continue.

"I didn't believe Portals existed. Once, talking about lore he felt was being lost, Father mentioned them. He believed every legend and story had a kernel of truth, and said it was best to be prepared for anything that might emerge from the gates of hell."

His niece flinched more noticeably, with a tinge of disgust.

Leo rested his forearms on his knees and looked up into her cross face. "I don't believe as he did. You know this."

"I know you aren't as backward. But, never mind. Continue, please."

"Portals were supposed to be women who stood with one foot in this world and one in the next. The dead could return to life through them, or angels or demons could enter the world as mortal beings, throwing off eternity and all its many burdens." He paused. It was probably better to tell her everything, including the parts he still didn't believe. "Father cited the belief that it was possible for a god to use a Portal to enter the world."

"It doesn't sound like you believe it."

"I don't know that I do, but Father did."

"Have you told her?" Anger and accusation edged into her voice.

"No. Lichtenberg will tell her."

"Lichtenberg? The guy who lives upstairs? Why?"

"He's an Observer. He knows more about it than I do."

"An Observer lived in this building all this time, and you

didn't think you should tell me?"

"I didn't think it had anything to do with you. I thought it was about me and your father. And you didn't tell me you were a seer."

"It wasn't any of your business. An Observer spying on me and my friend is definitely my business."

"I apologize. I don't like that he's here, either, but he's useful and knowledgeable."

"And he probably wants to put Jo in a cage to poke and prod her to see how she works."

"No. I don't think so. For whatever reason, he seems to care about her. He wants to be certain she's safe."

Vesna snorted. "You mean 'in a safe.'"

"I promise you that won't happen on my watch. Is she in?"

She shook her head. "Helena's funeral is today." She pulled the cat out from behind her and brought her up to her face like a baby. "Why is it dangerous to Jo to be a Portal?"

"She's a threshold that can only be crossed once. It would be her life for the one she brings in. Father believed in God and Jesus, but didn't believe the Bible was complete and accurate. He said if Mary had been a Portal, she wouldn't have lived."

Vesna stopped petting the cat and watched as she jumped to the floor, indulged in a lengthy stretch, and disappeared into the bedroom. "So what do we do?"

"We let Lichtenberg tell her. We let her aunt teach her how to protect herself, and we find whatever demon has possessed one of your friends."

"I can see if someone is possessed. There isn't anyone."

"Lichtenberg thinks it's a revenge demon."

"Oh." Vesna grimaced. "I can't see those." Leo could almost hear the gears spinning in her head, trying to work out a way to protect her friend. "I should get her to leave Ljubljana. Let you and Lichtenberg find the demon and dispatch it back into whatever it came out of."

"How far are you willing to take her? She's a lighthouse. I can't see auras, and even I can sense what she is."

"As far as we need to. Antarctic cruise. Whatever."

"I appreciate your loyalty, but she can't live there, or at least I doubt she'd want to. She needs to know what she is, and she needs to learn to control it."

"Her aunt will be here on Saturday. Maybe she has some family ritual to protect her."

He leaned back into the enormous couch. "I doubt it. From what little I could find, the last Portal died in the 1930s."

Vesna sat up. "There's really nothing you can do?"

"Unfortunately, Lichtenberg is more likely to be able to come up with something."

Disgust flitted across her face again. "That's not very reassuring."

"Vesna, you know as well as I do that our family would never have tried to help someone like Jo in the past." A horrifically vivid image of Jo's face, agonized and wreathed in flames, raced through his mind.

She nodded. "Well, thank whatever gods there may be, none of those backward idiots is around now. But you — you have to figure something out." Her agitation washed over him.

"I agreed to look for the Vessel. The sooner we locate that and determine who the demon's using for a mule, the faster I can guarantee Jo's and everyone else's safety."

She nodded.

"And you…," he added, "keep an eye on her. At the very least, don't let her go wandering around by herself."

CHAPTER 19

The ride back to Ljubljana was quieter than the ride up had been. Jo had more questions for Maja, but they would have to wait until they were alone. Gregor didn't seem to want to push Jo to talk. She was grateful for his consideration.

Aside from a few answers, she wanted nothing more than some tea on Vesna's couch with a cat curled in her lap, followed by a very long nap. But that was not an option. Not with Maja and Helena's killer still roaming about town. She still had Maja's funeral to deal with, which should be a hoot as Maja had pledged earlier to offer nonstop commentary for it.

Jo had half-expected to see Investigator Klančnik with an officer in tow at Helena's funeral, or wake. Whatever it had been. Apparently in life, the pieces don't fall into place quite as easily as they do in a Nancy Drew mystery.

The teahouse was dark as she crossed the courtyard to climb the stairs to her apartment. They would close until the funeral, when they would hold a small reception at Maja's mother's request. The whole staff agreed that Jo needed a little break; only the women understood how much she needed one, and why.

Jo scraped her keys into her lock. The door behind her opened, and Vesna's face peeped out of the door of her flat.

"Jo, would you join us?"

"Us?" Jo turned the lock back on her own door.

"Uncle Leo is here. He came looking for you."

Maja would have to wait.

———

Jo settled into the opposite corner of the couch from Leo, who was not wearing the monk's habit she expected. He looked disconcertingly normal in dark jeans and an oatmeal sweater. Cleopatra jumped into her lap, kneading and turning around on Jo's belly pooch before settling down and purring quietly.

Leo waited for the cat to finish her ritual before speaking. "I'm worried about you." He moved closer to Jo on the couch.

"You and everyone else, apparently." Jo leaned back into the leather.

"This is all new for you. Maybe it feels like a game, but I can assure you there are things you are not prepared for." Leo made the same mom-face as Vesna, but Leo's involved more stern eyebrow action.

"I don't think it's a game. If I did, I'd have taken my marbles and gone home by now."

"Vesna told me Maja has been to see you more than once."

"Yes. My aunt thinks she might be my new spirit guide. Apparently those come with the territory."

"Have you learned anything from her?"

"No. We really haven't had much of a chance to be alone since yesterday morning. I asked her to check out any rumors that might be circulating in Dead Ljubljana, or whatever you want to call it." Jo shifted, and Cleopatra dug a claw into her thigh.

"Let me know when you speak with her. I think it's related to the museum."

"Why?"

"Something was stolen from one of the exhibits the night of Helena's murder. A doll or figurine. Did you see it at the museum? Was anyone especially interested in it?"

"I did see a doll, but I wasn't looking for anything particularly weird. I mean, that was before..."

"If you think of anyone... In the meantime, I think you need to stay home and not get any more involved. I'm not sure what we're up against, and you don't know what you're capable of yet." He patted Cleopatra's head. "Or what your limitations are."

"You sound like Vesna."

"She's right, then."

Vesna brought a tray with tea and cookies from the kitchen. She sat on the edge of the chair next to Jo's end of the oversized couch. "How was the funeral?"

Jo nodded as Vesna handed her a cup of tea. "Weird."

Leo and Vesna both waited for her to continue. "I mean, Helena was not exactly a conformist, so no surprise she would have unconventional ideas about how she wanted to be mourned."

"How unconventional?"

"She wanted a party. Rosé champagne and canapés. A room filled with people she'd slept with, plus a family member or two." Jesus. She hoped there wasn't a crossover between the two groups.

"Didn't you go with Gregor?" Leo seemed dubious. "Helena doesn't seem … his type."

Jo shrugged. "I don't know. I didn't ask him that."

"How long will you keep the teahouse closed?" Leo took a sip of his tea, grimaced at it, and reached for a small pot of honey on the tray. "I'll never understand the appreciation for tea that tastes like grass clippings."

Jo admired his deft change of subject.

"We'll reopen on Monday. Jo's aunt is arriving tomorrow so they'll have time to catch up." Vesna did not make a face upon tasting her tea.

"Good. Sounds like you'll be busy all weekend. That should keep you out of trouble." Leo took a sip of his honey-laden tea, also without making a face.

———

Vesna closed her door, and Jo said goodbye to Leo at the top of the stairs. "You promise you'll call if you find out anything?"

"Yes. And please, call me after you talk with Maja." He turned and started quickly down the stairs with a wave.

"Leo."

He stopped and turned around.

"What does it mean when the stone you gave me vibrates?"

"Why? When did that happen?" He walked back up the steps to the landing and towered over her.

"Today. At the party for Helena."

"At her brother's house?"

She nodded and put her hand in her pocket. The stone was still, cool to the touch, and fit right into the hollow of her palm.

"I don't think it means anything good. Please, stay home and stay away from Helena's family." He turned and walked more slowly down the stairs. She could almost see the huge black cloud of concern above his head.

Maja was leaning against the wall next to Jo's door. Her blue hair clung wetly to the plaster, but the wall was dry when she straightened up and spoke.

"Guess we better debrief or whatever. Not sure if it's interesting."

"So none of the deads want anything to do with the museum or the Roman house. Apparently they stay far away from all the ancient Emona stuff, at least since they started the renovations in the basement at the museum — and especially since Helena was killed." Maja leaned back in her chair. She was corporeal enough to tip it, but soundlessly.

Jo shook her head. "The demon was trapped in a vessel that came from the Roman well in the basement of the museum. They had an exhibit case of items… Fuck. Olga. Olga was the one looking so intently at the stuff in the case."

"What could Olga possibly want with a Roman demon?"

"The doll had these creepy ass eyes. Like they were following you, but they were just scratched into the clay. Olga was fascinated by it."

"Sorry." Maja straightened her chair. "Why would Olga want to kill Helena, or me? That doesn't make any sense."

"Maybe not. Nothing else makes much sense to me either though."

Maja laughed. "I'm pretty sure it wasn't Olga who hip-checked me into the river."

"You said you didn't remember everything."

"Not everything, but whoever or whatever came at me was bigger than Olga. Bigger than me. Maybe Olga's fascination was a MacGuffin, or whatever it is you call it."

"I think you mean red herring. But yeah. Possible." Jo's phone vibrated in her jacket pocket.

Faron had texted her. "Meet me at the tea house? 10 mins. Urgent."

Jo thumbed a reply. "Y. Everything okay?"

"Not exactly."

Maja peered over the table but couldn't see the screen. "Who was that?"

"Faron. I need to go downstairs."

"Want me to come?"

"No… Yes… Does it matter? You're going to anyway, aren't you?"

"Most likely yes. It's not like I have a lot to do."

———

Faron met Jo at the door of the teahouse just as she was turning the lock. He had Ivanka in tow, and Maja disappeared as the two approached. Jo waived Faron and Ivanka into the shop and closed the door behind them, the bells jangling against the wood.

"What's up?" Jo ran her hand through the top of her hair.

Faron took Ivanka's hand. It wasn't a possessive gesture, but one that made it clear they were more than friends. "Can Ivanka stay with you tonight?"

"Sure, I guess. But why?"

Ivanka shifted away from Faron and stepped toward her a bit. "I had an awful fight with my mom, and I just… I can't go back. Not tonight, at least." She looked down at her ratty black Converse sneakers.

Jo looked at Faron. "Can't she stay with you?" She doubted it would be Ivanka's first overnight there.

"No!" Ivanka lowered her voice, "That's the first place she'd look."

Indeed. "That bad, huh? Do you have your stuff?"

"Veronika's bringing it later." She looked down at her feet again.

Jo had an overwhelming urge to pull the girl's chin up with a crooked finger so she could look her in the eye when she spoke. "Do you guys want to go up now?"

"No. We're going to meet Veronika at her friend's place." Faron was the one in charge here. Jo wasn't sure she liked it much, but maybe he thought Ivanka needed a protector.

"I can stay—" She started to say "at Milo's" but caught herself and backtracked. "I can stay at Rok's tonight. You two can stay here. Just no smoking — anything — inside." She gave Faron a raised eyebrow for emphasis.

Faron nodded. "Are you sure? About staying with Rok, I mean."

"Yeah. The flat's tiny. I need to confirm with him, but if not, I'll crash at Gregor's. Still have your key?"

"Yep." He patted his pants pocket.

Faron and Ivanka left. Jo sat down at the table nearest the door and called Rok.

"Ah, Jo. Is all well?"

"Yeah. Sorry to bother you, but can I crash at your place tonight?"

"Always."

"Thanks. Seven-ish?"

"Then." He hung up with a soft click.

The screen on the phone went dark, and she replayed the conversation with Maja. A flash of the doll's freaky face. Helena's amber eyes. The air in her chest felt heavy. How was she supposed to figure all this shit out? Less than a week ago, she didn't know any of this existed. She would be more than happy to go back to that ignorant bliss.

A knock on the window brought her back with a start. Staring down at her from Matjaž's bearded face were the same amber eyes that had drawn Jo to his sister. She stood and opened the door for him.

"I saw the light. I didn't realize you were closed." He looked into the empty shop.

"We're closed until after Maja's funeral." She ran her hand through her hair again, hoping to smooth it into place.

"I was very sorry to hear about Maja. I didn't really come for tea though. I wanted to talk to you." His expression changed, his mouth and eyes tightening.

"Sure. Have a seat." She stepped back and gestured toward the table where she'd been sitting. "You said you don't drink tea. Can I offer you a glass of water? I also have an employee coffee stash."

He sat, folding his long legs under the small table. "No. I'm fine, really."

She sat back down opposite him. "What's up?" She slid her hand into her pocket again. The stone was cold and still.

"I want to apologize." He looked her in the eye, without pretense or guile. "About how I spoke to you at my house."

She sat back in surprise. "You really don't need to do that. It's been—"

"No. I do. You were being kind, trying to comfort, and I was rude. Especially after how my mother spoke to you. Polona filled me in. I'm sorry about that too."

"I … you really don't need to apologize for your mom. She's a grownup. Thank you anyway though." The way he looked at her, the nakedness of it, reminded her so much of Helena. No need for a poker face when you were blunt or honest all the time. But Helena hadn't been completely honest with her. Her fling with Faron had been a lie of omission.

"Polona was going to intervene, but your Gregor

maneuvered you away."

She chuckled. "Yeah. He knows me pretty well. I wouldn't have made a scene … well, maybe not … but your mother caught me off guard." She wasn't exactly proud of her occasional lack of filter. "I didn't know Helena had talked about us, about me, to anyone in her family. We didn't, um, talk about that kind of thing much." She looked down at her hands, weirdly embarrassed to be alluding to sex with his sister. She thought of Ivanka's downcast face and looked back up at him. He was smiling wryly.

"She didn't usually mention her… friends. To Mother, at least. But she talked about you often. Not everything, mind you." He must have noticed the brief flicker of horror across her face.

"Oh." She wondered if he knew about Faron. She was glad he hadn't brought it up if he did.

"Anyway. Helena was intrigued by you. She once said she thought you'd be better for me than for her." He laughed awkwardly, as if he hadn't meant to blurt that out.

She wondered how much he could see in her face. She was sure she hadn't been good about hiding that she was attracted to him. She was also sure she couldn't act on it. That might not be as bad as Helena with Faron, but it still seemed wrong. She was flattered that he'd said it, though, even if he hadn't meant to. She was a little embarrassed for him and a lot confused about how warm she felt all over in his presence. It just wouldn't work, or do. Shit.

He put his hand on the edge of the table. "I should go. I'm sure you have stuff to do."

"Yes. I mean no. I don't, really. I mean ..." What did she mean?

He settled back into his chair. "Have you eaten?"

She thought through her day. Other than champagne at the funeral and tea and a cookie at Vesna's there had been no food. "I haven't."

"May I buy you dinner?"

Shit. Rok. Faron and Ivanka. Maja.

Rok wouldn't care when she showed up. He hadn't even asked why she needed a place to crash. Faron and Ivanka could take care of themselves. Maja, well, Maja would wait. She had to eat, didn't she? And maybe she could pump him for more information about Helena so she could figure out what the hell was going on.

"Sorry. I just thought we could continue our conversation."

"No. I mean, yes. Yes, you can buy me dinner. I just need to run upstairs and get my bag and a jacket." She didn't want to tell him she also needed a clean pair of underpants and a toothbrush. What would that sound like? She also needed to call Rok. "Give me five minutes."

———

She and Matjaž walked down Breg to the Indian restaurant. She wanted to sit outside, but the proprietors had decided it was too cold or damp and the tables were stacked to the side under tarpaulins. The host seated them in a private corner, apparently thinking they were on a date.

"Wine?" The server, dressed in a spangly embroidered tunic, offered Matjaž the list.

"Hm, I prefer beer with Indian, but I'm game if you'd like to get a bottle." He was looking at Jo.

"I'd prefer beer."

They ordered their drinks and looked at the menus.

Despite not eating all day, her stomach was too full of butterflies to leave room for hunger. The fantastic smells from the kitchen were enticing though. It always took her too long to decide what she wanted, so she often ended up ordering the same things. She looked up at Matjaž as he pored over the menu. "Thali? Then we can get a few things without ordering too much food."

"You seem to know more about this than I do." He smiled, his eyes crinkling at the corners.

"Indian's my favorite, though I mostly make it at home."

"Of course. You're a chef." He smiled at her.

Sexy. Charming. Fuck. "Um, no. I'm a cook. A decent one, but not a chef. That implies a whole other level of mastery. I sling tea and make fancy sandwiches."

His face darkened for a moment. "Yes. I had forgotten about our conversation at the reception." He recovered quickly and smiled again, but it just barely made it to his eyes.

She hadn't meant to cast a pall, but it was impossible not to reference the fact they'd met the night of his sister's murder. For a brief moment she had almost felt normal again. No escaping for the wicked or something like that. She sighed.

"I'm sorry. I didn't mean to be a downer."

She shrugged. "And I didn't mean to sigh out loud. It's been a phenomenally shitty week. I think we are entitled to some honest emotion."

"Yes. You're right." He closed his menu and slid it under hers on the table. "I'm going to ask you to order for us. And I'm going to enjoy the food and your company and we can talk about whatever. Please don't feel like you need to spare me reminders."

"Same." She smiled back at him. He was very much like Helena, and he was very different.

———

The waiter covered their table with small dishes filled with spicy vegetables, a creamy chicken stew, sauces, rice, and a couple slabs of garlicky naan. Jo scooped a little of everything onto her plate and tore off a piece of naan to eat.

Matjaž watched her as she put the saag-covered naan in her mouth. "Are you supposed to eat with the bread?" He set his fork down on the table.

She chewed the bite and nodded. She swallowed. "Yes. I mean that's how people ate when I was in India."

"I guess the bread keeps you from getting your fingers covered in food."

"Yeah. I thought it was probably filler, too. Bread is less expensive than meat or vegetables." She took a sip of her beer.

"It's very, um, intimate." He scooped up some rice and saag with a chunk of naan and dripped some onto his beard. He wiped his mouth with his napkin.

"There's that. My aunt always said not to order spaghetti or tacos on a first date, because it was too messy. I prefer food a little messy. People tend to fuck like they eat." Why? Why had she said that? Her cheeks burned.

He laughed, but it was kind. "I don't think I've ever seen anyone make themselves blush that much. And, I've never thought about it that way. I think you might be onto something."

That didn't help. Her chest was as hot as her face. She took another sip of her beer. Time to change the subject. "So, tell me about your business?"

He smiled. "There's not much to tell. I work with an architect, and we specialize in historic renovation. Mostly here, but in Austria and Italy as well."

"It sounds interesting."

"It can be. We've worked in some beautiful places, but sometimes it's really humbling trying to keep time and water at bay."

"Water will always find a way."

"Yes. It will. Usually the path of least resistance. I've spent a lot of time in crypts and cellars slogging around up to my knees in the water that's trying to find its way to the surface. But what about you? How does an American wind up in Ljubljana? Why here?"

"Have you seen this place? It's beautiful." She waved her hand in the general direction of the door.

He laughed again. "It is. But I didn't think Americans in, what, the early 1990s? — even knew this country existed."

"I have to admit that I didn't. Well, not really."

"So, how then?"

"I ran away from home."

"How old were you?"

"Eighteen. Just. I dropped out of college and took off to India with a guy from my photography class. We were going to be nomads and convince National Geographic to hire us."

"That's when you were there?"

"The first time. I've been back a couple times with Rok, a friend." Why did she need to qualify that?

"How did you get to Slovenia from India?"

"On a train."

He smirked at her. "That's not what I meant."

"India didn't agree with Turner. He got sick all the time and decided he'd rather be somewhere in Europe. So we headed east. Interesting trip. He had a friend, a poet, he'd met at a writer's thing in Chattanooga — that's where I was in college. He thought this friend would put us up here. No such luck, but I liked it and wanted to stay for a bit. He liked the poet's girlfriend a lot, and the two of them wound up going back to Tennessee — or so I heard."

"And you just stayed?"

"I didn't want to go home."

"No one was worried about you? The war, all that."

"There's just my aunt and my cousin Michael in the States. She sent me money occasionally and told me to do what I needed to do."

"Parents?"

"My father drowned when I was a kid. My mother's alive, but she's, well, she and I ... I haven't seen or spoken to her in years. My aunt raised me after my father died."

She said it nonchalantly. Over the years, it had just become a fact, like the fact that her eyes were blue. Even so, she could still feel a little dig in her chest, a little tingle in the scar on her cheek where her mother had thrown a plate at her in one of her rages. Jo took another bite of naan with rice and chicken. Recent events explained a lot, but the answers she was getting had thrown her childhood into stark relief against all she'd thought she knew about everything.

"I'm sorry. I didn't mean to…"

"It's fine. I'm fine. It was a long time ago." A different existence, even.

"And then you were here and got married?" He took a sip of his beer.

"You mean my son? No. I was never married." Helena must have mentioned Faron after all.

"How did you get citizenship then?"

"I enrolled at the university to learn Slovene, then I finished my degree. I had some help from Gregor and his family."

"I thought Gregor might be Faron's father."

"He isn't."

"You studied photography at the university, yes?"

"Umhm." She had her mouth full. "How did you know that?"

"Helena went to one of your shows, at ŠKUC, I think."

She almost choked. "She never told me that." She hadn't thought about that show in a long time. She hadn't taken photographs in a long time either.

"Yeah. She said she was surprised when she'd met you and put the name together. How many American photographers are there in Slovenia?"

"Not many, but I'm not a photographer, not anymore." Helena had a few other omissions.

"And Faron's dad?"

"Do you really want to know that?" She really didn't like to tell people. She always got the look.

"Yeah. How did you meet him?"

"He was my mentor, Dušan Črnigad."

Matjaž almost choked on his beer. "The Dušan Črnigad?"

"Yes."

"Does he know?"

"Of course he knows."

"And he was … involved?"

"No. He'd already been offered a job in New York, and it was a pretty easy way to get himself and his wife as far away from me as possible."

"Does Faron know?"

"Yes. I wouldn't hide that from my kid."

"I'm sorry."

"Sorry that some other guy was a douchebag? That's not necessary. We were fine." With a whole lot of help from Gregor and Vesna and Rok. Faron had been raised by a village.

"So you ran away from home to get away from your mom and ran smack into an asshole?"

"I've never really thought about it that way but, yeah." She shrugged.

"I'm impressed that you're fine."

"You do what you have to." She finished her beer and looked at him, really looked at him, the embarrassment forgotten. "Isn't that what you're doing now? Isn't that what most of us do?"

He met her gaze steadily and nodded yes. "I don't know what to do next though."

"Finish dinner?"

He laughed. "I mean after that."

"I don't know what to tell you."

"And you, tea mistress and lapsed photographer, what will you do?"

"Mourn my friends. And avenge them."

Matjaž froze, a bite of saag halfway to his mouth. He rested his forearm on the table and stared at her. "You don't mean that, do you?"

"I do. I'm going to find out who killed them and make sure they pay."

"Isn't that a job for the police?"

"The police don't seem to be getting very far very fast."

"Still. We're talking about someone capable of murder. I … I would hate to see you get hurt."

There was a connection between them, as sure as if they'd

had their wrists bound together. A thousand times fuck. She really, really did not need this.

"Listen," she said. "Would you or wouldn't you do everything in your power to make it happen if —" She paused, then forged ahead. "If you were certain Helena would know that you'd avenged her."

He stared at her. "She wouldn't know. Vengeance would only be for me."

That's what she used to think. "Maybe. Maybe there is more beyond this than any of us know."

"Do you really believe that?"

"I'm not sure what I believe right now. I know that someone killed Helena. I don't know why, and I don't know who. But I think the same person killed Maja, and if there's something I can do about it, I intend to do it."

CHAPTER 20

Matjaž insisted on accompanying her, so they walked in companionable quiet through Tivoli toward Rok's apartment in Šiška.

Matjaž broke the silence. "How did you meet Rok?"

"Here in Tivoli. I was teaching Faron how to ride a scooter, and he wiped out on one of the paths. He scraped his knees up pretty badly." Faron's knees still bore the scars, and she still felt guilty that he hadn't been wearing kneepads. "He was four, maybe newly five. I picked him up and carried him to a bench, dragging the scooter. There was a lot of blood. Rok was passing by, and he stopped to see if we were all okay. And then history or whatever." She smiled to herself, remembering the furtive sex after Faron had fallen asleep. She'd had to put her hand over her own mouth not to scream. "But I've spilled all my secrets. What about you? No girlfriend? No boyfriend?"

Matjaž laughed. "Not a girlfriend. Not for quite a bit."

"So there was someone?"

"You might say Helena got her wild ways from her older

brother."

"Oh." Girlfriend was probably not the word then.

"I gave all that up a while ago to focus on work. Mostly, anyway." She could almost hear him smile in the gathering darkness.

"That's not much of a spill."

"I'm not sure what you'd like to know."

"Oh, I don't know." What did she want to know? "I think I'm just trying to figure you out." Jo stopped on the path. The air was damp and smelled of rotting leaves. Tivoli's main paths were lit, but they were off the paths, taking a shortcut onto Vodnik Street. She could almost make out his face in the gloom. "You are so much like her. And so much not."

"More not than like, I think. Helena is, was…" He took a breath that caught in his throat.

She put her hand on his arm. Aside from a handshake, it was the first time she'd touched him in any way, and she felt a crackle in the contact.

He took another deep breath. "Helena was happy. She loved her life. She was completely honest, and she was a chameleon, all at the same time."

She wasn't exactly sure she'd use the word honest to describe Helena, but Helena was his sister. She wrapped her arms around him, her face squished against his chest. "I am so sorry."

He returned her embrace and put his chin on the top of her head. Like Milo. The gesture was jarringly familiar, and she had to fight the urge to pull away and run. Maybe Gregor was right. Maybe she had barbed wire inside her.

Matjaž ran his hands up her arms to her neck and held her back to kiss her. A hungry, open-mouthed kiss.

Her body responded before her mind did. She kissed back, pulling him into her by his waist. When her brain checked back in, she pushed him away, gently and with restraint. She wanted to shove him, not because he'd been untoward, but because she couldn't process it all.

"I'm sorry. I didn't mean to …"

"Fuck. Please. Don't apologize." Jo stepped back trying to gather her thoughts and slap down her emotions so she could say what she needed to say. She took a breath. Then two. Matjaž stood there, like the nice guy he was, waiting for her to speak. Damn him.

"I … fuck, I'll just be honest. I want to fuck your brains out. I have since the moment I met you at the …" She winced thinking of how, when, they had met. "I just can't. You're her brother. It's just wrong." She threw her head back for punctuation. She just wanted to wail. For all of it. For Helena, for this fucking weirdness that had descended on her unbidden, for Maja, for him. For everything. She just wanted to go back to Saturday morning and stay in bed.

He stared at her. She couldn't tell if he was amused or angry, so she asked.

"Not angry. Maybe amused. And the feeling about wanting to fuck your brains out is mutual. Except when I met you I thought you and Gregor were an item."

"Hm. That's kind of our shtick." She bent over with her hands on her thighs and looked up at him. "What do we do now? I can't do this. You. I can't do you."

"I'm going to walk you to your friend's apartment and go home and take a cold shower. And I'm going to hope you reconsider your position. I'm not sure what you're going to do."

"That makes two of us." She grabbed his hand and headed down Vodnik toward Rok's block of flats. He'd lived in the same apartment as long as she'd known him. The building was a square, ugly vestige of communist architecture at its worst, but Rok's apartment was a hidden Aladdin's cave tucked into the concrete high-rise boxes.

Matjaž walked her up to the front door. She stood on the step, evening out the height difference for a moment. He kissed her again, a chaste goodnight kiss. He ran his hand down her arm and squeezed her fingers. "Please. Think about what I said, and please don't put yourself in danger. Let the police do their job."

She watched his silhouette moving through the orange glow of the security light at the edge of the parking lot and into the darkness of the street beyond. She watched until she couldn't see him anymore.

She pushed the button for Rok's flat. The door buzzed, and she hiked up the stairs to his apartment.

He met her at the door in a kimono. Aromas of pot and curry and incense drifted out onto the landing. She could hear Gogol Bordello turned down low on the ancient sound system in his living room.

She pounced on him. She pushed her way into the apartment, taking his face in her hands to kiss him as hungrily as Matjaž had kissed her. She kicked the door closed with her foot and backed Rok into the living room. She let go of his face and untied his kimono. Still kissing him, she kicked off her clogs and started peeling off her clothes. She pulled away long enough to yank her shirt over her head, then she pushed Rok down onto the Moroccan wedding blankets that covered the couch. She climbed on top of him, her knees burning against the scratchy wool.

She wanted to hurl herself against him, to break herself, or him. Break something. He responded with the same intensity. He stood, holding her legs under her thighs, their bodies still connected. He carried her the few steps to his bedroom and threw her onto the bed, separating them. She reached for him and he crawled into bed on top of her.

She screamed. Clawed her fingers down his back. She wailed and cried until they collapsed together. Her face was wet with tears. He had red smeared across his cheek. Jo looked at her hand. She must have scratched him harder than she thought.

He raised his head and looked at her. "Better?"

"Oh my god. I'm so sorry." She tried to wipe off the blood on his face and succeeded only in spreading it further.

He rolled off her and leaned on his elbow. He shrugged as best he could. "There have been worse injuries for worse reasons."

She laughed despite her chagrin at having wounded him.

———

Rok sat naked on the edge of the tub while she dabbed the scratches on his back with a paper towel soaked in vodka. He barely flinched.

That was going to leave a mark, she was pretty sure. She was naked, too, except for her bra, which neither of them had managed to get off. She put the cap back on the vodka and sat down next to him. He turned so their thighs were touching from hip to knee.

She lowered her head to her knees, still holding the bottle and the paper towel in her hands. Rok took them from her gently and put them in the sink. He ran his calloused hand up and down her back, warming the skin and soothing her.

"You are going to be okay." He massaged her neck.

"I think you have too much faith in me." She didn't raise her head.

He sighed at her.

She sat that way, staring at the ugly yellow linoleum in his bathroom with his warm hand on her back until she felt like she had enough blood in her brain to think straight.

"Thank you." She sat up.

He laughed. "Thank you."

———

Jo woke up to her phone ringing. She reached around next to the bed and then remembered she wasn't at home. She sat up on the edge of the bed. Who was calling at … what time was it anyway? Where was her phone?

It was in the hallway, in the pocket of the coat she'd shed inside the front door. She got to it just in time to miss the call. Who called at midnight, other than Aunt Jackie getting the time mixed up? She picked up her coat and continued along the trail of discarded black clothing that led to the couch. She gathered everything up and walked back to the bedroom, where she deposited it in a heap on the edge of the table Rok used as a desk. Her phone chirped with a voice message.

It was Leo. She should call him in the morning. Setting her phone on top of the pile of clothes, she climbed back into bed and curled into Rok. She wanted nothing more than to fall back into a dreamless sleep. Instead, she stared at the ceiling thinking of all the horrible things that fucking doll may have unleashed until the dark blue light of dawn found its way between the gap in the curtains.

———

Jo gathered her things. She put on the clean underpants and brushed her teeth with the weird baking soda and chalk mixture Rok had in his bathroom. She put her coat on and slipped back into his room to kiss him goodbye. He was awake and pulled her into bed with him. He kissed her back, greedily.

"Where are you needed so early?" His voice was warm with sleep.

"I need to do prep for Maja's thing at the shop, and Jackie gets in tonight. And I need to see my priest friend for confession."

He laughed. "He may enjoy your mea culpa about last night."

"That is not something I need forgiveness for, I hope." She tousled his hair.

"No. It isn't." He hesitated.

"What?"

"I'm leaving today."

"I thought you weren't going to Nepal."

"I changed my mind."

"Um. We've kind of ruined your celibacy preparations." She ran her thumb over his eyebrow.

"Yes. There are other things I still need to take care of there."

"Okay." She had hoped he would stick around. It would have been nice having someone nearby who understood what was going on.

She sat up on the edge of the bed, and he curled around her, resting his head against her hip. It was probably for the best that he go to Nepal. She couldn't just stay burrowed here in his cave and forget about everything outside. Fuck. It wasn't a curse, this new superpower. It was a duty, which was a lot worse. To turn away from duty would be selfish and cowardly.

"Are you afraid?"

His question surprised her. Rok waited for her to speak. "No. Maybe?"

"Maybe?"

"It's so much bigger than me. I feel like I have this huge responsibility, and at the same time I feel like a chess piece."

He nodded. And waited.

"But I know there are some things I have to do."

He nodded again. "Tread lightly."

———

Jo walked in the cold and mist through Tivoli back to the central city. Tread lightly, Rok said. Not be careful. Not beware.

Tread lightly. Just like Rok to be her very own Cheshire cat. She caught herself humming "Time Bomb" and felt Maja walking next to her.

A lone runner was crunching gravel, moving away from them in the fog. Then the park was empty except for the two of them, one alive and conflicted, and one sarcastic and dead.

Maja's voice carried a tease. "So, how was your evening?"

"Complicated."

"I'll say."

"Just how much can you actually see?"

"I know you went to dinner with Matjaž. And I know you spent the night at Mr. Bear's flat."

"And?"

"And nothing. I'm not interested in amateur porn. Besides, central Ljubljana on a Friday night is great for people-watching — alive and dead."

Snappy patter with Maja felt good, but Jo had things to accomplish.

"I think Tomaž is our murderer."

Maja stopped. "What happened to your theory about Olga?"

"I gave it a little more thought, and you were right about that. There's no reason Olga would kill anyone. But she is part of Tomaž's web of connections. Tomaž, who was sleeping with Helena and with you." She told Maja about the stone Brother Leo gave her and how it started quivering and humming when she'd stood near Tomaž at Helena's wake.

"It has to be him."

"I don't know. He's an asshole, but a killer? He's too big a chicken. And what about all the woo-woo shit going on at the museum? Maybe it's not even a person we should be looking for."

"Maybe. I need to call Leo. I need to do prep for Sunday's thing for you at the shop. I need a shower." Her hair smelled like sex.

"Are you going to my interment today?"

"Shit. It is today. I don't want to go. Is that terrible of me?"

"Not terrible, but who will I snark to?"

"You're still going?"

"Would you miss your own funeral?"

"If I had a choice? Probably. If you have something nice to say about me, say it while I'm alive. If you want to say something nasty, same."

"If I were alive, what nice thing would you say to me?"

They were at the exit of the park, walking up the long-hidden ramp by the modern art museum. Jo stopped.

"I would've said that you were tougher than you needed to be. And that I really did want to know more about you." And now, she would say she was sorry for all the life that Maja wouldn't live, for all the things she would miss. But she couldn't say it. It was raw and fresh, and to say it made it real.

She couldn't break open right now. Grieving her dead would have to wait.

Maja stared at her, blue lip trembling.

Jo hugged her, and it felt like hugging a statue — same as when she'd hugged her father as a shade. "I haven't been very good about taking my own advice. Or letting people in."

Maja hugged her back but didn't speak.

Jo held Maja a moment by the shoulders. "And I'm really pissed off that the best baker we ever had is dead, and now I'm going to have to hire someone else."

They both laughed, awkward in their shared discomfort, and continued on. They walked into the square in front of the museum, and Maja flickered out of sight amid the early morning walkers and their dogs.

———

Jo let herself into the shop. It smelled stale. They'd been closed long enough for the smells of kitchen and people to settle and mingle into a flat metallic funk, punctuated with vanilla, because everything in this part of her world smelled like vanilla.

She threw her bag and coat on the table inside the door and flipped on a few lights. She stood in front of the new mural and followed the lines of the waves as they washed the burning crates back toward the suggested land at the edge of the wall. She imagined them crashing open on the beach, spewing burning boxes of tea into the surf. She could almost hear the sizzle and pop of the seawater extinguishing each little fire. The water always wins.

She remembered clambering over the rocks on the Irish coast with Rok on one of their many adventures with Faron in tow. She'd stood on the edge and turned to look back at Faron on the grass. Rok had laid out a picnic to make the most of the first bright sunshine of the trip. A rogue wave had smacked her from behind, knocking her face first into the rocks and bracken between her perch and the edge of land. She felt for an instant like she was being pulled back into the sea, but she found a foothold. Rok had helped her up onto the grassy jut of land and removed a clump of seaweed from her hair. She was banged up and soaked to the skin. Wiping the blood off her chin, he'd said, "Never turn your back on the sea."

She couldn't trust the sea. She couldn't trust her friends and family to not be supernatural weirdos. She couldn't trust herself not to be a supernatural weirdo. She couldn't trust lovers and friends not to die. She sat on the nearest chair and wept until she was dry.

She could trust herself. She had to. And Vesna. And Leo, even though she barely knew him, and his world seemed way weirder even than hers. She trusted Faron and Gregor. She hadn't told them everything, but not because she didn't trust them. She just didn't want to involve them. And she trusted Rok, at least to be there and bandage her wounds. But he clearly wasn't up for a fight, if that was what this was going to be.

Her phone rang in her pocket. It was Leo.

"Are you home?"

"No. I'm at the shop. I was going to figure out what we need for Sunday. Do some prep. Maybe go to the market. Then

Maja's funeral." So much for not telling him she had rejected his house-arrest idea.

"Can I join you? We need to talk."

"Sure."

She touched the red button and slid the phone back into her pocket. She rummaged in the kitchen for her coffee stash and started a pot of Turkish coffee on the stove. The ritual of it was calming. Coffee, a little sugar, and water in the chipped enamel ibrik she kept hanging with the utensils for coffee emergencies. Bring to a boil. Add another spoonful of the powdered coffee and stir it down.

She let the grounds settle while she pawed through the bottom drawer in her office desk for her chipped mug. She poured the coffee into it, trying to leave as much of the grounds as possible in the little flared pot and taking care not to burn herself where the flames had licked the long metal handle.

She splashed some milk into the mug and sipped from it while she surveyed the contents of the reach-in, mentally putting together a menu for Sunday.

The bells on the front door clanged against the wood. She poked her head around the kitchen door. It was Leo dressed in his black cassock, towering over the tables of her little shop. He cut an impressive figure, reminiscent of Jeremy Irons in The Mission. She guessed Leo would not welcome the comparison.

And to be honest, Leo was much better looking than even young Jeremy Irons.

"Coffee's hot." She held an empty teacup out for him.

"I would've expected tea."

"I try not to get high on my own supply."

"I'll pretend I know what that means and happily accept your offer of coffee."

She poured the rest of the liquid out of the ibrik into the teacup, leaving the coffee grounds sludge behind. She poked her head around the door again. "Milk?"

"Please."

She carried her mug and Leo's teacup of coffee out to the table where he sat. He was so tall the tables looked like children's furniture.

"I thought you would call me back this morning."

"It's been a … it's been a difficult start to the day." She knew her face was probably still blotchy from crying. Her eyes still felt sticky and swollen.

"I can see that. Are you okay?"

She hated for anyone to see her like that. Jo gave him a lopsided smile. "I guess. As okay as I can be. It'll be nice to get to a place where I don't feel like I'm standing on the edge of an emotional precipice all the damn time." She had been trying to sort out and catalog her feelings lately, with no success. She seemed to have no problem spilling them all over him. "It would just be easier to feel nothing."

Leo set his cup down and looked at her. Her skin flushed under the intensity of his gaze. She reminded herself he had taken a vow of celibacy. But it wasn't just that. He looked through her. He looked at her like he could see the atoms swirling in her cells.

"I don't think that is something you would wish for if you had truly experienced emotional emptiness."

She leaned back in her chair. "Fair enough. I don't want to be empty, I'd just like to go back to where I was a week ago. I think I fully understand the concept of ignorance being bliss now."

"How you feel right now, wanting to not know? That's why I do what I do, and it will be what you do now too."

She cocked her head at him.

"We protect others from knowing about what is really out there."

"But people actively seek that. They ghost hunt. They track Bigfoot. They watch for UFOs. People seem to want to know exactly what's out there." She flapped her hand at the front door indicating everyone in the world beyond the two of them.

"They think they want to know. Those things are all just barely ripples on the surface of an unfathomable sea."

"UFOs?"

"I only deal in what's of this planet. That's enough."

She laughed. It was more than enough.

Leo continued. "Dabblers. They dismiss old gods even as they experience gooseflesh when they walk into a place of power. They dismiss the darker things as monsters under the bed or things that go bump in the night. Knowing would be too much for most people to bear."

"Werewolves, vampires, and whatever else there is — all that is really out there?"

"Yes, but not as they are imagined and romanticized by novels and movies. Old magics are not pleasing to modern eyes."

Jo let out a long slow breath. Her morning wasn't really improving. "Thank you for the lesson. I think. But that's not why you're here."

"Maybe partly. There is much you don't know, and that worries me. Vesna says you are headstrong."

Jo laughed again. "That was polite of her."

"She did not use 'headstrong.'"

"I bet. So why are you here?"

"The doll needs to be recovered and returned to the well."

"Have you been in the basement of the museum? The well is as dry as this shop. They excavated around it and the stones are stacked in a well-shaped column lit from within. There's no mortar, just gaps. There's no well there, really."

"It isn't quite that literal."

"Okay. So the first problem is where is the doll?"

"Good question. Does Maja have any news?"

"No. Not beyond the fact the dead of Ljubljana have no truck with any of the Roman sites since the well was excavated."

"That says we're on the right track."

"Yes, but not where it is or who stole it."

"You have a hunch though, I can tell." He leaned toward her and put his clasped hands on the table, his elbows just off the edge.

She could smell the church on him, incense and wood polish, like it was coming out of his pores. "Do you think being able to talk to dead people increases your sense of smell?"

"What does that have to do with anything?"

"You. You smell like incense and beeswax. It's almost overwhelming." And it inspired thoughts she should not have about a man of the cloth.

Leo leaned back and laughed his cello laugh.

Jo blushed and felt angry with herself because of it. "What's so funny?"

"I don't think it has anything to do with being able to talk to dead people. I think that's just you. Vesna said—"

"Vesna seems to have said a lot."

"She did, but you should know it was all in kindness. To her, you are family. Maybe more so now, and she's worried."

The angry knot in her stomach loosened slightly. "I just don't like the idea that I am such a topic of conversation. If you want to know about me, I'd rather you just ask me."

"Vesna felt the need to warn me you might be … a temptation."

"Did she?" The knot tightened right back up.

"And did you not just allude to such things?"

"Thinking of them and acting on them are very different. I do have some fucking self-control." She flopped back against her chair.

"As do I." He leaned back in his chair and folded his hands

together in his lap.

"So there." She looked up at him. "I do suspect someone. Tomaž. He and Helena were sleeping together. And he and Maja. Maybe he just became unhinged or needed to cover his tracks or something."

"Sex, power, money. We humans are fairly predictable."

"Is that always it though?"

"For people, pretty much. For gods and monsters? It's usually just power. Or vanity." He leaned back. "I'll send someone to his home and see if the doll is there. If it is, I have means to have it removed and returned."

"How will they know if it's there? I imagine he won't have it sitting out on the coffee table with the latest issue of Assholes Quarterly or whatever he reads. But I could go. They know me."

"No. You should stay far away from them, for your own good."

She bristled and thought about Ivanka, still curled up in her bed upstairs. With her son. She had every reason to go and get this sorted out as quickly as possible. "You can't go. Jesuits don't go door-knocking like Jehovah's Witnesses. Don't you think that would tip him off?"

"I'll send someone."

"Whatever. I've got stuff to do today anyway, including another funeral and picking my aunt up at the train station." She was up to her eyeballs in this. Why couldn't he trust her to do something as simple as doll reconnaissance?

"Do you still have the stone?"

She felt for it in her skirt pocket and produced it, holding it out to him on the flat of her palm. She wrapped her fingers around it and put it back. It had become her equivalent of a security blanket.

"Keep it with you. If something malevolent is hanging around it will alert you."

"How?"

"Depends on the thing." He looked at her for long moment. Enough to make her skin warm again.

"What?" What was the purpose of hiding things from her now?

"Please promise me you won't do anything foolish."

———

Jo finished the menu plan and taped the prep list to the front of the reach-in cooler. She dragged the market bag out of the office. A quick trip to her usual vendors in the Saturday market, then she could go boot Faron and Ivanka out of her flat so she could shower and dress appropriately. Gregor was going to drive the five of them to Žale. They'd be a little squished, but it wasn't far and no one really wanted to take the bus out there.

She walked down Breg and crossed the river at the Cobblers' bridge. She preferred walking through Staro Mesto on Saturdays. Prešeren Square was a crush of tourists and locals on foot and on bike, usually being serenaded by at least two street musicians not playing the same song, or even the same type of music. Pushing through all the buskers and selfie-stick wielders was not her idea of a good time. She was on a mission, in and out.

Her first stop was at Zsofia's stall. The tall Hungarian woman always gave Jo a good price on local fruit and a few things imported from Italy. October brought apples, old varieties she'd never encountered in the States. They were small and tart and good for cooking. It was time to make more apple butter and some chutney for cheese and chutney tea sandwiches. She bought a few kilos and covered the bottom of the roller bag with open cardboard baskets. The apples' sweet, earthy fragrance perfumed the bag and flooded her senses. She had a flash of lying under the apple trees at Dušan's family's farm. He had spun some folklore yarn about fucking in the orchard being good for the fertility of the trees, and she had wound up with rotten windfall in her hair. And Faron. She suspected the trees were doing just fine.

Zsofia took the folded euros from her and nodded thank you. Onward. One more stop, to Josip to put her meat order in for the week. He'd bring it early Monday. She had a standing order with Jakob, her milk guy, so she waved at him across the crowded cobbles. His untidy dreadlocks bobbed as he waved back.

She wove her way back through the shoppers and the many merchant stalls selling flowers and carved wooden trinkets. The crowd, the cobbles, the air itself buzzed with the Saturday-ness of its existence. Suddenly there was a minor chord running beneath the thrum that Jo hadn't heard before. The hair on the back of her neck stood up, and she felt a need to get inside as fast as she could. Her heart was racing and sweat prickled at her hairline. She'd never had a panic attack before, but if this wasn't a panic attack, something was coming for her and she needed to get away now.

She moved as fast as she could without actually running or knocking anyone flat in her haste. The market bag bounced on the cobbles, threatening to pour her apples out into the street. The safety of her building's courtyard had never seemed so far away from the market. When she finally got there, her hands shook so badly she couldn't get the key in the teahouse's lock. She stopped trying and rested her forehead against the cool wood of the door. She took a deep breath. And another. Her hands still shook.

A polite cough behind her startled her almost out of her clothes. It was the mystery man from the apartment upstairs.

"I did not mean to start you." His English was heavily accented. German maybe. He took the key ring from her hand and unlocked the door. He held it open with his arm while she maneuvered her market bag inside.

She was still shaking. Her shirt stuck to her back with sweat. Inside, away from the scents of the river and all those people, the sour smell of her own fear was overwhelming. She stammered a thank you and wiped her sweaty palm on her skirt before offering to shake her neighbor's hand.

"You looked to be in distress."

She nodded. Words were hard to form, but her breath was less ragged now.

"Sit. I will get a glass of water for you." Her rescuer disappeared into the kitchen of her shop and returned with a tall, skinny glass of water.

She reached for it with her trembling hand.

"Perhaps it is better if I set it on the table for you first." He put the glass in front of her and took the chair opposite.

"I hope it is not too forward of me to ask you what has frightened you so."

She shook her head no. She took a sip of water, then downed the glass. "I don't know. I was in the market and there was this sound."

He nodded and waited for her to continue.

She had no idea why she was talking to this man. She'd seen him maybe a dozen times in the ten years she'd lived in the building. He was always leaving, and he rarely acknowledged her with more than a polite nod. But once the words started, they just kept spilling out.

"It was like a dirge but played just at the edge of my range of hearing, and so fast. Like insect wingbeats or the pulse from a techno dance club from the street."

He nodded. "The dead. They know you are here now. They have been waiting."

Her breath stopped. "What?"

"Jolene Wiley, you are a Voice of the Dead, are you not?"

CHAPTER 21

"Who the fuck are you?" Jo rose and spoke in one fluid recoil.

The man looked at her without surprise, still seated. She tried to focus, but her mind was racing. Who or what had she let into her shop?

"I am friend," he said, "not foe." He continued to sit, hands clasped on her table in her shop, moving neither toward her or away.

She lowered her gaze. "Can you prove that?"

"I can explain it. Please sit."

"I think I'll stand, thank you."

"As you wish."

She nodded, watching him, not blinking. She slid her hand into her pocket for the well stone. It was cool, unaffected by this man's presence. She relaxed a little inwardly but kept her guard. Trust but verify.

"My associates and I have an interest in you and your ability."

"Your associates? What are you, a fan club?"

"No."

"Then who are you?"

"I am Gustaf Lichtenberg."

She sat down. "Is that supposed to mean something to me?"

"There is no reason for you to know it, though we have been neighbors these many years."

She was chastened. "You seemed to like keeping yourself to yourself."

"I do. As do you."

Fair enough.

"Much has happened in the last week, and I am certain these events have been difficult for you. It is not in my nature to interfere, but there is much at stake."

She sighed. She got the distinct impression that a task or two had just been added to her woo-woo to-do list. "What do you want or need of me?"

His laugh was dry and quiet. "My assigned task is only to observe, but in this case, I felt the need to intervene. At least to the extent that I am able."

"Observe?" She smirked. "What are you, my Watcher?"

"No. We are not the Council or the Talamasca. Though Mr. Whedon and Ms. Rice made us slightly uncomfortable with the uncanniness of their depictions."

Yet another layer. This gift of hers was like a goddamned onion.

Her neighbor continued. "There are always some who take

it upon themselves to police the police, so to speak. People like you, like the Kos family, and like your old friend; people who have access to a great deal of power. We want to be sure that your interest remains in helping humanity, not in enslaving or destroying it."

How should she respond to that?

"This is a great deal of information to assimilate. There is more, but it can wait. The task at hand is to recover the Roman doll. It must be reunited with the entity it was created to hold."

"Leo told me about the doll. He's—"

"He's very foolish. If for any reason you come across the doll, you must secure it immediately and bring it to me. Brother Kos has greatly underestimated the situation." There was irritation in his voice, but he was trying to mask it.

"If the situation is that bad, why involve the newbie? I mean, let's be honest, a week ago I didn't have a clue about any of this crap, and now I'm up to my eyeballs in it. I'm not sure I'm your girl, Gustaf." She leaned back in her chair. "Besides, Leo all but told me to stay home and knit."

"Your answer lies within your question. You are in it now. None of us can rest until this business is settled, but the greatest danger now is to you."

"And why is that?"

"Your gift is unique. You are a channel between this world and the next. If the entity wishes to fully return to this world, you will be the door."

She shifted uneasily in her chair. "And what happened in the market?"

"The dead are interested only in their own problems. This is no different. This entity is an anomaly, as unwelcome in the next world as it is in this. To prevent its breaking through, the crossing is closed, and the dead are forced to remain in the space between. What you heard was the unquiet dead making their displeasure known to the only person who can hear them."

She dropped her head to her chest. What the ever-loving fuck could she have done to deserve this?

"Ms. Wiley, are you unwell?" He reached out, but she looked back up and drew back before he could touch her.

"I would rather you didn't. I'm still not sure what or who you are."

He dropped his hand and nodded curtly. "Perhaps you should ask Brother Kos about me. I assure you he will confirm that my associates and I mean you no harm. Unless of course, you intend harm."

He said it with a tone of finality that made her shiver. So there was a sheriff in town. It just wasn't Leo. All of this new authority in her life was making her itch. She doubted that her "new friend" was missing her discomfort.

"I have been watching you and your family long enough to recognize that you are not one to, shall we say, conform? I can assure you, we have no desire to bend you to our will. That is not my purpose. But please understand: there is a line, and action is swift whenever it is crossed."

"And my not bringing this doll to you, that would be crossing the line?"

He shifted uncomfortably in his chair. "Not as such."

"Then what would be?"

"Using it for personal gain."

"I don't even want to be in the same room with Creepy Barbie."

"Good. Then you understand me." He stood to leave, turning back to her before reaching the door. "Ms. Wiley, I know you don't think much of this intrusion into your life." He knew about events that occurred beyond his presence, of that she was sure. "You are more important than perhaps you know. I sincerely hope you will undertake this endeavor with the caution it demands. I would hate for our acquaintance to be unnecessarily shortened by your demise."

Who talks like that? Wouldn't a simple "don't get your ass killed" do?

He turned to open the door.

"Wait. Who did you mean by 'my old friend'?" Was Gregor a werewolf or something? She was past the point of being surprised.

"You don't know?"

"Clearly, or I wouldn't have asked you." Maybe she and her neighbor could go back to nodding politely when this was over. Maybe she could have her werewolf friend ask him to move.

"I suggest you ask Mr. Zorko how old he will be on his next birthday." He closed the door softly as he left.

Infuriated by yet another person in her life who refused to simply answer a bloody question, she got up to lock the door behind him. She wished she could sit back down to take all this in and ponder what the fuck would happen next, but she had a market bag full of apples to put away and a funeral to attend.

———

Jo stood with Damijan, Vesna, and Frédéric in front of the white marble Napoleon monument in French Revolution Square. The gold face of a French liberator looked out over them as they waited. Every gust of wind sent a new parade of gold and orange leaves swirling through the roundabout in front of them. The buzzing that had driven her from the market earlier still hung in the air, less menacing now she knew what it was. Her dress and hair blew around her in the stiff breeze. Vesna handed her a hair tie without saying a word. Jo took it from her and tamed her mane into an unruly bun at the nape of her neck.

Gregor's car pulled into the parking spot closest to the silent group. He got out and opened the back door, ducked out of view into the back seat and reappeared with a wreath of burnt orange and burgundy flowers. The trunk popped open with a flick against the fob in his hand. While he was moving the wreath, Jo and the others played a short round of "no, you, please" over the front seat. Vesna settled it, opening the front passenger door and practically pushing Damijan inside.

"You've got the longest legs. Hush." She closed the door before he could protest.

Vesna gracefully shimmied into the center of the rear seat. Jo climbed in beside her, and everyone else wedged in. Luckily it was only about ten minutes to Žale. The group of friends rode in silence. Jo looked out the window watching the familiar landmarks of Ljubljana moving past the car window like a succession of tableaux as she tried to take stock of all the pieces she had gathered, hoping to put them together and see how they fit. Maybe she would make one of those mystery walls with photos and strings when she got back. The problem was, the string connected to her was still dangling. What did Gustaf mean when he said she was a door?

Damijan interrupted the quiet inside the car. "Why are Maja's ashes being interred at Žale? I thought you said her parents were from Maribor or something?" He looked back at Jo.

"They live there now, but Maja's mother's family is from Ljubljana, and they have a plot here."

Damijan nodded, and they each went back to looking out a window.

She dreaded being in Žale. She had seen the sprawling cemetery complex with its grand entrance gate and chapels as Ljubljana's City of the Dead. She braced herself. There was sure to be an unholy racket of clamoring voices wanting to get a word with her.

Gregor pulled into a parking spot and put on the hand brake. They sat for a second before opening doors and unfolding themselves from the car. Gregor popped the trunk again to retrieve the wreath, and they walked, still quiet, to the entrance of the cemetery complex.

A glass-fronted message board near the old church had a list of the day's interments and locations. Gregor glanced at it and led the way through the grand monumental gate. The white marble glowed warmly in the early afternoon light. Jo wondered if Plečnik, the architect, had been going for the look of bleached bone.

Walking under the gate, she was braced for an onslaught that didn't come. They walked on. Maja's family plot was in an older part of the cemetery. As they joined the gathering mourners, Jo was startled by the utter silence. Were there no dead in the very place built for them? Was this all for the living? Maybe all the ritual and monuments and flowers and lanterns at the neatly tended graves were no more than a way for the living to give some import and meaning to the deaths of those they loved. The idea struck her as touching and strangely funny at the same time. She felt a case of church giggles coming on, and she looked down at the path in front of her.

The opening bars of "Time Bomb" played in her mind. Maja must be there, but she couldn't see her. A whisper in her ear confirmed it.

"Wow, boss lady, this is the first place I've seen in Ljubljana with no dead people except me."

Jo smiled to herself and resumed her count of the blades of grass at the edge of the pavement. When she got control of her emotions she looked up again and observed the two distinct groups of mourners. One group, obviously Maja's friends, sported hair in various shades usually seen in the plumage of tropical birds, and more tattoos and piercings than a convention of bikers. The other group, obviously family, was a mix: older women wearing lace-up shoes, younger women in Italian fashions, and men of all ages in suits that either itched uncomfortably or served as extensions of their own constructed personalities. Jo's group was kind of in the middle, neither family nor peers.

Maja's parents approached Jo, and her father extended his hand. "You are Ms. Wiley?" His English was rusty.

"*Dober dan, Gospod Demšar, Gospa Demšar. Pokličite mi 'Jo,' prosim.*" He visibly relaxed.

She had met Mrs. Demšar just once, when she'd come to the shop to discuss a gathering for Maja. She wasn't much older than Jo, but she was drawn and gray with grief.

"Thank you for coming." Mrs. Demšar looked into all of their faces in turn.

Gregor nodded, as did the others. Nobody was happy to be there, but they would do what should be done.

Maja hadn't been religious, as far as Jo knew, and there was no reason to think her parents were, either, so it was not surprising that there was no priest or minister to oversee the interment. Mrs. Demšar's brother, another Leo, spoke a few words about Maja's life and how we all return to the earth. Her mother dropped a handful of dirt onto the small wooden box nestled into the ground holding the ashes of her daughter's body, and she broke down. Mr. Demšar pulled her close to him as she shook with strangled sobs.

The air behind Jo was cold and dense. Maja was still there but didn't say a word.

As quickly as they had gathered there, it was done. Gregor laid his wreath near the open earth, and one of Maja's friends set down a solar-powered lamp covered in the signatures of her friends in silver magic marker. The mourners made their way to the entrance and dispersed, walking to their cars or toward the bus stop.

Maja's father stopped Jo. "Should we come early tomorrow to help?"

She shook her head. "We have everything in hand. Please don't worry about any of that." He turned to rejoin his wife, and she stopped him. "Mr. Demšar. I am so very sorry for your loss. Maja is … Maja was a good person. Far too young for us to be here today for this."

He nodded at her and walked away.

There were so many things she wanted to tell him: that Maja was okay, that she was there, that she had seen her parents' pain. That there is something beyond this life.

But she'd tried that with Matjaž, and she had a pretty good idea how it would be received here. A week ago she would have received it the same way. There wasn't much comfort in her new knowledge if she couldn't use it to actually comfort anyone else. There seemed to be precious little comfort about anything.

The friends rode back to French Revolution Square in a different kind of silence.

———

Frédéric made a pot of Irish breakfast tea and heated up the milk in the ibrik Jo had used that morning for coffee. Jo scanned the prep list for tomorrow's event while donning her apron, crossing the ties behind her back and wrapping them around to tie in a lopsided bow under her breasts. She pulled the baskets of apples out of the reach-in and lined them up on the counter. She would tackle the chutney while Frédéric baked a few Pullman loaves for the tea sandwiches. Once the chutney was going she'd make some brownies and shortbread for sweet.

Maja's mother had asked them to make Maja's favorite, potica, a walnut-filled, bready cake. The centerpiece of the Slovenian kitchen, potica had been commemorated on stamps, but it wasn't one of Jo's specialties and there wasn't enough room in their tiny kitchen to roll out the whisper-thin, table-sized dough. Vesna's mother had offered to make potica and bring it that afternoon.

Mrs. Kos was a formidable presence. She was in her late sixties, but she showed no sign of it. She looked fifty, tops, and could run circles around people a quarter of her age. She had an acid tongue that could cut to the quick if you met her disapproval. But her people were her people, and the category included those her children cared for. Maja was hers because she'd been Vesna's friend. Jo could imagine Mrs. Kos in her kitchen surrounded by a faint cloud of flour as she bent over her cloth-covered dining table, scowling an errant tear in the paper-thin dough back together and making sure that Maja's mother's wish would be fulfilled.

Jo's reverie was broken by a knock: Mrs. Kos herself was at the shop door. Out of habit, Jo patted her apron and walked to the front to let her in. Mrs. Kos was carrying the biggest potica Jo had ever seen. They could have fed half of Ljubljana with it.

It was nestled on a huge wooden serving platter and covered with tea towels. Jo took the platter from Mrs. Kos and set it on the nearest table to the door. Mrs. Kos hugged her and air-kissed both sides of her face, then stepped back and looked at Jo with narrowed eyes.

"You are different. It suits you." Mrs. Kos laid her hand on the side of Jo's face. It was an unexpectedly tender gesture.

Jo didn't want to ask what she saw that was different. Who knew what Mrs. Kos's take was on the family business? Instead, she asked her if she'd like a cup of tea.

"Of course. Is Frédéric here?"

"He's in the kitchen making bread for tomorrow."

Mrs. Kos brushed by her and strode to the kitchen. Frédéric received the same warm hug and air-kisses, plus an added tsking for not coming to see her more often. Jo figured that meant Mrs. Kos saw just about enough of her. Fred poured tea for all of them, and they sat down together long enough to finish their cups.

"Jo, would you like me to come early tomorrow to cut the potica?" Mrs. Kos set her cup gently back on its mismatched saucer.

"I think we can handle it. Vesna and Damijan will both be here. Tina is coming to help with dishes, even though she really didn't know Maja."

"Who is this Tina person?"

"New dishwasher." Frédéric swirled the last of his tea in his cup waiting for the inevitable reply.

"Another new one? What happened to Aljo?"

"He lasted almost a month." Jo smiled into her teacup. Longtime staffers joked that being dishwasher at Renegade Tea was akin to being the Defense Against the Dark Arts professor at Hogwarts. They'd gotten used to a parade of dishwashers young, old, and in-between, each taking a stab at keeping the wares clean. Mrs. Kos seemed to regard this cycle as a shortcoming, but Jo did not misplace the dishwashers or run them off intentionally. She and Fred had a running bet on the longevity of their pearl divers, and she was in the lead for the year. She'd bet short on Tina; she was a slip of a thing and apparently hated punk music. Fred went long, hedging on the common knowledge that it's always the quiet ones.

Mrs. Kos tsked them both again. "You two. It's bad for business to have such turnover."

Jo let it lie.

They finished their tea, and Mrs. Kos left with more air kisses and noises about letting them get back to their work. Jo loved her like a bonus mom, but like a mom, Mrs. Kos could push exactly the right button when she wanted to.

Fred's timer for the bread buzzed.

———

The night was clear, and over the city a low moon hung in a blue velvet sky nearly devoid of stars. Jo, smelling of vinegar and cinnamon from the chutney, stood outside the train station waiting for the GoOpti shuttle to deliver her aunt. When all this was over, if there was an over, she wanted to go out to Gregor's house in the country and lay in the backyard to watch for meteors. For years, she and Gregor had done that, sober or not — mostly sober in recent years.

They tried to solve the political problems of the world and answer the great cosmic questions as they lay out in the field behind his house on an old quilt or in sleeping bags, as the temperature allowed. She craved the perspective of floating on the sphere of the earth, staring out into the endlessness of space. Gregor said it made him appreciate gravity. She wanted to break loose of it and disappear into that milky river of stars, away from everything that had happened. Even her imagination provided no escape now. She could see the six crimson tethers that bound her to the earth, no matter how high she floated against the tension. Faron. Gregor. Vesna. Jackie. Rok. And? She wanted to pull that imaginary thread into her hand to see if there was a name on it. Instead, she stood at the station, staring into the bus lot, watching a yellow sign for pomarančni sok and "to-go coffee" flicker across the street.

The shuttle pulled up and disgorged a mix of tourists and returning locals. She could sort them as easily as if they'd been wearing badges. No Jackie. A man with two purple suitcases smiled at her. Definitely tourist. Slovenians rarely smiled at strangers in that face-cracking way that went all the way up to the eyes.

She pulled her phone out of her pocket and tapped the email icon. There were two messages. Spam and a message from Jackie. There were storms off the coast, and her flight out of Dulles had been canceled. She hoped to be there the next day, but it didn't look good.

Well, shit. She really should check her email more often.

CHAPTER 22

Leo sat in the chair next to his bed trying to read. His eyes moved across the words on the page, but his mind didn't follow. His thoughts were not in a place he was comfortable with. He should have stayed in Ljubljana, but he wanted to put some distance between himself and Jo. His niece had offered him her couch, but he'd felt the need to hide from her as well. Vesna could see his struggle in the colors that swam around him. She would know he was losing.

In his youth, before he had met Berta, Leo had planned to join the church. It was what his father had wanted. A son late in life, his father said, could serve as tribute for the God who protected the family in its work with demons and witches and the undefeated pagan gods. Leo believed that too. He'd seen the damage and the carnage. He hadn't yet realized how much of it was unnecessary.

Then there was Berta. Interest in the history of witch trials in rural Slovenia brought them both to the same book in the National and University Library. Berta was studying the persecution of women as witches. Leo had been tracing his family's legacy and growing increasingly disgusted by what he found in the records. A woman who was a better midwife or whose cows produced richer butter than her neighbors' was tortured, sometimes for days, and then burned. His ancestors had been responsible for fanning the flames of moral panics, hence for the deaths of hundreds of people, including children.

He turned away from his family and his faith. He turned instead to Berta. Marveling at her powers of reason, he embraced and adopted her scientific explanations for the seemingly supernatural. He knew there was more beyond the things her research had uncovered, but he wanted to believe that he could forget those things. He wanted to believe in the possibility he could have a life with her, a life that didn't involve the stench of demon or the fear of what he couldn't see in the darkness.

He'd returned to his family only to bury his father. He had stood at the graveside and with every shovel of dirt that rang against the coffin, he imagined his past being covered over. He'd held Berta's hand and walked away through the gates of the Ribnica cemetery and into his future.

He looked out of the window of his cell. The most decadent feature of his quarters at the monastery, it had been the picture window of a sitting room before the building was divided into sleeping rooms and flats. He watched the sun set beyond the mountains. The valley faded quickly from gloaming to darkness. Luka was coming up the path to the main house, his hands full.

There were two sharp raps against the door.

He crossed the room to answer. Luka stood on the threshold with a bottle of slivovec and a basket.

"Teja is worried about you and said I should bring you dinner and some company." Luka laughed. "I think she just wants to be alone this night to talk about me on the phone to her sister."

"There isn't anywhere to eat in here. Let's sit in the garden." Leo took his phone off the small table and slipped it into his front pocket. "It's nice that's it so warm."

He and Luka settled in at the wooden table and chairs tucked in a small walled garden he shared with a ragtag group of mystics, ascetics, and eccentrics. True monastery life had not been for him. Too much of his work had to be kept hidden. This loose commune of outsiders made a family of sorts that was more suited to both his personality and his unconventional life.

Luka poured slivovec into two heavy tumblers he produced from the basket. They toasted each other and downed the first glass. Leo poured the second round while Luka laid out a board of pršut, homemade butter, and Teja's hearty bread, still slightly warm from the oven.

"You seem far away, friend. More so than usual." Luka tapped his tumbler against Gregor's. "A burden shared is a burden halved."

Leo turned the small glass in his hand and watched the little lights strung along the fence reflect in the slivovec. "It isn't a burden you'd want."

"Perhaps not, but who chooses a burden?"

Leo took a deep breath. Luka could not offer absolution, but he wasn't a man to judge. "I've had cause lately to doubt the choices I've made."

"That is not such a strange burden. That is the stuff of life." Luka tore off a piece of bread and slicked it with the soft butter.

Leo chuckled.

"Has an event or a person brought on this doubt?" Luka handed him the buttered bread.

"I wonder sometimes if you can read minds."

"Only faces. You have the look of a man in love. Given your choices, as you say..." His voice trailed off as he finished his second shot of slivovec.

Leo nursed his shot. His gut told him he needed to stay alert. "It isn't an easy thing to hold."

"You still have choices."

CHAPTER 23

Jo had walked out as far as the train station. Might as well keep walking, she decided. She was heading in the direction of Tomaž and Katarina's house in Zelena Jama. Leo would be angry, but how could he expect her to sit on her hands? She didn't need Leo to be her babysitter, and she certainly didn't need Neighbor Gustaf taking on that role. She continued her walk, considering the possibilities she might face. If Tomaž and Katarina were out, she just could peek in the windows. If Tomaž was home, it was unlikely he'd be alone. The four people who lived with him would provide a buffer.

She would have to come up with a reason for being there, though. Something to say to Tomaž or whoever answered the door.

The front gate was unlocked, and she picked her way through the dark yard to the front door. It really didn't look like anyone was home, but she knocked anyway. She heard a thud from inside and tried to see through the rectangle of glass in the door. Tomaž's face appeared briefly in the window before he opened the door.

"Jo. What a surprise to see you." He stood there in his

stocking feet and shifted his eyes from her face to her feet to the doorjamb.

"Yes. Sorry, I should've phoned first, but I was in the neighborhood and thought I'd stop by to see if … if you wanted to do anything for the wake for Maja tomorrow. You know, since she worked for you too."

"Oh, that. Um, I hadn't thought of that, but you're right."

"May I come in?" Maybe she was wrong about him. Tonight he looked weak and run down. Sunken cheeks joined with the dark circles around his eyes to give him an almost skeletal appearance.

"Of course. Where are my manners? Please come in." He flipped on a light in the hall and directed Jo straight to the small, trendily appointed kitchen. It was clear that no one ever really cooked in it. It looked like something out of an IKEA catalog, but without the warmth. The well stone in her pocket began to vibrate. It felt like a hummingbird's heart against her leg.

Tomaž gestured toward a clear Lucite chair, and she sat down. "Would you like a cup of coffee? No, you're a tea drinker, aren't you?" He rummaged in the cabinet nearest the stove.

"Just a glass of water, thank you."

He set a glass of tap water on the table in front of her and took the chair opposite. He had the look of someone who really wanted to flee.

He worried the end of his right thumb with the index finger and thumb of his left hand and talked, more to the place mat in front of her than to her. "Did you have something in mind? For tomorrow I mean?"

"No. Not really. We'll handle the food, and we'll serve tea of course. Maybe you could bring wine and maybe send someone from the blue bar to serve it?"

"The blue bar?" He looked up at her now.

"The place on the river? With the lights?"

"Oh. Spotlight." He picked at his thumb again like he was trying to remove something. "Yes. I can have someone come over. I'll call tonight."

"Thank you." She moved her chair slightly and made as if she were about to leave. Relief washed across his haggard face, quickly followed by disappointment, or maybe fear, when she settled back down.

"Oh, did you hear about the theft at the museum the night Helena was murdered?" Her emphasis on "murdered" was not intentional.

"No. Was it in the papers?"

She was surprised he was such a bad liar. "I don't know. I heard about it from a friend. A Roman toy went missing, a doll or something that the museum excavated from the well in the basement. Such a weird thing to steal, don't you think?"

"Yes. That is strange." He sounded like he was reading from a poorly written script, and he kept stealing glances into the darkened living room opposite the kitchen.

She got up to leave for real and stretched out her hand. Tomaž clasped it weakly with both his clammy hands, then he practically frog-marched her to the door.

He was attempting to close it when she turned. "Aren't Katarina and the girls home?"

"No. They are all out at a school thing for Ana." He looked back into the dark interior.

"Tell Katarina I said hello, and I'll see you all tomorrow."

———

Okay, that was weird.

Jo walked along Kavčičeva back toward downtown.

Two things were clear. The doll was there, and Tomaž couldn't lie his way out of a wet paper bag. He was also deeply afraid of something in the house. Someone? Was it the doll? Did it have its own powers over him or something? Maybe it was ordering him to kill people.

The streetlights dimmed and flickered, then went black. The air stilled around her, and the scent of rotten cabbage wafted over her. Light still poured from the windows of shops and flats.

Not a power outage.

A Rancid lyric throbbed in her head. "Black coat, white shoes..." The stone hummed in her pocket, and Maja was with her.

"Boss lady, I really don't want to freak you out, but you need to get off the street, like now." Maja all but pushed her toward the nearest mini-market, flickering in and out of perception as they neared the door and the people inside. "Go!"

Jo opened the door. She couldn't see Maja, but she knew she was there. The stone quieted as soon as the door closed behind them. Jo rummaged in her sweater pocket for her phone and found Leo's name in her recent call list. She was about to hang up after the fourth ring when his voice greeted her as politely as could be expected from someone dragged from sleep.

"Jo?"

"Yes. Were you asleep?"

"Hm."

"Can you come get me? Shit just got weird. I'm in the mini-market on Kavčičeva. The one closest to the train station."

"It'll take me a bit. I'm not in Ljubljana."

"Where are you?"

"Škofja Loka, but I'll be there as soon as possible. What happened? Why are you out by yourself?"

The mini-market customers were staring at her. She had been speaking loudly in English. She lowered her voice and switched back to Slovenian. "I was at the train station so I went by Tomaž's. All the lights on the street went out, and Maja shoved me in the nearest open door."

She heard a hard-whispered "*prekleto!*" then, "Did she say what happened?"

"No, and now there are too many people around to talk to her."

"Okay. Don't leave the market. I'm on my way."

She clicked the phone to sleep and kept staring at the blank screen. A tiny, ancient woman with her hair wrapped in a gaudy floral scarf touched her arm.

"Are you all right, Miška?"

Jo stared at her. Dušan was the only person who'd ever called her that pet name. She'd hated it: "mouse-lette" suggested she was easy prey. "I'm sorry. What did you say?"

"Are you okay?"

"No. After that. You called me Miška."

"I don't think so. You're very upset. Is there anything I can do?"

"No. A friend is coming to get me."

"You should wait for him inside." She squeezed Jo's arm with ice cold fingers and moved past her down the aisle before Jo could ask her what she knew. She ran after her and looked around, but the woman was gone. She hadn't moved fast enough for Jo to lose her in a fucking minimart.

Jo really needed to talk to Maja.

The market didn't have a public bathroom, but there had to be one for the employees somewhere. She walked to the checkout and tried to look pained. It wasn't too difficult. "I'm so sorry to ask, but do you have a bathroom, I'm really nauseated and I don't want to throw up in your store." She faked a little heave.

"Yes. Yes. Please don't be sick here." The cashier dragged her to the back of the store and pushed her through a door to a broom closet-slash-toilet that looked like it was bombed during the war.

Jo nodded a thank you. She wedged the poorly hung door closed and ran water into the cracked and caked basin. She flushed the toilet for good measure. "Maja, what the fuck is going on?"

Maja appeared in front of her, solid and almost nose to nose in the cramped closet. The air chilled around her. "No idea. The dead people in the street went running when the lights went out, and that woman you were talking to? Dead as me."

"I figured that out, but I don't even know her." Jo slumped against the wall, or at least as much as she could, given the parameters.

"Me neither. Maybe you're past that point where it's only people you know?"

Jo wanted to slump right to the filthy floor. "I'm so not fucking ready for that." That woman had to be dead for a long time if she could appear plain as day in a shop full of people. Not a comforting thought.

———

The scent of rotting cabbage and lilacs hung heavy in the air. Gustaf picked up his pace. The demon had to be nearby, and it had to be wreaking havoc. Demonic beings held the belief that the odor of antique flowers could hide their evil, a thought that never ceased to amuse him.

He turned the corner into the empty plaza. The only light was from a burek stand that was open late for drunks wandering home. The vendor was turned away from him. She wore huge over-the-ear headphones and she danced about the small space as she cleaned. The lights on the street beyond had gone out, throwing the plaza into darkness except for the slice of light from the stand.

Gustaf picked his way around the edge of the square. He

reached the concrete staircase that led up to the second floor of shops and travel agencies. He pulled his hand back quickly.

The demon had been there. The traces of anger and vengeance it left in its wake confirmed his fear: they were dealing with a revenge demon. Revenge demons had singular motives, motives that often caused them to lash out in unpredictable ways. And anyone standing between a revenge demon and its goal was fair game.

Who was it seeking vengeance for? That would lead them to it, perhaps, but he already knew its end goal. If it got to Jolene Wiley, it would cross into this world permanently and unleash its punishment unbridled. He shuddered. Of all the things he dealt with, demons were perhaps the only thing he truly feared. Gods were malleable in their way. There was an ego to flatter, and though they had the upper hand in most ways, they were only as strong as the belief in them.

Demons fed on the endless supply of human suffering and cruelty, and that made them impossible to destroy. The best scenario was to capture or recapture them and secure the Vessel. His personal goal was to salt the earth with the interred containers of every demon that lingered in this world.

He worked his way around the edge of the square. Ms. Wiley was supposed to meet her aunt at the train station. He didn't like the idea of her roaming about the city on her own but understood she was not going to stay home and knit, as she'd put it.

The lights came on with a blinding suddenness.

There was a body on the concrete near where he'd been standing. He went to the figure and crouched down to check for a pulse.

Nothing.

Dark bruises had already blossomed on the skin of the man's throat, and he stank of cabbage and the damned cloying flowers.

Gustaf stood and pulled his phone out to call Marta. The woman in the burek stand started screaming and calling him a murderer. Her cries were enough to draw a crowd. He wasn't going anywhere anytime soon.

———

Leo made a grand entrance when he finally got there. Not only was he wearing his cassock, but he had the biggest fuck-off wooden rosary at his waist. He also had a look on his face that would have read as murderous if it hadn't been for the whole cassock thing. A woman buying tampons and condoms crossed herself after he walked by and put the condoms back.

"Are you okay?" His expression softened when she looked up at him.

"Shaken. No. Scratch that. I am fully freaked the fuck out."

"The lights are back on outside, but there is the distinct smell of rotting cabbage and lilacs."

"I noticed the cabbage earlier, but it's not like that is particularly unusual in these parts."

"No, but with the lilac, it's a demon trying to cover the smell of its workings."

"You mean magic? Like lilac is demon air freshener for turning people into toads?"

"What demons do isn't exactly magic. It's … it's too complicated to explain right now. But yes, they do try to cover the scent of it, especially when they are being sneaky."

"I am never going to think of lilacs the same way. I think I preferred associating them with powdered grandma boobs."

Leo laughed, and a different woman dropped the box of condoms she was holding. He was going to get everyone in Zelena Jama inadvertently knocked up in one night.

"Let's get you home. It's the safest place for you to be. You said you put wards on your flat?"

She nodded and followed him out onto the street, where his beater was parked illegally. It didn't look big enough for him to actually get into it.

"I didn't know you had a car."

"I don't. I borrowed it."

He could have driven the car with his knees on either side of the wheel and probably would have been more comfortable if he'd ripped out the front seat and just sat in the back. She felt a little sheepish for both dragging him out of bed and making him drive a clown car to rescue her. Fuck. She also didn't like being a person that needed to be rescued. That chafed more than the guilt.

"Was the doll there?"

"I didn't see it, but the stone you gave me went apeshit in my pocket. So I'm going to guess yes. Are you going to go get it?"

"I will arrange for it to be returned to its proper resting place."

Jo looked out the window. That thing didn't need to rest anywhere, if whatever it held was responsible for both Helena and Maja being "not alive," as Helena had put it. Leo seemed to think it was a demon. If someone had asked her even a few weeks ago if demons existed, she would have asked where they were getting their supply.

There was a commotion at one of the business plazas as they passed. She watched the blue lights of a police car bounce off the concrete and glass, thinking about Helena and how all this had started.

"Probably a drunk sleeping it off in the open or something." Leo pulled into the roundabout by French Revolution Square. He parked the car and looked at her. "Why did you go there, to Tomaž's? I thought I was clear this morning about you not being anywhere near him."

"I thought you were being overprotective. I just want this to be done."

"I'm trying to make sure you don't get killed, Jo. Did Lichtenberg talk to you?"

She couldn't tell if his anger was directed at her or at Gustaf. "He did. He warned me that I should only use my powers for good and…"

"He didn't tell you about being a Portal?"

"A what?" There had been something about a door.

"Jo, you aren't just a Voice of the Dead, you're a Portal. Supernatural things can use you to get into the world."

"Isn't the demon or whatever it is already in the world?"

"Yes, but it can't possess someone for very long. It needs

someone like you if it wants to stay."

"And what happens to me if it finds me?"

"You…" He looked at her, pained by whatever it was he had to say. "Nothing good, Jo. Nothing good happens to you if it finds you."

Jo bent at the waist and rested her forehead on the dashboard. Leo put his hand in the small of her back. "Are you okay?"

She sat up, and he pulled his hand away. "I'm not sure I know how to answer that question anymore. Define okay."

"I'll walk you home. I know it isn't far, but…"

She wanted to argue but didn't have the energy to lose. They walked in silence through the throngs of people out for a Saturday night in the old town. It was a stark contrast to the dark empty streets beyond the city's center. The stares were numerous. She had long gotten used to the Slovenian tendency to look longer than was usually considered polite in the States, but it was beyond that. She and her cassocked friend made a strange pair.

He walked her through the quiet courtyard and started to follow her up the stairs.

She stopped. "I've got this from here. Thank you."

"I really should walk you up."

"I'll be fine." And she didn't need to be alone with him in her apartment. Ever.

He nodded but kept looking at her. "You should put wards on the shop too. And probably the entrance to the courtyard."

"Will that drive away customers?"

"Do you want those kinds of customers?"

"I don't know. Maybe I've had an entirely vampire clientele until now and we'd go out of business."

He snorted. "Vampires don't drink tea."

"Good to note. Thank you, again, for coming to get me, and I'm sorry I woke you up." He stood on the cobbles of the courtyard. She was two steps up, evening out their height, maybe a bit in her favor. If he were any other man she'd ever been attracted to she would have touched his face. "And I'm sorry I didn't take your warning more seriously."

He looked down at his feet, then back at her. Jo couldn't parse his expression. "I should go. Call me in the morning before you leave the apartment."

She nodded. "I'll be in the shop all day."

"Still, call. There aren't any wards on the shop."

She nodded again and turned up the stairs. She heard him pause, then turn on the cobbles to walk away.

"Leo?" She turned back on the stairs. He stopped.

"Why did the dead run from whatever happened on the street? Why would they be afraid? I mean, they're already dead, right?"

"I keep forgetting how much you don't know. Vesna was right about you acting like you've got everything under control."

"Despite my earlier statement about you and Vesna having a Jo-themed gabfest at my expense, I'll take that as a compliment. But I will admit I have no idea what dead people would be afraid of." She stepped back down onto the cobbles.

"They don't have much to fear except their own troubled thoughts, and that's enough to make many of them who won't or can't cross mad."

"But that's not why Maja saw them all run for the hills when the street lights went out."

"It isn't. Usually, the dead want only to make right what they couldn't in life and to cross into what the next world is."

"Heaven?" She looked up into his face.

"That's what I believe, but there are still mysteries."

"My father said the same thing."

Leo nodded. "Some of the dead never cross. They linger here too long, and eventually whatever the energy of our souls is fades away to nothing."

"Jesus. How long does that take?"

"Depends on the soul. But there is a more sinister reason the dead don't cross. And a reason they would flee from a presence."

"I was really hoping fading into nothingness was as bad as it got."

"I wish it were too. But demons and some other supernatural beings have the power to murder the dead."

Her mouth fell open.

Leo continued. "They absorb soul energy, or they sever the connection the dead have to this plane. I'll be honest, I'm not really sure how it works, but it isn't good. The dead have no desire to be anywhere near a demon or anyone else who's more than human."

"Except me."

"Except you."

———

Jo knocked on Vesna's door to ask how her date with Igor went but she wasn't home. Maybe breakfast had turned into an all day affair. She went back down to get the mail and walked back up to her flat.

She opened the door to her apartment and her phone rang.

The stone in her pocket felt like a burning coal against her hip.

———

A photographer circled the body behind them. The flashes punctuated Marta's sentences.

"He's connected to Wiley." Marta motioned at the corpse with a jerk of her head.

Gustaf had thought he looked familiar but didn't want to move the body before the police arrived to get a better look. "How did you know that?"

"I interviewed him about the first murder."

"You didn't think he was involved?"

"No, but I thought he might give me a clearer picture of her. There's something about that woman I don't trust. She's a terrible liar, for starters."

He nodded. "She probably thinks you'll lock her away if she spoke the truth."

"The thought had occurred to me." Marta watched the crime scene team work. They hadn't laid down a single evidence marker. "So what happened here?"

"I suspect the same thing that happened to Ms. Belak."

"But why him?" She said it like she didn't really expect an answer.

"My best theory is the demon was out looking for Ms. Wiley and came across someone connected to her."

"How would a demon know they were connected?" Marta looked incredulous.

"We leave traces on the people we care about." He turned to go.

Marta caught his arm. "I can't just let you walk away. You're my only witness and you were seen with the body. You'll have to go to the station."

"I don't have time for that." He resisted the urge to pry her fingers off his arm. He needed to find Jolene Wiley before the demon did.

"I really don't care. You may deal with all this paranormal nonsense, but I have to deal in the real world with real paperwork and real superiors who expect me to do my job."

"I understand that, but I must find Ms. Wiley. This proves she is in danger." He looked at the man's body. He lay on his side, as if he had fallen asleep on the concrete.

"Where do you think she would go?" Marta's phone buzzed in her pocket. She answered and watched Gustaf as a man's voice strung together times and addresses in her ear. The line of her mouth tightened with each sentence. "I think I know where she's been."

"This will be a long night." He looked up at the moon coming out from a passing cloud. He'd stopped praying a long time ago, but just now he wished he believed there was someone, or something, out there who would intervene on Jolene Wiley's behalf.

CHAPTER 24

Jo slid her finger across the screen to answer the call. A woman wailed into the other end of the connection.

"Who is this?" The stone in her pocket started to vibrate as well as burn.

"Faron. She … she … she took Faron."

Jo froze in the doorway. "Who is this? Who took Faron?"

"Ivanka. My mother. She took him. She took him away."

Jo's heart sank into her stomach. She turned and ran down the stairs back out into the cobbled street, her phone pressed hard against her ear. "Ivanka, take a breath. Tell me where you are."

"At … at … at Faron's, at his flat."

"Don't move." She pushed her phone into the pocket of her jacket and took off at a run toward Trnovo.

The night closed in around her, and there was only a tunnel of street lamps and lit faces staring. She pushed around pedestrians and in front of cars at the few intersections between her place and his. Her heart tried to beat its way out of her chest, ten thumps to every footfall of her boots on the pavement and cobbles. Her lungs were burning, but she didn't stop until she was standing at Faron's door.

Ivanka stood, shaking, still holding her phone in her hand, in a trashed room that smelled of rotted cabbage and old lady flowers. If Faron was dead, she was going to figure out how to dismember a demon.

"What the fuck happened?"

Ivanka jumped at Jo's voice. "It was Mom, but she's not right. She was at the door and I opened it and she threw me against the wall. She grabbed Faron and left." Ivanka rubbed the back of her head as she spoke. There was blood on her hand when she dropped it. "He fought her, but she was so strong."

Katarina? Jo could kick herself for being so stupid. The stone had warned her at the funeral, but she'd still thought it was Tomaž because she disliked him so much and felt so sorry for his wife. And now she had Faron.

"Let me look at your head." She had to get Ivanka help and go.

There was a knot, which was good. Better out than in, but the skin was split and bleeding profusely.

Jo sat the dazed girl on the couch and went in search of a towel.

She crouched in front of Ivanka. It was pretty clear the girl was in shock. Jo took Ivanka's hand and pressed it to the back of her head with the towel.

"Look. I think I know where they may have gone, but I won't be able to get there as fast if I take you with me."

Ivanka nodded. She was crying now, but not sobs.

"I'm going to call the police to come to you. Tell them someone broke in and attacked you."

Ivanka nodded again.

Jo pulled her phone out and tried to wake it up to make the call. It made its low battery sound and she watched the screen go black. "Fuck."

She pried Ivanka's sparkly red phone out of her hand and dialed the emergency number. She handed the phone back to Ivanka and nodded. "Tell them."

Back on the street, she stopped. She needed to get back to Tomaž and Katarina's. Adrenaline would not be enough to get her there fast enough on foot. She said a silent prayer to whatever gods might be listening and ran back to the street in hopes that a taxi would appear.

The whatever gods were on a coffee break until she got to Slovenska, where she hailed the first cab she saw.

———

The driver left as soon as she tossed him a handful of wadded up bills from her pocket. She could only imagine what he thought of the frenetic woman who'd been in his back seat.

The street lights were out, and all the houses were dark. She made her way through the gate and to the door.

It was open. The house reeked of demon magic, or whatever it was, and something else. The air tasted like copper pennies.

The moonlight illuminated the IKEA kitchen enough to see that someone was splattered all over the cabinets and dripping from the counters and ceiling.

Jo made her way to the table, trying not to step in anything on the floor. Please don't let it be Faron.

A tattered bit of shirt collar was stuck to the table. It was pale gray, maybe white, similar to the wrinkled shirt Tomaž had been wearing. She stepped back out into the entryway, staring at one of the Lucite chairs that was designed to disappear into the decor. It was now completely visible.

Someone else was in the house.

There was a cough, then a stifled cry. She turned toward it and moved along the edge of the wall into the living room. The doll was on the floor near the couch. She crouched down slowly and picked it up. She jammed it into the pocket with the well stone as she moved in front of the windows toward the hall she thought led to the bedrooms.

She nudged the first door open with the side of her boot. Bathroom. And too small to hide in. The door across from the bathroom was closed; she moved next to the wall and turned the knob slowly. The door creaked as it moved away from the jamb.

A sharp intake of breath came from inside.

Someone, or something, was in the room. She doubted that Katarina, or whatever Katarina was now, would hide from her.

"Who's in here? I'm not going to hurt you."

A young girl darted toward her. Veronika lunged out of the shadows attempting to stop the girl — who had to be Ana, the youngest daughter — before she reached Jo. Ana evaded her sister and tackled Jo in a hug, but she didn't speak.

Veronika stood and stared at her. Her face was white, and across her cheeks was a pattern of dark spots too big to be freckles.

Jo stretched out a hand, and Veronika ran to grab it. Jo wrapped her arms around the girls, and for a few seconds they clung silently together.

She stepped back from them. "We need to get out of here." Ana nodded up at her, but Veronika continued staring into Jo's face as if she didn't understand her words.

Jo crouched down, her knees screaming at the demands she'd placed on them within the last hour. "Ana, do you have a neighbor you like?"

The girl nodded again.

"Okay. Let's go outside, and then we can go to your neighbor and call someone to help."

Both girls nodded at that.

Jo walked them out, blocking the view of the moonlit kitchen with her body as well as she could. Out on the dark street, she asked Ana which house the neighbor lived in. The child pointed across the street at a house identical to theirs except for the flicker of candlelight spilling out of the windows.

She crossed the street with the girls. Before they got to the gate, Jo stopped and turned back to Veronika. She put her hands on the girl's shoulders and looked directly into her face.

"I have to find Faron. Ivanka is okay. She is with the police. Go inside and have your neighbor call the police."

Veronika's gaze moved down and locked on Jo's boots.

She gently tilted the girl's chin back up. "Veronika, I don't know what you saw, but I know it was awful. That was not your mother. You need to take care of Ana and call the police."

Jo waited for her to nod, but she didn't. Ana pulled on Jo's jacket and pointed at the neighbor's house.

A man stood at the gate holding an old-style candleholder by its loop-shaped handle. The candle's vanilla bean scent drifted into the night air around them; it was a welcome, if jarring, reprieve from the smells of the Novak house.

Jo looked into the man's face. It was kind and concerned. She had no choice but to trust him with the girls. She had to get to Faron.

"Something has happened to Mr. Novak." Jo stammered, realizing it would be impossible to explain what had taken place across the street. "Can you take the girls inside and call the police?"

"Yes." He reacted to the shock in the girls' faces with his own and looked back at Jo. "What happened?"

"I don't know. It's bad. Please take them. Please call the police."

"And you? Are you okay?"

"No. I have to find my son."

———

There were no taxis roaming the residential streets in Zelena jama, and her phone was dead. She mustered the strength she had left, and she ran. She ran as fast as she could, cutting through alleys and breezeways, following the most direct route she knew. She had reached the edge of the park at Tavčarjeva when someone reached out and grabbed her.

She fought hard but could not wrest herself free. She'd been dragged into the park before she felt the penetrating cold seeping into her arm where her assailant gripped her. She swung around to get a look at the shade who was trying to stop her.

She gasped.

"Milo?" His ponytail was half undone, and his neck was black and blue. Her knees started to buckle, but he grabbed her other arm and held her up.

"What did you do?" His words weren't accusatory but defeated.

She couldn't speak. Her head was pounding, and she felt the blood racing in her ears from the run. She stared at him. This could not be real. She resisted the urge to wail.

"I … she came out of nowhere. I was walking to the burek stand, and the lights went out. And there was this woman, but not a woman, and then this smell. And I couldn't breathe. She kept asking me where you were." He looked at Jo. "I don't understand."

Jo put her hands on her thighs and bent over. "I don't either." She couldn't catch her breath and couldn't even begin to find words of comfort for him. "I have to go."

"Go?"

"It has Faron."

"I'll come with you."

"No. You have to go somewhere else. Somewhere safe. Away from here. She can still hurt you."

"You always want me to go away."

"No." This was so unfair. "It really isn't that. I can't protect you."

"I'm already dead. What more could happen?"

"I don't understand all of this, but I know this. She can still hurt you. She can take your soul. And I can't protect you." She cried with rage at the idea that he could disappear forever and that it would be because of her. "I'm so sorry. I'm so, so sorry. I have to find Faron. And you, I can't …"

He put his hands on either side of her face and brushed his cold lips over hers. "For goodbye." And he was gone.

She reached out to where he had been standing and ran her hand through the air. What the fuck could be the point of killing Milo? He had nothing to do with this except to be with her.

Maybe this thing was trying to break her. Maybe it thought she would just lie down like a doormat and let it waltz on through into this world if it took everything she had.

She had news for this fucker. She wasn't letting anything in.

———

She had to stop to catch her breath again near the cinema behind the Slon Hotel. Someone really should have warned her that she needed to train for this dead whisperer thing. The breezeway was empty except for the sound of her ragged breaths. "Time Bomb" drifted past her, and Maja appeared next to her.

"What are you going to do?" Maja's blue hair was haloed by the light from the kino signs.

"I'm going to take the doll back to the well."

"Now? The museum's closed. Are you going to break in?"

Jo nodded. "I guess I'll have to. I have no idea where Katarina is, but she might follow me there if she thinks I'm going to throw her Barbie back into its hole."

"Let's go then." Maja started off down the tunnel.

"No. I need you to go to Leo."

"Why? He can't even see me, and you shouldn't go by yourself."

"I don't have time to wait. Were you not there? Didn't you see what she did to Tomaž?" Jo's throat was tight, and her voice was pitched an octave too high. She tried but couldn't even say Milo's name yet.

Maja nodded. There were things the dead couldn't unsee either.

"And besides," Jo said, "you can't be near Katarina."

"Why?" Maja's sassiness was back. "It's not like she can kill me again or anything."

"But she can. Leo said demons can take your energy, your soul, even after you're dead. Fuck, Maja, I can't let that happen to you."

Maja was still staring at her.

"Go. Go to Leo. Knock shit over. Throw shit. Do whatever you have to do to get his attention."

Maja disappeared, and Jo took off again down the tunnel, winded and shaking but not stopping.

———

The front door to the museum was not an option for Jo's less-than-stellar cat burglary skills. Anyone on French Revolution Square could see her. She walked down the side street between the museum and Križanke, where she found another entrance to the museum offices and tried the handle.

The door opened. It was dark inside, and the garlicky smell of burnt electrical wires stung her nose.

Katarina had gotten there first.

Jo pulled her keys out of the pocket, along with her stone. She held down the button on the mini LED light and moved the small circle of intense blue light around the walls of the entrance corridor. A white box with its wire guts hanging out was next to the door on the inside. There were scorch marks on the wall.

At least she didn't have to worry about the alarm or the police. The image of Milo's shocked face rose unbidden in her mind. She couldn't let anything like that happen to Faron. He had to still be alive.

She found her way to the museum lobby. Her eyes adjusted to the low light of moonlight streaming in through the glass wall that separated the exhibit rooms from the courtyard.

She walked down the dark ramp to the basement. The wall of glass to her left afforded a view down into the courtyard and above to neighboring rooftops. Now that she could see it clearly, the waning moon seemed especially bright. She stepped past the solid wall supporting the ramp and the building for a clear view of the stacked stones of the reconstructed well. Lit even at night with a watery green light, it was much spookier than it needed to be.

There was movement near the well on the raised middle section of the floor. She stepped back behind the wall. Maja was next to her, whispering. "Leo's at the rectory. I threw a book at him, but I don't know if he got the message."

"Why are you here? Go."

Maja's blue lip trembled. "I don't want you to die too."

"Maja. I have no intention of dying, but I need you to get out of here. I can't protect you."

Maja nodded and disappeared.

Jo wasn't a fighter, not in the physical sense, but she'd be damned if she'd let a fucking demon kill her son. She peeked around the wall. Roman jugs and vases were set in smooth depressions in the clay, small placards next to them. Beside the well lay her son, looking much younger and more vulnerable than his twenty years. Bending over him was Katarina, her hair wild, grasping a knife as if to sacrifice him. But to what?

Jo took off at run down the ramp, grabbed the first piece of Roman crockery she saw, and hurled it at Katarina's head. Bullseye.

She hit the mark, but apparently ancient pottery didn't have much stopping power. Katarina turned on her, eyes dark and flat in the green light from the well. There was no murderous rage in them, just a nothingness so complete that Jo had to look away. Katarina advanced on her, leveling her knife like every movie street fighter Jo had ever seen. Jo backed away until she was pressed against the glass partition that separated the dark basement from the ramp above her head.

Jo prayed again. Aloud. "Look, I don't know who or what might be listening, but I really need some help this time. If it has to be me or Faron, take me."

The sound of her words stopped Katarina, who looked around in confusion as if to see who Jo was talking to. The momentary pause was long enough for Jo to grab the nearest object: a metal sign holder holding a placard stamped with a bright red arrow. It seemed the right weight: not too heavy to wield, but heavy enough to clock Katarina more effectively than a two-thousand-year-old jar. Jo ran to the right and edged her way around the room in hopes of putting the raised floor section between her and Katarina so she could reach Faron.

But Katarina was impossibly fast. Jo looked at her again. It was Katarina, but not Katarina. The eyes, the speed, the not-talking — she really needed to get this doll back into the well. She could feel the sickening weight of it in her pocket.

Katarina lunged at her. Long, manicured nails raked over Jo's face, just missing her eye. Jo swung the sign hard, a bit above waist level. It smacked into Katarina's arm, and the knife and the sign both went flying.

So much for keeping the sign as a weapon.

Katarina hadn't stopped her advance. Jo continued to back away. Her eye was watering, and the skin on her cheek felt like she'd been bitch-slapped with a porcupine. She lost her footing on the uneven ground and turned her ankle. There was a distinct pop, and pain radiated up her leg. She hobbled the best she could, backing around the well and the platform where Faron still lay. Jo's heart was racing and all she could think of was the goddamn M*A*S*H theme song.

No, no. Oh, no. That was bad. Her father did not need to be there.

Katarina lunged at her again, arms outstretched at the level of Jo's shoulders. If Katarina got her, it was over. The thing inside her would snap her neck or do whatever it was demons did to people like her.

Jo had backed as far as she could go. There didn't seem to be a way out. She turned and tried to run in an effort to fake the demon out, but the pain in her ankle screamed at her to sit the fuck down. Katarina ran after her, unhampered by such considerations. Panicking, Jo went for a Hail Mary: she pulled back her arm and flung the doll at the well. Katarina screeched and wheeled back toward the green light.

Jo seized the opportunity and tackled her from behind. They went down hard together, and Katarina's chin caught on the edge of the raised bit of flooring. It was the first time Jo had actually heard a bone snap, and she didn't ever want to hear it again.

Katarina wasn't moving.

Jo scrambled up and limped back around to Faron. He was breathing, but his breaths were shallow. She shook him gently and his eyes fluttered. As she was positioning herself to pull his arm around her shoulders, she heard water began to bubble up from inside the well. The gentle bubbling quickly became a steady geyser.

Her father stood in front of her. "Jolene, you've got to let it in."

"Let what in? Why would I let anything in?"

"It's the only way."

Whatever had been inside Katarina was now a black hovering mass, a mist made out of thousands of eyes and wingbeats. Looking at it hurt her brain.

"No!" She lunged at her father's shade to push him away.

The inky cloud engulfed her father, and he disappeared in a flash of fluttering wings.

Before she could wrap her brain around that, the mass rushed at her. She dodged, and when she turned again to face it, it crashed into her from behind. She went sprawling onto the step and into the room beyond the well, the room filled with shelves of Roman pottery and glass. The blow had knocked the air out of her, and she tried to get it back. Every inhale felt like one of her ribs was trying to escape. A low hiss came from everywhere at once. Water was pooling around her, and the taste of floor and blood filled her mouth. She slid down off the step to try to roll over.

It was on her. Its weight flattened her against the floor. It pinned her, all the while beating its wings and casting about wildly as if it were searching for a crack. Her face was submerged in the quickly rising water, and she couldn't push herself up.

Her lungs burned. This was it. She was going to drown in a few inches of water, and that would give the demon access. It had beaten her, and it would take out everyone she loved.

Where was the doll? The thought echoed in Jo's mind like an amplifier in an empty hall.

She closed her eyes for what felt like half a second and felt another presence in the room. The pieces started coming together. The god's broken head from the exhibit, the feeling of menace she'd had on the bridge — from the start it had been trying to get to her, and that was what her father had come to tell her. She was the pigheaded woman from the poem who wouldn't dance with anyone.

A warmth rose from her feet, up her legs and into her chest. Achelous was putting her on like a pair of pants, and she was being crowded into a corner of her own body. She fought it, pushing back mentally.

But she had to let him take her. It would be the god or the demon. It would be her or Faron. And everyone else. She stopped fighting, and the warmth spread through her, the demon still fluttering angrily against the back of her neck.

For the next few minutes, it seemed like she was watching herself on a monitor from another room. She was aware of a being whose essence was far larger than she, yet constrained within the parameters of her body. It sprang up from the floor and threw off the dark cloud of eyes and wingbeats, dashing it against the raised platform. Then she, or it, or whoever, fished the doll out of the water and spoke in a voice that sounded like Tom Waits howling from the bottom of a mine shaft.

"Return to this Vessel. These are under my protection."

Markings she'd never noticed on the back of the doll were glowing.

The demon's screech sounded like ten thousand nails on a chalkboard inside a tornado. She wondered if her ears were bleeding.

An explosion of light hurled her back against the well. She slid down to the floor, a heap of dirty clothes, bruised flesh, and a cracked rib or two. She was alone in her body again, but she had to struggle to stand. Water was getting into her mouth, and it tasted like muck and metal. She pulled herself up against blocks of the well. Faron was floating freely, his face slipping under the black water. The green light sputtered a final time and then died, leaving only moonlight shining through the glass wall to light her way back to the ramp.

So this was what dead weight meant. The weight of her own clothes and boots and her unconscious son pulled at her, threatening to take both of them under. The water was now too deep for her to touch bottom. She went under again, clutching a handful of Faron's shirt.

The voice from the well was inside her head, urging her to let go, to let the water carry her to him. He had helped her. She wouldn't have to worry about this happening again. Her gift would be hidden. It was her choice.

How easy it would be to just let herself sink down. No.

She was not going to die now. She was not going to let Faron drown. It took everything she had to swim to the ramp with his unresponsive body. Again and again, she reached out, thinking she'd made it. It couldn't be more than twenty feet, but her waterlogged boots couldn't find a purchase underneath her. She reached out one more time and finally touched glass. She slid along it until she banged her knees hard against the concrete of the ramp. Then she crawled, heaving Faron up ahead of her until they were both completely out of the dark, lapping water.

As her boot cleared the surface, the water began to recede,

back down the ramp and into the basement. She lay flat on the cold concrete looking up through the glass and the open courtyard at a few stars visible despite the city's light pollution. She was still clutching Faron's arm. Every breath hurt. Definitely a broken rib. Maybe she wouldn't rush in like the cavalry next time.

Please don't let there be a next time.

She puked onto the ramp, then closed her eyes. She took a long breath that pushed painfully against the cage of bone holding her chest together. When she opened her eyes again, Helena was looking down at her. It looked like her neck had straightened up a little since Jo had last seen her. Now her head seemed to be cocked like a bird's when it's listening.

"I have to go back for Katarina." Jo didn't even have the energy to sit up.

"Katarina's dead, honey." Helena rested her cold hand on Jo's cheek.

Jo closed her eyes and exhaustion took her.

CHAPTER 25

Leo stood over the unconscious bodies of Jo and her son. He'd checked twice to make sure they were both still alive. The scratches on her face were painful to look at. He could only imagine how they felt. A perfectly round hole the size of a tea saucer was missing from the front of her shirt, and the skin it exposed was raw and blistered.

Marta Klančnik was at the top of the ramp with Lichtenberg. They both turned to look at him when he glanced up at them. He disliked the idea of bringing another person into what Lichtenberg referred to as the Veil, but he saw there was no other way to clean up the events of the night without drawing more eyes and raising more questions.

Lichtenberg could handle that. He and the investigator could say it was a meteor or aliens for all he cared. Leo wanted to get Jo and Faron out of there. Marta had forced Vesna to wait outside. Never before had he heard such language used by a woman who looked as demure as his niece, but Marta had prevailed. The courtyard lights were off to attract less attention, but Marta had turned on the lights inside the museum, and the light spilled out through the glass into the courtyard.

Lichtenberg's voice drifted down the ramp. "…She can't be connected with this."

Marta sighed loud enough for him to hear. "What the hell am I supposed to do with three crime scenes, three dead bodies — one of which will have to be scraped together off kitchen cabinets — stolen artifacts, and," her voice rose as she turned toward him again and looked down the ramp, "two unconscious witnesses you say I can't question? And why the hell is there a priest here again?"

Another woman wearing a dark T-shirt and jeans and a man in dark blue scrubs joined Marta and Lichtenberg.

"Marta, this is Dr. Struna. She will care for Ms. Wiley and her son."

Marta threw her hands up. "Okay, get them out of here." She started to walk away and then turned on Lichtenberg. "There'd better not be any extra paperwork in this for you and your Board or whatever the hell they are."

Lichtenberg nodded.

Leo knew he was lying. The Observers were all about documentation.

Dr. Struna, Lichtenberg, and the man in scrubs made their way down the ramp.

Lichtenberg looked down at Jo then up at Leo. "How badly is she injured?"

"I'm not sure. They've both taken a beating."

The man in scrubs leaned over Faron and took his pulse. He nodded at Dr. Struna, who squatted next to Jo and felt her pulse, then stood. "I'd prefer to do a more thorough examination here before moving them, but given the situation…" Her voice trailed off as she looked up at Leo. "I assume you can carry her out to the ambulance?"

Leo nodded. He squatted down and tried to get his arms underneath Jo as tenderly as possible. She moaned but didn't wake when he lifted her. He tried not to think about all the unseen injuries she could have. The man in scrubs carried Faron, and they followed Lichtenberg and the doctor up the ramp and out through the museum to the waiting ambulance. Vesna rushed to them.

"Gustaf, did you see her chest?" Dr. Struna nodded her head back toward Jo.

"Yes. I'll be curious to see who she is when she awakens."

Dr. Struna sighed heavily. "If she wakes up. People don't usually survive divine possession."

The ambulance looked like the kind of panel van furniture movers would use, but when Dr. Struna opened the back doors, the inside was all ambulance. She pulled down two gurneys for Leo and the assistant to put Jo and Faron on.

When the patients were strapped to the gurneys, Dr. Struna stepped up into the van and pulled one of the doors closed. "Gustaf," she said, "I'll take them to my surgery first. Call me when you know where we need to take them from there." She pulled the other door closed and thumped it from the inside.

The van took off down the cobbles toward the roundabout at the end of the square.

More police cars arrived. Lights and sirens sliced through

the night.

Marta came out of the museum's front entrance and shooed Leo and the others off to the side. She spoke to them in the shadows. "Everyone needs to get the hell out of here." She turned to Lichtenberg, "I'll do my best to make your ridiculous cover story stick."

CHAPTER 26

Sunlight filtered through a lace curtain pulled closed over the window. Pain shot through Jo's back and side as she sat up in an unfamiliar bed in an unfamiliar room. There was no clue as to how she'd gotten here from the museum.

A few bars of "Whatever Lola Wants" drifted through her thoughts.

Helena appeared at the foot of the bed and walked around to sit next to her. Her head was situated properly on her shoulders now, and her dress was clean and dazzlingly white.

"I'm dead."

"You're not dead." The corner of Helena's mouth curled into a sly smile.

"But, you're…"

"That's a long story. For later."

Jo rubbed her hands over her face. Every inch of raw skin where the Katarina-thing had scratched her burned and throbbed like she had just rubbed her wounds with salt. "Where's Faron. Is he okay?"

"He's fine. He's with Ivanka in town."

"And Milo?" It hurt, in a very different way, to say his name.

Helena touched her face, the cold of her fingers soothing the sting. "He must have crossed. I haven't seen him. I'm sorry."

Jo looked around. "This is Gregor's house?" She didn't want to talk about Milo, or what had happened to her father, with Helena.

"Yes. His mother's old room, apparently."

"I've only been in here once. To help him go through her things after she died."

"It's, um, quaint." Helena ran her hand over the bumpy chenille bedspread and flicked at the lace at the window.

"Who's here besides you and me?" She wasn't ready to face anyone else, alive or dead.

"Vesna and a tall, gorgeous Jesuit who may be the first person who's made me wish I were still alive…" She shushed Jo's attempted interruption. "I know, love. Gregor, of course. Oh, and your Aunt Jackie."

"Wait. Where's Maja? How are you even here? I thought you crossed or whatever."

"Nope. The door was closed when I got there, so I stuck around and made friends and found out how to, um, freshen up a bit."

"But Maja?"

"I offered to stay in her place when her door opened."

"I didn't get a say in any of this?"

"Don't be angry. I think being your sidekick was more than your little baker could handle. She told me to tell you, boss lady, to take it easy for a while. And not to be too hard on Mr. Bear? I have no idea what she meant by that."

There was a soft knock at the door, and then it opened. Helena remained visible.

"You're awake. I heard you talking." Aunt Jackie crossed the room to the bed and sat on the side opposite Helena.

"I'm glad you finally woke up. I was getting worried." Jackie took her hand.

"Finally? What day is it?"

"Wednesday."

"Oh shit. Maja's wake. The shop ..." Jo moved to get out of bed. Jackie put her hand on her shoulder to stop her.

"All taken care of. You should trust your team more."

Jo sank back into the bed. "Guess so. But what happened? How did I get here? Where's that fucking doll?"

"I just came to check on you. I think Leo is the one to explain all of this. Are you hungry?"

Her stomach growled. She hadn't thought of food until Jackie asked. "Yes, I'm starving."

"I'll bring you something." She closed the door behind her.

"She made chicken with dumplings. She said it's your favorite." Helena stood.

Jo grabbed her hand before she could go. Helena turned back to her with a question on her face.

"Why did you stay, really?" Jo couldn't put into words why

Helena's return as her guide unnerved her, but everything about it screamed trouble.

Helena laughed. "I have a mission."

"Is this mission for you or for me?"

"Later, dear. You need to heal up and eat your dumplings."

———

Getting dressed was hard, and she wasn't even sure that fresh underwear and a kimono counted as dressed. She was happy to be upright and sitting at the table with most of her family. Vesna and Jackie wedged her into a chair with pillows to support her back and keep her from slouching, which made her ribs sing with pain. She had crutches, but she couldn't use them because of her rib. Instead, someone had to walk on her right side to help support her sprained ankle. She hated being dependent on anyone else, even if it was temporary.

She was halfway through her third bowl of chicken and dumplings for the day. Gustaf Lichtenberg had shown up while Vesna was helping her shower. He stood at the counter, nursing a cup of coffee. She had questions, but nobody seemed willing to answer any of them. If she heard "later" one more time she was going to pitch a dumpling at someone.

"How do you feel?" Leo sat next to her but didn't offer to touch or comfort her.

She swallowed a mouthful of broth. "Better. I mean my body feels like I was wrung out like a sheet, but my head is starting to clear. Are you going to tell me the rest of what happened now?"

He nodded. "But first, why did you go to the museum alone? What in the name of God were you thinking? I told you that you're a Portal, that you needed to stay away from the demon."

She jerked with surprise. She should've known he'd be angry. She looked around at the people she loved most in the world. All but Jackie were looking at her the same way Leo did: with reproach.

Jackie was glaring at Gustaf. "She's a what?"

Gustaf set his cup on the counter and stared at Leo. "You shouldn't be so angry at her. You're the one who nearly got her killed with your fairy story about returning the doll to the well."

Jackie stood up then and marched over to Gustaf. "She's a Portal? And you didn't get her the hell out of town as fast as you could? You and the Board can go … go fuck yourselves!" It was pretty rare to see Jackie that steamed. She sat back down and fumed without saying another word.

Gustaf had the sense to look abashed. Vesna shot him a look, too, but nudged Jo to continue her story.

"Gustaf said something about being a door, and Leo said the doll had to go back to the well. He specifically told me he would take care of it, but I had to find Faron after Katarina took him. I thought if I went there with the doll and chucked it into the well, she would come to me. I didn't expect her to get there first."

She looked down at the last dumpling in her bowl. She pushed it around with the tip of her spoon. "I just wanted it to be over." She could not have imagined what over would look like.

Leo took a deep breath. "You do realize that it won't ever be over for you?"

Jo looked him in the face, but before she could form a question, there was a knock on the door. Gregor got up to answer it.

"Your gift isn't going to go away. This will not be the last time you are visited by the dead or by danger. You cannot act in such a cavalier manner. You have a duty." Leo's stare burned through her. She imagined all the molecules in her body trying to cover their nakedness against the intensity of his gaze.

Finally, someone else had said it. It was a duty, and one that meant her life would never again be like it was. There was no going back to slinging tea, or at least not just slinging tea.

"That being said, if you hadn't gone, it's almost certain Faron would be dead and more people besides." Leo let out a sigh with the last word.

Jo choked down the last dumpling. She had to swallow hard. Leo handed her his glass of water and asked her what happened at the museum.

Jo filled in her portion of the story. Or at the least the parts she was ready to talk about.

Gustaf laughed. "I was right. You were possessed. I didn't see how you could have bested a revenge demon any other way."

Jo felt like she was sliding down the rabbit hole again. "So how does a revenge demon wind up trapped in a Roman doll in a well in the City Museum?" Jo's question was directed at Lichtenberg.

Leo answered. "You know the story of Jason and the Argonauts?"

Jo nodded.

"And you know it's believed that Jason traveled the Ljubljanica on his return with the Golden Fleece?"

"Yes, but what does that have to do with revenge demons?"

"Do you also know the story of Medea, Jason's wife?"

A small light dawned in Jo's mind. "Medea was a revenge demon?"

Lichtenberg answered. "No, but when she killed her sons, she created one. It must have found its way to Emona and been imprisoned here by followers of Achelous. He would not have protected you otherwise."

"He didn't protect me exactly. I had to drag myself and Faron out of the flood he created in the basement." And he hadn't wanted her to leave. She shivered at the thought of his voice in her head and the promise he had used in his attempt to make her believe.

"Gods are imperfect, despite their wish for us to believe otherwise." Leo spoke with a finality that said this portion of the story was over.

"It makes sense now that Katarina or the demon would go after Helena and Maja. But why Milo?" She knew the answer already. But she still didn't want to believe it.

"Once the demon had complete control, it no longer cared about Katarina's revenge fantasies. It wanted to stay here permanently." Gustaf walked to the table and sat down across from her. "It only wanted to get to you."

"Couldn't it have just kept walking around dressed up as Katarina?" Vesna looked from Jo to Gustaf.

Gustaf said, "Human bodies can't hold the demon for very long. It survives by consuming first their pain, and then their life force. When the body dies, the demon is released again to find a new host."

Katarina would have died anyway. There had been no way to save her. The demon had taken more than her life, though.

"Why did it take Faron?" Jo watched the gray man's face. She still didn't trust Gustaf.

"Two reasons, I think. First, to lure you, the Portal, to it. Then, if you hadn't come, it would've sacrificed your son to Achelous in hopes of gaining his protection." He picked up his cup to take a sip but set it back down again.

So the god hadn't wanted her son. It had wanted her. It was not here to protect a demon.

"So how did I get here?"

"Maja did as you asked. I'd just gotten to my room at the rectory when a book about Roman Ljubljana came flying off the shelf at my face." He gestured at Vesna and Gustaf. "I called Vesna, and the two of us found you and Faron unconscious on the ramp to the basement."

Gregor returned to the kitchen with Marta Klančnik in tow.

"What are you doing here?" Jo was having trouble keeping everything straight in her head. Was Marta part of Gustaf's group?

Marta sat down in a chair Gregor produced from somewhere. "I keep asking myself the same question."

Leo laughed his basso laugh. "When she got to the museum with Gustaf, she thought Vesna and I had broken in and tried to kill you and Faron."

Marta winced. Jo found it hard to believe she was comfortable with all this. "So, Investigator Klančnik, what do you think really happened?"

"I've been told a demon possessed Katarina Novak and killed four people and tried to kill you and your son. As much as I would prefer that weren't the truth, it seems to be what happened. My report says Katarina and Tomaž Novak were involved in stealing and selling ancient artifacts. Helena Belak observed Mrs. Novak stealing something at the museum, and one of the Novaks murdered her. Maja Demšar overheard them talking about the murder at her work, and she was killed to silence her. Mr. Novak was killed in the process of making a homemade explosive for the purpose of breaking into a safe or something equally ridiculous, and Katarina was killed in a freak accident at the museum during another robbery." Marta looked like she'd just a reported an epidemic of cows flying across the moon.

"And Milo?" She felt a little shard of ice dagger its way through her heart. None of them were innocent exactly, but Milo had done absolutely nothing except care for her. That was the only reason he was dead.

"An unfortunate mugging unrelated to the rest of the night's events." Marta looked at her with what might be described as pity.

"Is anyone going to believe that?" Jo doubted it.

Marta shrugged. "Your guess is as good as mine, but I doubt anyone would prefer the true version. Would you?"

"And the doll?"

"It has been returned to Achelous's protection in the river, encased in a great deal of concrete." Lichtenberg dusted his hands as he stood. "And now I shall take my leave."

Marta stood.

Jo pushed her bowl to the center of the table. "Are you leaving too?"

"No. I came to get your statement. I agreed to file a fantasy story for Brother Kos and Mr. Lichtenberg, but I still need your story for the reports I am now required to file with the Board." She pursed her lips.

Jo doubted that Marta would dislike her any less now that she knew the truth. No police officer was going to rejoice in more paperwork.

CHAPTER 27

"Are you sure you're up to this?" Gregor was walking her out to the back garden.

"Yes. I've been thinking about it since I waited for Jackie at the train station when she missed her first flight." She tried to conceal the wincing, but her ankle and ribs reminded her with each step that they'd prefer she stayed in bed.

Everyone except Gregor had left for the day. Gregor's partner, Janez, would be in London for a few more days. Jo was grateful she didn't have to make up more stories to explain her convalescence in Mrs. Bregant's old room. Jackie suggested she attribute her injuries to a fall down the stairs from her flat. That didn't really explain her face, but it covered her other injuries pretty well.

Gregor had dragged two reclining lawn chairs out into the garden from the shed. He settled her on the one he'd decked out with pillows and blankets, then he lowered the back so she could lie flat and look up at the stars.

He lay down on the chair next to her and pulled a blanket around himself. He found her hand and squeezed her fingers.

They looked up into the sky, letting their eyes adjust to the darkness. The Milky Way swirled into focus. A meteor streaked low in the darkness near the horizon.

"Did you make a wish?" He squeezed her hand again.

"I did. I wished—"

He stopped her. "You aren't supposed to tell anyone your wish."

"I have to. I wished you'd forgive me for not telling you what was going on."

"I was angry. And hurt."

"I'm sorry. I didn't want you or Faron to be involved. I almost got him killed. And I can't imagine what you thought when Faron and I showed up at your house addled and broken and in the care of strangers."

"Well, Gustaf wasn't a stranger, but I was surprised to say the least."

"I bet."

"Did you not trust me?"

Tears were running into her ears and hair. "I always trust you. It was you I thought of at the museum. You and Faron and Vesna. And Rok. When I thought I was going to die."

"I would've never let you go there." His voice was hoarse.

"Things are different now, though. I mean, I'm different."

"You're still Jo. You're just Jo, who can talk to dead people."

She laughed. "I keep waiting for it to sink in that really there is something out there after we die. I would have thought that knowing would be comforting, but it isn't." What was out there was much worse than not knowing.

"I'm not comforted knowing there's a whole unseen world around me all the time. It completely fucks with being a good atheist." Gregor laughed.

She squeezed his hand. "If it's any consolation, I don't think there's a god with a capital G. I think it's like there's another layer of beings, but they aren't any more perfect than we are."

"Something else happened at the museum, didn't it?"

She really couldn't hide anything from him, not for long, anyway. "I don't know if I'm ready to talk about it yet."

"I'll be here when you are. You know that, right?"

"I do. I did. I really thought I was protecting you."

"I thought it was supposed to be the other way around."

"You can't do that forever." The stars were blurry now as the tears came faster and hotter on her face.

"Jo. What did you see?"

"I thought I hated him."

"Tomaž?"

She nodded in the darkness. "But those girls. Veronika's face. They will never be the same. He didn't deserve that. They didn't deserve to lose both their parents. And Milo." And her father. Nothingness was what she had believed became of everyone, but now Nothingness was sinister and wrong, and she couldn't do anything about that.

Gregor sighed wearily. "I don't know what to say, Jo."

"It's like I killed him." She wasn't sure whether she meant Milo or her father. It didn't matter. It was true for both.

He got up and sat on the edge of her chair. "You don't really believe that, do you?"

"I didn't save him."

"You saved Faron and yourself."

She looked away from him. "I almost didn't do that." The god's voice echoed in her head, and she felt the water lapping at her, trying to pull her under again.

He put his hand on the unmarred side of her face and turned her toward him. "But you did do it. Faron's alive. You're alive. I don't know what happened down there. I don't understand being possessed by gods I can't believe in. But you won. You came back."

Her throat was too tight to speak. She nodded.

Gregor brushed his thumb under her eye. "I don't know what I would've done if you hadn't made it."

She nodded again. She wanted to sob, but everything felt corked up inside. It was ironic. The woman who wouldn't let anyone in, now couldn't let anything out.

Gregor looked at her, then looked up at the Milky Way. Jo looked up too. Her eyes had fully adjusted now, and she watched the luminous thick river of twinkling stars. "I think up there in some alternate universe, you and I are an old married couple."

Jo choked out a laugh. "People think we act like one here."

"We're family."

"Speaking of family." Faron's baritone voice drifted down from the deck. "Can I join you or is it a party of two?"

"I'm freezing. I'll go make some cocoa. Come down here

and keep your mother company." Gregor and Faron passed each other at the foot of her lawn chair. Gregor clapped her son on the shoulder.

Faron sat down on Gregor's vacated chair. "How're you feeling?"

She shrugged. "Can you help me back up?"

He leaned over and adjusted her chair so she could sit. She was glad he couldn't really see her in the darkness. Her face was puffy, and she winced again when he got the chair back upright.

"Still hurts?"

"Yeah. Guess I can't hide it very well."

"You don't have to. Everyone here knows what happened."

"I'm supposed to be the mom, remember?"

"You make it hard to forget." He looked down into his lap.

"Why didn't you tell me what was going on with you?"

"Would you have believed me?"

"I would've tried to."

"I also didn't want you to get involved. I thought I was protecting you." Her throat tightened again. God, she would be glad when she could get back some emotional control again. If that was even possible. "That didn't work out too well."

"You couldn't know that thing would take me."

She should have known that if it wanted her and couldn't get her it would go for someone she loved. "Maybe."

"But we're good now."

"I think so. What about Ivanka?"

"We're figuring that out."

"What about her sisters?" She couldn't say their names without seeing the spray of blood on Veronika's pale blank face.

"Not sure yet. They may go live with Olga."

"Olga? Really?"

"She's their aunt."

"Really? She's Tomaž's sister?"

"No, Katarina's."

"Hm." That explained the prudish outfits. The last thing you'd want is your sister's lecherous husband coming on to you.

"Are you really okay? Ivanka told me Veronika won't talk about what happened at the house."

"Honestly?"

"Please."

"I don't think I am okay, but I think I have a lot of tethers to keep me from completely losing my shit."

"And the dead people thing?"

"Jackie said that's for keeps. At least that's something you don't have to worry about. It's just the women."

He nodded his head and looked off into the dark fields. "That's something, I guess."

"Is there something you need to tell me?" Whatever gods there were better not fuck with her kid again.

"Nope. It's just strange that it's only supposed to be women."

Gregor came back with three steaming mugs of cocoa with whipped cream on top. He handed them around and sat next to Faron on the lawn chair. He pulled the blanket up and threw it over his and Faron's lap.

"So what happens now?" Faron took a sip and got whipped cream on his nose.

Jo brushed it off. "I think I'll heal up a bit more. I'm definitely not ready for the stairs at the flat, even with Jackie's help." Her stomach sank at the thought of it. "And I'm not quite ready to go back to work looking like I was mauled by a tiger." She pointed to her face.

Gregor sat his cup on the edge of the chair. "I think you should definitely stay here for a bit. Then I think you need to get away for a while and recuperate inside."

She shook her head. "When I'm mobile enough, I want to go back to work. There'll be too many questions if I disappear. Besides, there are dead people everywhere. It's not like I ever get to escape that."

"But Gregor's right, Mom. You and Rok should go on one of your treks or something."

She paused and looked up at Gregor. "About that."

They both looked at her and waited.

"Rok isn't exactly what he appears." More layers. More tethers. With each new revelation, she had to wonder if she was tying or cutting them.

Faron cocked his head at her. "He's not a vampire or something, is he?"

"God, no. But according to Gustaf, on his next birthday Rok will be 371 years old."

"What the fuck?" Faron blinked at her in the darkness.

"He probably would've moved on by now, but he's attached to us, to me and you." She nodded at Faron. "Or he was. I don't know when or if he's coming back."

"You weren't the only one keeping secrets." His tone was wearier than a twenty-year-old's should ever have to be.

"I wasn't. But no more. I promise." The things that happened, with her father and with Achelous, weren't secrets exactly. They were just stories she wasn't ready to share.

Gregor picked up his mug and they all toasted, though Faron didn't look her in the eye.

———

Jo scraped her spoon through the last of the ice cream in her bowl. She was pillow-wedged between Vesna on one side, reading a book with her legs stretched across the chenille comforter, and Helena curled up on the other side, gazing out the window.

Jackie was grocery shopping. Gregor had failed to convince her that he and Vesna had the situation in hand until Jo was ready to go back to her flat. Jo wanted Jackie to stay, but it still bothered her to think about how much she hadn't known. Maybe if Jackie had told her, she would've been able to do more. She had too many things to dwell on and not enough to distract her from them.

She licked ice cream off the back of her upside-down spoon. "I never got to ask you about the date with Igor. Spill."

Vesna smiled broadly and laid the open book across her lap. "Nice. Lovely actually. He took me for a breakfast picnic in Tivoli."

"And?"

"And what? We ended up spending the day together. We'll see each other again when you're able to go back to your apartment. He thinks you fell down the stairs because the stupid landing light went out again."

"Convenient."

Vesna nodded. "It doesn't explain the scratches or that burn on your chest, but with any luck, no one will think too much about it."

Jo brushed her fingertips over her sternum. It didn't hurt now, but there was going to be a hell of a scar. "Well, no one will see the burn."

Helena laughed at that.

"Should I make a complaint to my negligent landlord about the light, to make it official?" Jo put the spoon back in the empty ice cream bowl.

"I wouldn't ask Gregor to play pretend any more than he has to." Vesna thumbed absent-mindedly through the book.

Helena plucked a small card from the flowers on the bedside table. "Give him time. He loves you, and you almost died. The supernatural stuff is merely icing on the cake, as you would say."

"I wondered who sent those." Jo tried to take the card from Helena. She supposed that all Vesna could see was the card floating about in the air.

Helena held the card out of Jo's diminished reach for another second, then she relented and put the card on Jo's lap.

Get well soon. — Matjaž

"You should call him when you're more … mobile." Helena's mission was becoming painfully obvious, but hooking up with her brother, or anyone else, was a nonstarter. Jo wouldn't be dragging any more innocent bystanders into her life.

Vesna got up and took Jo's bowl. "You should rest. Want me to help you get situated?"

"I might read for a bit."

"You should get her to leave too." Vesna nodded her head toward where she assumed Helena was on the bed, then left, closing the door softly behind her.

"Yes, you should rest. I'll play Girl Guide later."

"I don't think you're supposed to dictate my life. You're just supposed to help with the dead whisperer stuff."

"Oh, honey." She patted Jo's thigh, and the cold from her hand went to the bone. "There is so much you don't know."

LOOKING FOR MORE FROM VICTORIA?

The complete *Voices of the Dead* series is available now from 1000 Volt Press.

Our Lady of the Various Sorrows - Voices of the Dead: Book Two

Like A Pale Moon - Voices of the Dead: Book Three

Strange as Angels - Voices of the Dead: Book Four

Sign up for the Notes from the Dead Letter Office at victoriaraschke.com for information about upcoming book releases, author events, and an exclusive *Voices of the Dead* short.

THE ZOMBIE CHURCH IS REAL

The Trans-Universal Zombie Church of the Blissful Ringing is a real organization and registered religious group in Slovenia. The church supports the rights of refugees and regularly works to combat the rising tide of white supremacist nationalism in Europe. They also run a pro bono clinic in Nova Gorica, Slovenia, that mostly serves patients with chronic illnesses like diabetes and high blood pressure who can't afford ongoing treatment but aren't deemed ill enough to receive free emergency services.

You can support their work at the clinic by sending donations by mail to:
Hiša dobrot
Vipavska cesta 104
5000 Nova Gorica
Slovenia

Or by international transfer to:
SWIFT: BAKOSI2X
SI56101000053803567
Refrerence: CHAR
Banka Intesa Sanpaolo d. d.
Pristaniška ulica 14
6502 Koper
Slovenia

To learn more about the church go to their public, English language group page on Facebook.

ABOUT THE AUTHOR

Victoria Raschke writes books that start with questions like "what if you didn't find out you were the chosen one until you were in your forties?" When she isn't holed up in her favorite coffee house to write, she can be found at the nearest farmers' market checking out the weird vegetables or at her home where she lives with a changing number of cats and her family who supports both her writing and her culinary experimentation — for the most part. Her first book, *Who by Water*, was published in 2017.